TINA,
MAFIA
SOLDIER

TINA, MAFIA SOLDIER

MARIA ROSA CUTRUFELLI

Translated from the Italian
by Robin Pickering-Iazzi

First published in Italian in 1994 under the title
Canto al Deserto: Storia di Tina, soldato di mafia.
Copyright © 1994 by Maria Rosa Cutrufelli
English translation copyright © 2023 by Robin Pickering-Iazzi
Translator's note copyright © 2023 by Robin Pickering-Iazzi

First published in English in 2023 by
Soho Press, Inc.
227 W 17th Street
New York, NY 10011

Library of Congress Cataloging-in-Publication Data

Names: Cutrufelli, Maria Rosa, author. | Pickering-Iazzi, Robin, translator.
Title: Tina, mafia soldier / Maria Rosa Cutrufelli ; translated from the
Italian by Robin Pickering-Iazzi. | Other titles: Canto al deserto. English
Description: New York, NY : Soho Crime, 2023.
Identifiers: LCCN 2022032811

ISBN 978-1-64129-424-9
eISBN 978-1-64129-425-6

Subjects: LCGFT: Novels. | Classification: LCC PQ4863.U75
C8713 2023 | DDC 853/.914—dc23/eng/20220708
LC record available at https://lccn.loc.gov/2022032811

Interior design by Janine Agro

Printed in the United States of America

10 9 8 7 6 5 4 3 2 1

Above the lava rocks, amidst the broom
withered by the sun, I, ancient olive tree
am weary of singing to the desert.

—SANTO CALÌ

I can't speak about Sicily
because I love her and it scares me.

. . .

I want to say that in your land
anger runs thicker
and the almond of pain ripens.

—ROBERTO ROVERSI

TINA,
MAFIA
SOLDIER

CHAPTER 1

The separation was sharp, obvious, desired. Two contrasting worlds—the city and the Villaggio—contiguous yet light years apart.

The Villaggio arose to make a space for hope, for modernity. And to achieve this aim it seemed necessary to separate the modern from the ancient, the past from the future. To create a break.

The Villaggio was the new. It flaunted its still flawless asphalt, the perfect, white street markings. To show off the goodness of the new was necessary, so that the laceration would transform into an opening toward the world. So that the arrow of development would shoot from the unfathomable depths of the cut and land solidly in the future.

The Villaggio was the dream of the new. On the small plain at the foot of the town—the ancient Piano Notaro, feudal lands belonging to a large estate owner—the streets intersected according to an orderly design of geometric simplicity. At each street corner stood the sign with its name: Via Cortemaggiore, Piazza Caviaga, Viale Enrico Mattei, in honor of the man who had insisted on building AGIP—the Petrolchimico refinery—in Gela, on the southern coast of Sicily.

Cortemaggiore, Caviaga . . . Names from the mainland, foreign names. Perhaps that was why the buildings had those smooth stark facades, without any terraces, without balconies—there was a link between those two things.

"Just like at San Donato Milanese," my friends maintained. To me, who had never been to San Donato Milanese and therefore couldn't confirm or deny it, the whole thing sounded strange. Those Milanese must have been strange, too, building their homes so they looked onto the interior, without the caprice of a curly balustrade, a pot-bellied curve to soften the street's profile.

"Not even a little balcony to look outside, nothing, are you sure?"

"Of course. Why would they need to look outside? To see the fog, the rain?" Then with an eloquent, definitive gesture, "All of the buildings look like this. All of them just like this."

The people who'd entered those buildings as renters or owners couldn't sit outside in their undershirt on the terrace, or enjoy watching others on the evening stroll from a balcony. Nonetheless, they showed off their pride of ownership and boasted about their good luck. Life was decidedly more comfortable there, in the "Villaggio of the masters," as the people living in town called them. A self-sufficient nucleus, which had to be one of the creators' intentions. There was more than enough water—they could even wash their cars in the street—public services, a church, a health clinic, a fully equipped beach open only to the residents.

In town, water was available only for a few hours each day.

At a distance of two, maybe three kilometers, Gela perched on its hill, unstable on the slope toward the sea, unhealthy and malarial on the slope to the plain, looking down at the Villaggio, sheltered behind her archaic poverty, ensconced in the pride of a splendor that lived only in the quotations of her professors, or erudite notaries.

"Aeschylus came here to die," my uncle, an Italian and Latin teacher at the high school, invariably reminded every guest, every foreigner. "There must have been a reason," he would insinuate, with the hint of an allusive smile. "One of the most powerful cities in Sicily. That's what Gela was when Agrigento still hadn't been founded."

FOR A WHILE, AT the beginning of the sixties, the flames of Petrolchimico also seemed to become part of the landscape, to renew the town's forgotten glory.

People who arrived from the Ionian Coast, after leaving behind the Mountain, La Montagna—as Etna is called, a womanly volcano with generous hips and slow lava flows—after leaving the citrus groves of Catania's green plain and crossing the stony peaks and the scorched high plains of Caltagirone, caught sight of a glow, dispersing mists there on the horizon, while little by little a futuristic geometry of pinnacles, pylons, and a rotundity of immense cylinders rose into the sky. The towers shot long tongues of blue smoke straight up in the sky, piercing the horizon. They spewed a persistent, invasive smell that announced the approach to Gela while it was still hidden from view many kilometers off in the distance.

But in the face of the wide opening of the future, what did it matter, that smell of rotten eggs that stung people's eyes and burned their throats? Petrolchimico's flames promised work and a comfortable life, while the flames of the Mountain on the island's other shore offered only earthquake tremors and storms of lava grit.

Gela still lived on fishing—though little—and raising cotton and tomatoes, cultivating its great, sunny plain, the "Geloi fields," the Roman Empire's breadbasket. Thirty-five thousand inhabitants holed up around the piazzas and the few kilometers of the main street, which bore the name of Vittorio Emanuele. A custom. An homage. A name that is repeated with regular monotony across the entire island. A street named Vittorio Emanuele runs from one end to the other of towns barricaded between the mountains or sloping down toward the sea. The alternatives are few: Corso Umberto I, Corso Principe di Piemonte, Via Garibaldi, Via

Roma. If nothing else, the Unification of Italy locked the islanders' toponymic imagination in the rhythm of obsessive celebration.

BY THE BEGINNING OF the seventies, Gela's population had already doubled. Petrolchimico's settlement had brought work: twenty thousand jobs promised or dreamed up, two thousand five hundred actual plant jobs in 1970 and an indeterminable number of related jobs. Young couples or single males attracted by the miracle of industrialization and the salaries ("northern" salaries, people said, to indicate the considerably high pay) flowed in from every ridge like thawing river waters. A hunger for the good life exploded, a voracious consumption, a desire for revenge for the eternal abomination of poverty. At that time, Gela wasn't a mafia city.

Of course in those days, there were people throughout Sicily and Italy and the world who could say: The mafia doesn't exist. Because you saw the blood, but not the men. The men stayed invisible, cloaked in their silence.

But Gela wasn't a mafia city. It wasn't completely devoid of mafiosi, but there were just a few, small stuff, enough to not belie local folklore.

The town and the Villaggio still faced each other, distant and alien. The Petrolchimico employees, who were the inhabitants of the Villaggio, could go to work and return home without passing through Gela. They could tranquilly ignore the town, live in a kind of suspension, an island in the island. But it was perhaps only the comparison between the two realities that made the protected life in the Villaggio enviable.

Back then, in the 1970s, I lived in the historic part of the city, in a house—not old, but already in disrepair—near the seashore promenade. A place to land, a needed break. When I was a little girl they had taken me away from Sicily, and I wanted to return to Sicily during that time of passage from the life of a student to the life of a working woman. I only chose Gela because an uncle on my mother's side lived there, as well as a cousin I had played with when I was little, during vacations or holidays spent according to the ageless Sicilian habit of exchanging visits from one city to the other, from one town to the other, from one continent to the other.

I remained in Gela three years, without ever being able to get used to that harsh dialect, or to life hemmed in tightly between the sea and the main street.

When I would drive out of town in my Fiat 500 to clamber up the road toward Riesi and my first job substitute teaching, there was just a single arrow indicating the wide entrance of perfect asphalt leading into the "Villaggio Macchitella." All around it, empty no man's land. Already then, off in the distance, desolate, threatening outlines of illegally constructed neighborhoods ran by, with asymmetric silhouettes of unplastered houses, never finished, with their black, empty window frames of gaping brick. Along the sides of the road were abandoned fields, parched scrub and exposed tangles of wires unfurling endlessly in all directions. Tubes and cables the same color as the dusty land, the houses, and scorched grass—or a pale silver.

In the silence of that summer heat wave, I used to hear a vibration rising from that silver, almost a faint song or the soft, hypnotic lament of a marranzano mouth harp, a deep resonance that seemed to gush from a source hidden in the bowels of the scorched earth, a subterranean spring that accompanied me along the entire road together with the waves of heat wafting from the dried asphalt crust.

THAT WAS TWENTY YEARS ago. Since that summer, I had never returned to Gela. Now I'm here, at the entrance to the town, looking at the transformed landscape from the window of the Fiat Uno I rented at the Catania airport. For an instant I'm bewildered.

The abandoned fields along the side of the road aren't there anymore, nor are the long tubular ribbons that unfurl, modulating a song of their own in the desert of dried twigs. A shapeless mass of illegal houses, over twenty thousand, has submerged everything, pushing down the hills right to the sea. A tide that rose from the inland and swept away Enrico Mattei's dream. The future, broken into black circles of oil sludge on the beach.

A familiar and unknown city. That's the impression, that's what I see beyond the dusty windshield. All of a sudden my undertaking seems impossible and absurd. I'll never manage to track down Tina in the chaos that's in front of me. Unable to tolerate the notoriety, after being the object of malevolent, dangerous attentions, she disappeared down there, in the streets of Gela, the protective womb of an immense Kasbah.

But precisely this temptation brought me back to the island. I know, or presume to know, which way to take to unravel the thread of Tina's life. I'll have to descend into the town. I, too, will have to disappear into the labyrinth of buildings that fill the horizon, resembling a precarious set of children's building blocks, irregular cubes stacked willy-nilly one on top of the other, one behind the other, denying all vital space, erasing all freedom, and blocking any avenue of escape.

I START DRIVING SLOWLY ahead again, my eyes ready to recognize and remember. An imprudent operation. I should know how risky it is to measure the changes of a familiar place. Right away one is inside a different scale of measurement, inside our very own rhythms of lived time.

For this reason, perhaps, as the warm June wind scatters my cigarette ashes inside the car, Gela appears so young and cruel. I feel it well before it becomes reality. Because Gela is actually young; one third of its population is younger than eighteen. And the males outnumber the females, as befits every frontier town.

"The males? They think they rule the world. Well, yes,

you need a male figure to represent people," a little girl spelled out condescendingly while being interviewed on the street for one of the usual special reports on Sicily.

Young and cruel. It's a cruel landscape that I find hard to recognize and doesn't correspond to the map of my memory anymore. Today only the width of a street separates the Villaggio from Scavone, a neighborhood of public building projects and illegal houses that earned the nickname the Bronx. The other day the carabinieri discovered an abandoned mafia hideout in the shared basement of one of these condominium buildings, a few meters from the Villaggio, with weapons, a kilo of high-powered explosive, a two-way radio tuned to law enforcement frequencies, three wigs, a fake license plate, and a master list of extortion revenues, victims, and money collectors.

The distance between the Villaggio and the town doesn't exist anymore. Not even in certain minute differences in their pasts. The houses in the Villaggio, the newer ones, have conquered the open-air space of terraces, though contained and minimal. They're narrow, with rigid, practical railings that ignore the Mediterranean suppleness of the balcony. I see them, all lined up in formation one on top of the other, one after another. They're advancing to stand up to the aggression of the Bronx.

CHAPTER 2

Twenty years ago, I was leaving (for the second time), and Tina was being born.

Sitting on the backseat of the car, in perfect order inside a transparent file folder, is the dossier that I compiled on her, cutting out newspaper articles, taking notes, photocopying news items. There are also some photographs. I like one of them in particular. It shows her laughing, her hands gripping the handlebars of a motor scooter. I like it precisely for that hearty laugh, her face tilted toward her shoulder instinctively trying to hide from the camera shot, granted nevertheless with an expression of childish mischievousness, of elusive, playful provocation. Tina *'a masculidda*. Tina the little tomboy. Loose pants, a striped top on her shapeless, slightly awkward, adolescent body. She must have been fourteen or maybe fifteen years old, and it was her debut, the first time she appeared on the pages of a newspaper. Attempted robbery. But that wasn't what made her newsworthy, though ultimately young girls who pursue exploits of this kind are rare compared to boys.

Tina was the recognized boss of a band of juvenile boys. That's what was really worth a photo and an article. A young girl and a band of little gangsters, unaware of the fragility of their age.

Sitting next to the driver's seat, my cousin Mimmo points his arm out of the window right where I need to turn.

"Here, I said." He straightens his hair, ruffled by the wind. He wears it long and combed smooth back in an old-fashioned style, so he doesn't seem either old or young, despite being forty. A look that suits him. Most of all it suits his way of being a doctor, fussy and paternalistic, but with an outward vein of cynical impatience.

It's a Sunday in late June, almost six o'clock, but the town is still sleeping or lazily dragging out the day behind the windows, which are closed to keep out the hot, heavy air. I park in a deserted courtyard and head toward the first of two small white and red buildings that mark the border between the Bronx and the Villaggio. Probably the same blurry building that you can make out in the right corner of the photograph: a perfectly squared wall, dark plaster, a piece of asphalt street.

And yet when the photograph was taken, Tina didn't live here anymore. In truth, she lived here just a short time. It hadn't even been a year since the entire family—her father, mother, older sister, and brother, who was just a few years younger—had moved from a hovel downtown to the public houses in the Bronx, at the time of the tragedy. Or rather, the incident. That is, when her father died, in that brand new apartment, just inaugurated, the armchair and chairs still covered in stiff, crinkling plastic. He died, shot directly in the face by two shotguns. Three shots exploding from weapons loaded with shrapnel: buckshot mixed with gunpowder and pieces of iron.

"THAT WAS THEIR DOOR," Mimmo says. "That's where the Cannizzaros lived. Tina and her family. Now, I don't know. Maybe it's still empty . . . But I doubt it, as we're starving for homes."

There are just two doors on the sandstone landing, well-lit by a side window. The door Mimmo had pointed out is right in front of a blank wall where the stairs make a sharp turn. No nameplate, no name written on the doorbell. The other door is open, and a male voice invites us to come in, welcoming us loudly with warm greetings.

The Cannizzaros' neighbor is a handsome, strong old man, with thick white hair and a lively expression. He's in his undershirt, sitting in front of a game of solitaire spread out on the table in the combined dining and living room, and doesn't get up when we come in.

"You'll have to excuse me, doctor." Now I notice the

crutch leaning against a chair and the empty leg of his pants, the material hanging limply as if the heat had sucked the flesh out.

"Disability pension," Mimmo whispers to me, "with a successful conclusion, for once."

The old man isn't alone. His wife is already bustling around in the kitchen, preparing coffee for us. A young, silent woman is pushing a baby carriage back and forth to lull to sleep a tiny, sweaty baby with two tufts of wet hair on his head, his little arms limp with the total exhaustion of early childhood.

"There's room for everyone."

The apartment is large. The man's blue eyes, sparkling triumphantly, underline the point, while he raises an authoritative, hospitable hand to invite the world, to welcome all progeny. There's room for everyone, as well as for his two married daughters and his grandchildren.

It's not a poor home, I think as I look around, compensating for the indiscretion with compliments. The impression the home makes suggests the metropolitan outskirts, a looming poverty held at bay by furniture, decorations, ornaments, and furnishings. The living room is suffocated by pieces of furniture. The table, in the middle of the room, takes up much of the space, almost touching a brightly polished credenza and small sideboard, and a corner shelving unit that holds the television and video recorder. On the top shelf sit six hardcover encyclopedia volumes, whose titles

I can't quite make out. Everything is well cared for but arranged ineptly, with a timid hand that reveals the uncertainty and confusion of someone who still doesn't feel like the owner of objects and spaces, and doesn't know the new rules of the game of living in a home.

Taking up an entire wall, in a sumptuous frame about ten centimeters tall, is a poster made from a photograph in which a very handsome, very serious young man wearing a carabiniere uniform shines, with the luster of arms and insignia.

"My son, when he took the oath. My daughters are also married to two carabinieri."

Pride in his tone of voice, in the rapacious haughtiness of his eyes.

As if responding, Mimmo, who is sinking into the flowery upholstered couch, sneers, "You could play cops and robbers in this building."

He breaks off, leaning to the side to briefly caress the baby, whose little legs are spread wide apart like a frog, moving restlessly in the baby carriage. He turns back toward me: "A killer lives in the apartment above. A famous killer. Good people and evil scoundrels, carabinieri and murderers, side by side, door to door. That's how it is in this building. That's how it is in the whole neighborhood."

The old man doesn't comment. He's suddenly drifted away from our conversation, chatter that doesn't interest him or have anything to do with him. His extraordinarily bright eyes, steadily fixed on Mimmo, have turned curiously dull; communication has been broken, consensus suspended. His wife has set down the tray with our coffee and taken a seat at a corner on the other side of the table.

"It used to be better than paradise on earth here," the old man blurts out of the blue. "Better than paradise on earth. Then those people arrived . . . You, sir, know, you know them, sir."

Which people? My mind jumps to the killer living on the floor above. So I had imagined his ostentatious lack of interest, that absent look on his face. Or maybe the old man still remembers the neighbors he had in the past, the man who was massacred at his front door.

"Sure, I know them. But what are they doing?" My cousin makes light of it. "They aren't doing anything, nothing bad. And they're clean and tidy."

"As for being clean, they're clean," his wife confirms.

But the old man shakes his head forcefully. "There's no pleasure anymore. There's no pleasure with those people below, on the first floor, that everyone has to pass by."

"Squatters," Mimmo finally explains. "The apartment went unrented for too long. So they forced open the door and settled themselves inside. An entire family."

"There's no pleasure anymore," the old man repeats resentfully. "And it was better than paradise on earth. Better, believe me."

The disgrace gives him no peace. His chest puffs up and

his shoulders rise in the effort to launch his protest and keep it high in the air, clearly visible, oozing with passionate hate. The man's disability, that crutch leaning against the chair, seems harder to bear and more evident amidst the throbbing emotions and repressed energies. The old man is the master of the scene. His feelings invade the home, fill the space, keep it subjugated. Compared to his captive vitality, the two women are only dull, silent extras.

"That's better . . ." The man sighs, calming down little by little, almost as if Mimmo's impassivity is rubbing off on him. An impassivity that has nuances of complicity. In this home, Mimmo treats everyone with familiarity, and is treated the same in turn. He's the family doctor, an important laissez-passer for me too. I know how it is, and I have taken note. After his brief introduction—"my cousin"—no one asked me any questions. It's not courtesy but simple control of curiosity, a normal exercise in this area between people who are friends, who respect each other. And no one asks about the reason for this visit, which is certainly an unusual one. "I was in the area." That's enough, at least for the moment. A convention, a recognized, accepted formality. Form isn't an empty shell, far from it. It enables you to manage situations. That's the essential thing.

But now Mimmo gives me a prodding look, encouraging me to come into play. He says, "My cousin, she's writing a book. Your neighbors, the Cannizzaros, you remember them, don't you? She's writing a book about Tina."

"Tina?"

Sugar has already been put in the coffee, and though I take it unsweetened, at this point there's no way to not drink it. A small sip and I put the cup back on the saucer.

"Tina?" Hostile, rebuffing: "She was called Cettina."

A NAME FOR A little girl, for a sweet little girl, that really didn't fit her, falling off her on all sides like certain little flounced dresses that her mother resigned herself not to put on her anymore and to replace with pants and a t-shirt.

A name that got in her way like the long hair hanging down on her neck. She just had to go to the barber's when her father went there, to get rid of that encumbrance. Cettina would see herself in those long mirrors under the neon lights, in the white bib towel that covered her, hanging almost down to her feet, and feel the same as all the other boys. It was beautiful to break free from that hairstyle. Cettina would have liked to make her own name slide away right along with the hair the barber shook out of the cloth at the end of her haircut.

But at eight years old, there wasn't any way to escape that shrill, clear diminutive. Even if she hid behind her cousins' clothes, in their old pants, jackets that reached her after unnervingly long peregrinations from one boy to another, from one growth spurt to another. At a certain point someone would call her *Cettina* and an entire scaffolding swayed unstably at the impact. Her body dislocated and piece by piece was swallowed up by the swamp of an unruly submission.

Spoken on her father's lips alone that name didn't jar, ridiculous and sickly sweet, a touchy spot always waiting in ambush in her imaginative soul. "A night wasted when you make a baby girl," her father would pronounce, repeating the age-old saying, but then he would take her along with him to the café and guide her hand on the billiard stick. Together, they'd roam through the bare countryside and dusty dirt roads, scars of a slightly lighter shade that furrowed the pale belly of the plain. He liked to take her along with him, that little girl with tomboyish eyes and a flair for adventure. They were often together on the long rides he had to take for his work as a metal scrap dealer, squeezed tight in the little three-wheeled Ape truck that bounced and squeaked at every gash in the asphalt and dangerously lurched at every stone. He took her alone out, into the world, and not Saveria, with that air of the busy older sister caught up in the most minute domestic duties. And not even Francesco, too babyish, too whiny. In fact, when he saw them arguing, "Let it all out, let it all out," he'd say, stirring her up. "Hit him now, because when he's big he'll be giving *you* a beating."

Then all of a sudden, the little Ape truck stood abandoned, and she found herself in a fast car, a new house, wearing her own clothes bought in her exact size, with a father who was brusque, worried, and distant.

Eight years old and she couldn't get used to her name.

Just like Cettina couldn't get used to the new house. Sure, if they asked her, she claimed she was happy. She boasted about it with a sort of arrogant vainglory. So much so that her cousins, wavering between envy and admiration, commented under their breath, "Haughty girl."

But Cettina felt she had to show how proud of her father she was. He was a man who knew how to take care of his family and had lifted his children out of that hole of just a few square meters and without any windows, where all six of them had lived and where only their grandmother remained, attached to her way of life, like all old people.

There was no lack of windows in the new house. In fact the light was too strong, too invasive and hot. The muffled sound of footsteps on the sidewalk was far away. She vainly strained to catch the sound of feet shuffling by, which at night, just beyond the doorstep of their old home, used to accompany her sleep. That silence tightened around her chest, provoking a sense of estrangement, malaise. Cettina would open the door and find herself facing a sad hallway, an empty ramp of stairs. The street no longer came directly into the house and the house no longer opened onto the street.

That's how it has to be, her father said. That's how it has to be, Cettina repeated to her cousins and friends from her old street, listing the advantages and comforts of their new accommodations. Then she'd list them over again to herself to find some confirmation and deceive her doubts. Because what good was having a telephone, for example (her mother had been the one to have it put in, after long haggling, furious arguments with her father), if afterwards no one could answer when it rang?

"But what did you all get into your heads? To let everyone know about my own business? Do you want to let the whole world know when I'm home and when I'm not here?"

He was a cautious man, and he certainly had good reason to be so. Even if all his caution wasn't enough to spare him from an unexpected, violent end.

"RIGHT ON THAT EXACT day I was at the hospital. You must remember, sir."

"But I still hadn't gotten my degree then," laughs Mimmo.

I haven't even opened my mouth yet and already the old man steps in, establishes limits, builds walls. But I can't go along with him and submit to devious sparring, to deferrals and competing allusions. I have no alternative. In order to understand (more than to know, which is a different complicated matter) I must be direct. Circling around reticence is long, complex work, and requires a comprehension of the powers at play, a capacity for identification with others for which I lack the strength to dig down deep inside me. Better to take the field straightaway.

"But his terrace borders yours. You could see him every day, know his habits . . ."

"He didn't have any habits. Sometimes he came home and others he didn't."

"To kill a father with a family that way," I intimate, a bit hypocritically. "They butchered him. But why, in your opinion, was he killed?" I ask, though I know it's useless asking.

"Who knows. We never found out."

The old man lifts up a playing card on the table. He examines it and slowly puts it back in the deck.

"Maybe just because he had found some copper that others had their eye on. Who knows. Maybe he was killed only over a little bit of copper. People kill for this, and even less, for little two-bit deals."

"Was he a boss?" I persist.

"A boss? Maybe that's going too far."

"I heard he was tied to a mafia family, to a clan."

"If he was, it was a losing clan, seeing as how they were able to kill him."

Mimmo leans forward on the couch, looking as if he's about to intervene, but then he stops himself and settles back again. From that distance he limits himself to staring at us, his eyes attentive but neutral, like a mere spectator. That look says his job ends with the courtesy of an introduction; he can't do anything else and must not. And not only because he lives here and his interference, each hint of insistence, could seem uncalled for. The fact is that these are the rules, and Mimmo sticks to the rules of a quiet life. My cousin really doesn't have the makings of a transgressor.

Yet he helps me graciously. Feeling a certain satisfaction,

he plays the role that I've invented for him, which is to say the role of a guide in my descent into the circles of a closed, distrustful world wound tightly around itself to prevent anyone from penetrating it. I know full well that without a friend to vouch for me and be an intermediary, this door wouldn't have opened so easily.

The killer who rang the doorbell right next door, when Cettina was barely eight years old, probably had a friendly face too.

CETTINA DIDN'T LIKE THE girls her age at school—they were meek and malicious. She didn't like her teacher, with that mouth that not even lipstick could soften. Always repeating: sit down, sit down. Never another word, always: sit down, sit down. But Cettina couldn't stay seated in her chair for the whole morning.

It was November and it was raining. An entire day of rain, so very rare in Gela. Cettina hadn't gone to school—she hadn't gone for a week—and had wandered around the streets until lunchtime. She was having fun in that pouring rain that turned the sloping streets into waterfalls and then spilled, foaming, through the escarpment of the seashore promenade. An unusual, turbulent landscape.

She'd gone down to the beach and lit a cigarette under the awning of a bar that was closed for winter. Something that no one at home scolded her for anymore. Her mother didn't even notice, and by then Saveria didn't dare grab the

cigarettes out of her hand. Cettina bought loosies contraband, from the older kids, more as a point of honor than
out of real convenience. It was the bargaining, the money
changing hands, that gave her a taste for cigarettes.

The rolling paper had lost its scent and become limp, soft
under her fingers. Everything was soaked with water: the
rotten wood of her shelter, the sand, compact and shining
like metal. She breathed in the smoke along with the smell
of seaweed and some sort of acrid substance that the rain,
instead of diluting, made more bitter and penetrating.

When she felt too soaked, with drops of cold moisture
condensing under her skin, making her tremble inside, she
started to make the climb up to her home.

"Hey, you. What are you doing here at this hour?"

In front of the butcher's, she ran into Saveria.

"You didn't go to school? Well, so you skipped school."

For a while her sister kept prodding her, alternating
between reproaches and flattery. "You act so tough, but
you're brilliant," she'd tell her. She wanted to get it into Cettina's head that school was important. "Make me happy."

"Shut up!" Cettina yelled. She didn't bother to tone it
down. Only rough talk disarmed Saveria. "Shut up! At
school, they didn't even want you."

"But I got my diploma."

It was true. She'd completed fifth grade, by repeating
every class, one after the other. And in the end, she arrived
at a compromise with the teacher. She promised she wouldn't

enroll in middle school if they gave her the diploma for elementary school. Nonetheless, Saveria was proud of her perseverance and that small final success.

They kept on arguing the entire way up the street and into their home, even while Saveria cut the bread and started setting the table. Up until they heard the front door opening.

Cettina wasn't jealous of the attentions Saveria showered on their father, her way of running to take his soaked jacket and rubbing a towel over his hair, still black and thick like a boy's. Saveria was just doing her duty as the grown-up daughter and didn't receive anything in return.

The man rolled the towel around his neck, glanced at the table that wasn't ready yet, and slipped straight into the bedroom.

He didn't stop to joke with her. It had been a long time since he'd stopped to joke around. He didn't even look at her. In a bad mood, Cettina then switched on the television and, turning her back on her sister, her mother, and little Francesco, who was silently staring at her as always, started surfing the channels quickly one after another. She stopped, raising the volume, only when the music of some song blared out.

Maybe that's why not one of them heard the doorbell. Afterward, Cettina would go back through her memory time and again, straining in vain to remember the sound of that doorbell, and an uneasiness, the shadow of something like remorse, would upset her. Maybe if the television hadn't been on, she would have heard it, the doorbell. And she would have gone to the door. And her father would maybe have had more time to understand, to defend himself.

Instead, she hardly noticed her father out of the corner of her eye that day, as he headed from the bedroom to the front door. She thought he was going out again. He was going out, alone. Her bad mood got worse, and her fingers started drumming time with the music on the chair slats.

What happened next was fast and executed with professionalism. Few movements, essential orchestration. Cettina perfectly remembers that in that very moment Telecittà was broadcasting a game show with prizes and someone—a girl—was singing in English.

There were two men, both of their faces uncovered. One of them planted himself against the door, keeping it wide open, his weapon pointed down against his thigh. The other one, with a shotgun leveled firmly in his hands, immediately opened fire. One shot, two shots. In Cettina's glimpse of the hallway, it seemed like her father leapt into the air, rising off the ground and arching backwards. Then the other man raised his shotgun, still keeping his shoulders against the door, and fired another shot.

Her father fell down backwards. Along with him, the small table with the useless telephone fell down too, tumbling over on the floor. The glass vase fell down. The little ceramic animals bought at the market all fell down. The photograph of their wedding resting up against a heavy metal frame, empty, fell down. The frame fell down. The entire house fell down. And in Cettina's head the land shook clear to its foundations, deep inside, and in turn as it shook, it crumbled, giving way, each landslide starting another one that tumbled deeper and deeper into her own viscera.

As the door closed behind the killers, Saveria started screaming. Without realizing it, without even hearing the sound of her own voice, Cettina yelled too. She was yelling, "Ma, oh Ma!" even though it was her father's body lying sideways in the hallway. Even though Cettina was sure that all her love was for her father, who took her to the café, and bought her rubber shoes. Because she was his favorite child, the child he could never deny, even though she was a girl, hardheaded and strange. *Scunchiuduta*, feckless girl, he'd say to make fun of her. But now she was yelling, "Ma, oh Ma!"

The room had filled with unusual smells, the smell of something burning, like the smell hanging in the street during the fireworks on July 2nd for Our Lady of Grace, and a different odor, repugnant, that seemed to rise from the body that was knocked to the ground, its head exploded in a pool of blood.

Suddenly Cettina heard her own voice and stopped yelling. She looked at her mother. She was standing stiff and still in the middle of the room. "In this home . . ." she murmured, with a strange offended look in her eyes, which never lit on her husband's body, but roamed over the shiny furniture, the new armchairs, in a resentful farewell. "In this home, cops . . ." she murmured again, barely moving her lips, as if in warning.

Cettina understood. Or she thought she understood. In any case, she didn't need to know anything else, and she immediately knew what she had to do. On Telecittà the girl was still singing. Cettina pressed the button and silence fell on the room, a silence that was unsettling and opened up a deep, painful emptiness in her chest. But there wasn't time to descend into that emptiness.

From the bottom of the bedroom closet, Cettina quickly pulled out the weapons, a hunting rifle—the usual twelve-gauge with sawed-off barrels—and a handgun. *Beautiful*, her thoughts strayed, turning it over in her hands. It was a high-powered gun, a nine-caliber model 84 Beretta, with a thirteen-round magazine. Well cared for, glistening with oil. She rolled it up in a shirt, instantly stained with oil, and stuck it in her school backpack. The rifle stuck out, but was well disguised under a multicolored layer of knit tops.

Returning to the living room she stopped in front of Francesco, who was stammering. His face streaked with tears, the little boy stared at her with furious concentration, turning purple as he was swept up in the effort to free at least a sound from his tight throat. He made her angry.

"We don't cry here," she told him harshly. "Get over there, go over there with Saveria."

She had to hurry. But going outside, crossing that threshold blocked by her father's body, was a terribly difficult operation. As much as she tried, her eyes couldn't manage to take in the whole scene and find a way to escape. She had to deceive her eye, forcing herself to focus on certain points, and glide over things ever so slightly on the surface. She had to move with the care of a person crossing a street full of mud. Small oases where she could step. She could let her eyes light there and only there. Eyes lowered and steady, also to keep herself from being caught in the red spiderweb that was expanding on the wall. She climbed over her father's legs without seeing them, even though she moved them with both her hands, just slightly, that little bit needed to open the door again and go out.

She immediately forgot that contact. Her mind refused to retain the sensation of that material—damp with rain? with blood?—on the palm of her hands.

Outside it had stopped raining. Cettina didn't look back. She didn't look toward the windows and balconies to figure out which ones had cracked open and which had remained closed. Taking slow steps, her shoulders bent under her heavy backpack, she set out toward her old street, toward her grandmother's house. She walked along and forbade herself any thoughts. But from that compressed pain, which she pushed with desperate strength into some remote part of her body, a strange, prodigious idea was emerging, one that almost comforted her.

From now on, she promised herself, *no one can call me Cettina again.*

THE SHUTTERS ARE LOWERED but the last rays of afternoon sunlight come in all the same and make the overcrowded room too hot.

I have given up on rummaging through the old man's memories, and now he's discussing medicine and prescriptions with Mimmo while his daughter silently continues rocking the baby. His wife stands up, leveraging herself with the table. She's not fat; she has a heavyset Mediterranean body. Her breasts are a shapeless bundle sagging down to what was once her waistline. She gathers up the dirty cups on the tray and goes back into the kitchen. I follow her. She sets the tray down next to the sink and turns around to welcome me. She seems happy for some reason of her own to have drawn me away from the men.

On the terrace that faces the back of the building, she shows me the landscape. The usual compact throng of illegal constructions fade seamlessly one into another. The top floors, empty and roofless, appear like erratic battlements, a fanciful, crooked profile like a witches' village. Below us, to the right, an open space with dirty, straggly grass, piles of garbage, and the carcass of a bus. Toward the sea line, an abandoned construction yard: two large skeletons of cement homes, already old, already in shambles, the nighttime meeting place for drug dealers and addicts.

"In our land things start well, and then fall through the cracks. They always fall through the cracks. What a shame. They started out as two beautiful buildings, and instead they're a disgrace. A danger. They left them half-built due to permit issues." Her voice fades into a whisper: "The *pizzo*, protection money, that wasn't paid . . ."

She isn't at a loss for words, now that we're alone. In fact, I get the idea that she was just waiting for this moment. She dries her hands on a dish towel. She folds it, lost in thought, clearly contemplating a delicate question. I lean on the railing. I'm not in a hurry. I can wait calmly, patiently, for her to make up her mind. Finally she asks me: "But why precisely Cettina? There are so many other stories, stories that are more . . ." She gropes, searching for the right word, the best for communicating her doubt. "Stories that are more worthy, that's it. She's not the only one whose father they killed."

That's not the question I anticipated, but she's right. I find myself agreeing with her. If that were what interested me, I would be spoiled for choice. Heaps of stories, mountains of stories, at my disposal. There's an abundance of little girls, female adolescents, and young women whose fathers and brothers have been killed. First the father and then the brother, a natural order for unnatural deaths. And each girl reacts in her own way.

The old man's wife folds the hems of the dish towel over and over again while she tells me stories. There's the one who becomes a collaborating witness. That's the term she uses. Not collaborator with justice, but collaborating witness, as used in the jargon of police reports and court transcripts. Yes, a lot of girls become collaborating witnesses and talk;

it's their unarmed reprisal. One of them, instead, got it in her head to join the police force. She wanted to submit the application for the admissions exam and had even gone to ask for the information. But her brother, one of the survivors, threatened her. A cop in the family, the worst disgrace of all. The police dissuaded her just as hastily.

"Because her aim was to kill. She wanted nothing else. Within the law, but she wanted to take revenge. Shielded by the law, but the only thing she was looking for was a vendetta."

The woman breaks off. "How's the vegetable garden doing?" she yells at a neighbor woman who's appeared behind the fence surrounding a little garden on the opposite side of the street.

"This year we have zucchini," the other woman yells back.

"We have a bit of greenery, some vegetable gardens here." Thin strips of land that take the place of sidewalks. "Well, then," she persists, smiling awkwardly, "why precisely Cettina?"

Of course, why precisely this story out of all of them? Is it because there's something in the protagonist's personality that touches a sensitive spot, a dark side of me, something I feel vibrating deep within me? Because it lets me venture into the extreme limits of my imagination? Because it's not a story of mourning, but of challenges? What I seem to discern is an excessive capacity for pride, a will to exist, to go beyond simply taking refuge from desperation.

But I still don't know how to give form to my emotion and a reason for my choice.

"I don't know," I answer honestly. The woman lowers her eyes and smooths out the dish towel again. Faced with her disappointment, the incredulity hidden in that automatic gesture intended to deflect the embarrassment, I try to suggest something: "Maybe because at a certain point Cettina became Tina."

GOING BACK TO THE Villaggio, toward Mimmo's home, we pass by the church. A light-colored box, anonymous, in sixties style like all the rest.

"Modern," Mimmo defines it. "Sometimes they come down here for ceremonies. There's no church in the Bronx." He shrugs. "No schools, no churches. They tried to scrape something together, in a stroke of imagination they put an altar inside a garage, but it didn't work. A garage . . . Now you tell me, who dreams of celebrating their child's baptism or getting married in a garage. Even so, there are some people thinking about sprucing it up. The parish priest doesn't like people from the Bronx coming down to the Villaggio. He said, 'I don't want them getting married here.' Those exact words. What do you expect, the image . . . He cares about the image of his church too," he quips.

He looks closely at me and suddenly asks, "So, was the visit useless?"

There's a strain of sincere anxiety in his voice, the fear of falling short of his precise duty of hospitality.

"I'm sorry. You didn't manage to loosen his lips for an impression or at least a piece of news, nothing new or that might be worth the effort . . ." He unexpectedly smiles. "Do you remember uncle Menico?" he says.

"Minicu," I correct him. "Minicu. Don't force yourself to translate everything all the time."

After all, I'm Sicilian too. Even if my Sicilian is like the dialect you hear spoken in Little Italy, in the streets of New York. A language that stopped short and no longer resonates, echoing within. But I don't need any translations. And how could I ever forget uncle Minicu, the character in our shared family legends? Besides that, and not by chance, Mimmo has the same name: Domenico.

Uncle Minicu's father had promised him, "I'll give you ten lire." Ten lire for every word that came out of his mouth.

"Well, sometimes he didn't even manage to get to fifty lire. In an entire day. Maybe he was going too far, but silence, as you know, is a well-known Sicilian pathology." Now he's burst out in hearty laughter. "Quite a project you've sought out for yourself. Have you forgotten that we speak through our eyes, never our mouth? I'm sorry, my poor cousin. How will you do it? How will you find the words for your book?"

CHAPTER 3

A mirage, a posting station in the middle of the desert, the miraculous outpost of modernity. Located practically outside of the town in a large piazza besieged by dust, the Motel Agip, like the Villaggio, was the tangible sign of the existence of the "other" world, yet at one's fingertips, with air-conditioned rooms and convenient telephone booths in the lobby.

Now the air conditioning works only every other day and the rooms are infested with mosquitos, as evidenced by the wall above my headboard, spattered by red flecks, the remaining traces of a ferocious nocturnal hunt. But it's still the only motel in Gela that is considered worthy of the title. Technicians and managers sent on missions to Petrolchimico stay here, along with politicians and journalists passing through. No tourists, because tourism doesn't exist in Gela. More precisely, it doesn't exist anymore.

MALE VOICES, NORTHERN ACCENTS. I hear nothing else in the entrance, in the wide area of the lobby and in the hallways. In the elevator and on the landings, I only run into weapons and uniforms. There are at least two hundred law enforcement agents staying in the motel on a permanent basis, with an entire floor reserved for themselves. Police officers, carabinieri, military personnel. Permanent guests. Sent down here as reinforcements with the aim of reestablishing public order in a town "where the laws of the Republic and the principles of the Constitution have not been in force for years," as Gerardo Chiaromonte, then president of the Antimafia, had to say already, back in 1989.

At noon, in the bar and at the restaurant, I meet judges, lawyers, collaborators with justice, along with their respective plainclothes bodyguards, and now and then the public prosecutor. Three years ago, after the umpteenth massacre—a settling of accounts between rival clans—the court Tribunal was finally instituted in Gela too. Judges and the military: that's the new tourism that is filling the rooms in the motel.

"But the only law that works is still the law of gravity." Upset, Ignazio sips his iced mint. "One murder per day in Sicily. We've reached averages in recent years that are worthy of Colombian drug trafficking."

So the State goes on the attack and sends its army to

disinfest the infected provinces. But what can the army do against unemployment, the crisis of Petrolchimico (the "cathedral in the desert" has been re-baptized "the mammoth, outlandish settlement"), or the public administration?

"And without work, roads, water, sewers, gyms, schools, hospitals, I ask myself how any kind of order could exist, or resist."

Ignazio's eyes glance away. Instead of meeting mine, they prefer to wander off in the distance or focus so hard on the shiny counter of the bar behind my shoulder that they look strangely crossed.

In contrast, I carefully study him. His bald, suntanned head disorients me. If I had met him in the street, I wouldn't have recognized him. He was very young, back then. Just a boy, not very outgoing, who frequented the Communist youth federation and distrustfully listened to my all-too-radical, uncompromising criticisms, so extreme they went beyond all reality.

Those were the years of political migrations. There were many missionaries who came down to preach on the island, on the industrial oasis of Gela. The leftist Lotta Continua, Potere Operaio, they were all here. Trying to rob militants who drifted from one group to the other, never fully convinced, never won over once and for all.

I remember Ignazio, wise in debates and immune to revolutionary outbursts, so quick to flare and common in those times. Ignazio was wise and suspicious.

Now, I still feel his opposition, if not exactly hostility. He's sitting uncomfortably on the edge of the chair, as if he were keeping himself ready to jump to his feet and run away at any moment. A precarious position that reveals his scant, wavering helpfulness. Even his body seems contracted in a kind of deaf resistance that I don't understand at this point. We're off to a bad start, I think, my own body stiffening too, without my wishing it to.

"Why in the world didn't you stay at your uncle's house? Why are you staying here?" He questions me in a brusque, inquisitorial manner, pointing at the bar and the reception counter, barely visible beyond the glass doors.

"It's more comfortable for me. I'm freer."

It's true, that's how it is. The hospitality in my uncle's family home is too confining. A return to ancient constraints that would have prevented me from working, I'm sure of it, forcing my mind toward other, more private obsessions. And perhaps even for the aged teacher my presence, in this phase of life, proves cumbersome. Getting old also means settling into the fully experienced rhythms of everyday life, and impatience toward everything that doesn't form part of one's domestic habits. Naturally, my uncle extended the offer of hospitality, but didn't insist too much. Naturally, I declined with an acceptable excuse, almost the truth. "I have to work, I need concentration." Appearances are safe. Emotions? Who knows. But my uncle is too old by now to allow himself resentments and too much of an adult to fall into devastating traps.

Ignazio doesn't accept my explanation. "A motel is more comfortable?" he retorts with a hint of skeptical malevolence.

"I like it," I reply. "I like living in a motel. If I were rich, I'd always live in one."

Only now it comes to mind that when I asked him to meet me, he didn't invite me to his home, which would be normal among old friends. That was the first sign of hostility that I didn't give due weight. In fact, I felt a wave of relief. Both of us preferred that this appointment would be impersonal, not very demanding. A concession, on his part, made out of politeness, in the memory of an old acquaintance. Or for what other prudent reason? At which point in the past we shared did this acrimonious detachment, seemingly unalleviated by the passing years, begin?

But I don't want to renew a friendship, I tell myself, repressing a surge of resentment. Today what interests me about him is his job. Ignazio is a school physician. It's in that capacity that he had interactions with Tina and her brother. And who could know better than he those children who go from elementary school right to the streets, where they grow up among thefts, robberies, and trafficking? The same children from whom Cosa Nostra chooses its future soldiers, bringing them up and training them in a school that is much more demanding than any State school.

The area where Ignazio lives is like a fort under siege. I randomly tick off items for him while fishing back in my memory: arson attacks, assaults in classrooms, armored security doors to stem the violence. I don't need any notes to remember. At the elementary school in the Margi district, three unknown suspects held the teachers and janitors hostage for half an hour. They wanted to settle accounts with a prior offender who worked there, employed by the city. To say nothing of little children who went to school as if they were going off to war, with a handgun in their backpack or tucked inside the belt of their pants.

"Am I remembering correctly? It's all true. Right?"

"In some cases, it could be," reluctantly admits Ignazio. I have the sharp sensation that he regrets his initial outburst, the allusion to that "force of gravity" that makes men and boys drop on the streets of Gela, like fruit over-ripened in the sun. "Oh, God, yes," he continues. "But one mustn't exaggerate. And then, it's always a question of point of view."

"What do you mean by point of view? Either it's true or it isn't."

In his glass, the mint has an unreal emerald density. Quenching one's thirst with this thick artificial green liquid is a habit that through the years has been left untouched by change. I still have its distant taste on my tongue, a gluish film sweeter than almond milk. I could never drink even a sip of it again.

Ignazio is playing with his glass, tightening his fingers around it, passing it from one hand to the other. He keeps on avoiding my eyes. He finally bursts out, "But you! First you go away and then you come back just to tell these stories? Why's it necessary?"

That's it, then. I should have understood. The same old business: going away means betraying. And people who betray lose their right to speak. To abandon Sicily equals choosing a kind of exile from which you don't return. The root of suspicion and separation lies in my transitoriness, in my ambiguous nomadism. What necessity did I have to go away? At this point irritation gets the best of me.

"Oh, yes, you don't like that I tell stories about violence. It hurts the image of Sicily," I say, shifting to counterattack. "And what should I talk about instead?" An anger that I wasn't aware I harbored inside makes my voice rise unintentionally. This time I don't feel like justifying myself, offering reassuring explanations. "About Sicilianicity, the Greeks and Normans? Or else about granitas, the pignolata pastry of Messina, marzipan fruits and vegetables, or the flagellants of Holy Week . . . Are these the stories I have permission to tell? Tell me. Come on, out with it. You tell me what I should talk about. What can I talk about without offending the Sicilian soul?"

Ignazio's face is a mask of hard indignation.

I add, somewhat treacherously, "Weren't you the one who knew how to look straight at reality?"

"Reality . . ." Caught up in my same emotion, Ignazio finally looks straight at *me*. And he laughs. "Sh-sh," he hisses. "Lower your voice."

Little by little I calm down too. The tension has dissolved.

"But sure. Maybe you're right. It's a question of point of view," I concede. However, I don't renounce making one thing clear: "My point of view is from the inside, Ignazio. I'm not an outsider." I persist with proud obstinacy, "I'm not from somewhere else."

I won't let him or anyone else treat me like a stranger to this land. And I'm not part of the ever-growing flock of pilgrims who set out in search of their mythic roots, either. I'm not a Black woman from America who returns to Africa to search for her origins and then upon arriving at her forebears' original point of departure, the longed-for source, realizes that the life there does not naturally become her own.

"This place is mine as much as yours."

Our lives—mine, his, and also Tina's, apparently so dissimilar—extend along the same coordinates of space and time. Even if at times the margins of my personal, private space don't coincide with theirs.

Now, my touchy friend sighs.

"It's that I'm sick and tired of hearing Gela described like a Wild West. All those 'screamer' headlines . . . I'm tired of being told I live in shit."

He sighs again, looking at the restaurant table where the strong young men in the bodyguard units, the men belonging to the Tribunal, and a shopkeeper who filed a police report against the extortion racket are already sitting down for lunch.

"TEACHING IS SOMETHING ELSE altogether," says Ignazio. "You can get some results, perhaps. You've been a teacher, so you can judge better than I can. On the other hand, I know I have an impossible task. Working as a school physician, in these conditions, is the most frustrating job in the world."

Our table is somewhat isolated, in the corner that's used as a café. Nevertheless, it's as if we were in the middle of a piazza. Quick glances of furtive curiosity alight on us, lap over us, and slip away, then return, slightly more insistent, to size us up, pigeonhole us.

"How can I fight, all alone, against tuberculosis? Diseases of the past, we'd say, and instead . . ."

All of a sudden he seems to become aware of the curiosity—mild, discreet and nevertheless implacable—that besieges us. He grimaces with annoyance. He moves his chair closer and lowers his voice, as if he had to tell me who knows what kind of secret.

"I can't help getting mixed up in matters that aren't part of my job, taking initiatives that aren't up to me. At school we have a social worker. I should leave things to her. Instead, if I know the families, sooner or later I take an interest, I go talk with them. What do you expect, it's a difficult vice to shake." He sniggers. "I have the heroic soul of an irredeemable communist. So I throw myself into these feats of . . . what would you call it? . . . of civilization." He's goading me, but with benevolent irony, no rancor. "The stories I could tell you . . . Like the time with the woman butcher's son. 'My' woman butcher."

Her little boy wouldn't talk at school, couldn't socialize. So one day Ignazio makes up his mind and goes to see the mother right in her shop, a butcher shop located downtown: a huge knife sitting on the counter and five chickens dangling head down from hooks. On the other side of the street, the little boy is unloading something.

"And what the fuck do you want?" she says as a greeting.

He explains the situation a bit, trying to play it down.

In a fury she rips off her apron and goes to plant herself in the middle of the street, hands on her hips, yelling at her son:

"You wretched kid! Tonight I'll have your brother kill you. Tonight I'll carve up your legs like a chicken. You're failing at school cuz you don't talk. But you were talking at the fair, wretched boy. You were talking, cuz you got me to buy you shoes."

Ignazio shakes his unrecognizable bald head. "I could tell you so many things, stories . . . But what's the use?"

I could give him an answer. What's the use of stories if not to find the threads that compose single lives, to identify the sign that distinguishes each one in the great overall picture? What else, if not this? That's also what I would have told him twenty years ago. It was our way of talking. Our style.

Now I'm not interested in wasting time in philosophical exchanges, in vaguely exhibitionist verbal competitions. I have a precise objective, a single aim: to get inside Tina's life, reconstructing it piece by piece.

So I prefer to steer the conversation back to the pre-established track and return pedantically, diligently, to the subject of our meeting.

"Tell me about Tina," I prod him, cutting off any digressions. "Since when have you known her?"

"Since she was born. And her family too, and her grandmother . . . a longtime communist. To be more precise, in elections she gave us her vote. She was the daughter of a sulfur mine worker, a tradition that runs in the blood forever. She'd also come to the party headquarters to have paperwork explained, things of that sort. With regard to the rest, no scruples. She lives by receiving stolen goods. At least that's what people say. She was the one who trained her grandchildren to pull off robberies. Without admitting anything, one time she said to me: 'I have the right to get by too, don't I?'"

"The kids went back to her house, to live with her in her basement apartment . . ."

"And where else could they go?" Ignazio interrupts me. "Their father ending up that way, and their mother disappearing right after. Maybe in Milan, staying with a sister, to find work. Then she reappeared and got together with a traveling salesman. She lives with him in one of those illegal homes, in Settefarine."

So the glue holding together the family is the grandmother; she maintains the ties, the matriarch, the everyday point of reference. It's from her, probably, that Tina gets that domineering will to put herself at the center of everything. Or is it a spontaneous germination instead, an unexpected, surprising fruit?

"A terrible old lady, easily offended. A *cumannera*." Ignazio smiles. "*Scumannìa, scumannìa*." He stresses the accent on that by-product of the verb *to command*. Coined specifically, it would seem, to indicate the domestic tyranny of women, who can't access the tragic gravity that in Sicily is attributed to being in command.

"Everybody has a sacred fear of her. One time Francesco, the little boy, got lice. They ask me at school, what can we do, how can we tell that woman that her grandson has lice? Maybe she'll take it as an offence, she could imagine that we're accusing her of being dirty, who can tell her? In short, I go to see her. I go into that basement apartment where they're living on top of each other and I don't really know where to start. In the end, then and there, I manage to invent an excuse. I said the teacher didn't wash her hair and so she'd *mischiato*, spread them to the kids. So she says: Jesus, my grandson too? Because don't you see, she goes, how *brillato* my grandson is, so sparkling clean?"

In those days, Tina had stopped going to school. And Francesco didn't last long either.

"Something happened, a terrible thing that's still unclear. We never figured it out. And immediately afterward Francesco stopped coming to school. A coincidence? I don't know. But everyone—the principal, teachers, janitors—preferred to hush up the matter. Stupid kid stuff. Even though perhaps, given how things played out . . .”

IT WAS A FULL-BLOWN commando that showed up one Tuesday morning, around eleven o'clock, right in front of the elementary school's main door, standing wide open as usual, facing the little street that turns and descends toward the waterfront. A real commando, even though none of its members was over four feet tall.

There were four of them. One stood guard outside the entrance. Certainly a little boy standing at the elementary school door didn't attract attention.

Tina did practically all the work. For her accomplices it was an exciting pastime, but for her it was a vendetta, premeditated, organized, and planned.

“No more school. I'll handle it. I'll prepare a beautiful farewell, a beautiful thank you party,” she'd told Francesco, silencing his stammered words about punishments, bad grades, harsh words.

The teacher ridiculed him: “You can't come into the classroom wearing an earring.” His schoolmates called him 'u maccarruni, macaroni, because he struggled to get to the end of a sentence; old as he was, already nine, he couldn't pass the second grade.

While Tina walked all the way down the street that Tuesday, she was aware of the weight she carried tucked inside her belt. It was the first time that she'd gone out with the nine-caliber that had belonged to her father. Three years since his death and she hadn't let one day go by without practicing with the weapon that she considered her inheritance, jealously her own. She was perfectly familiar with it by then, she'd gained confidence handling it. The Beretta trembled, heavy in her little girl's hand despite the light alloy. But she had kept on training tenaciously. She would grip it as high as possible, the back of the handle between her thumb and index finger. Then there was aiming the gun, aiming with it unloaded and sometimes—not always, for fear of ruining the mechanisms—firing empty shots. Finally, she'd return to the first position, learning to control her muscles. She liked the handgun better than the shotgun, because she could hold it tight and feel it was her own as her fist closed tightly around it.

Every two or three days she cleaned it. She closed the door to the apartment, turned on the lights, and took it carefully apart on the table. Using the special gun brush, she lubricated the barrel, dried it, running another brush in and out, over again, then she re-applied clean oil. She never forgot to polish the smooth grips, with no grooves.

"Still at this stuff," her grandmother protested distractedly, shelling beans for their dinner.

Finally the Tuesday of the reckoning arrived. Tina walked along, carrying the by then familiar weight under her canvas jacket, while a light residue of lubricant on the gun grip dampened her t-shirt, then slid down, tickling her buttocks.

She remembered her father's shirts, always stained too, with an oily ring on the back. The memory made her skin more sensitive, while drops of sweat thickened as they mixed with the oil and slid down with a quick, indecisive touch of a caress.

The belt holding the holster was too stiff, and pressed against her stomach. A surge of nausea filled her throat. Was it fear? She wondered about it indifferently, without apprehension. She swallowed and lifted her chin, brazen, quickening her steps.

Ever since she had left the home in the Bronx, climbing over her father's legs, Tina had been impervious to emotions. Her heart was beating hard, but its pounding didn't reach her head. Her armpits were sweating, but it was like suddenly turning on a faucet, an automatic reaction that doesn't produce anxiety. Fear assailed her body, but her brain didn't register it. Tina was living with entirely numbed emotions.

The janitor yawned, bored. But his yawn stopped short and his eyes, still watering, shot wide open in front of the nine-caliber that the little boy suddenly pulled out from behind his back with a smooth movement that seemed right out of a textbook. Now he was holding it with both hands, arms held out straight, legs slightly apart.

Maccarruni, to my brother, Tina thought triumphantly, standing in front of the janitor's blanched face. She was delighted with her skill, the weapon's success, her clothes and her hair, cut like a boy's. The janitor certainly couldn't imagine that the person pointing the gun at him was a girl. A great advantage. A sure way to muddy the waters, make identification difficult. Everyone notices a female and remembers her. A male among males, though . . . The deception gave her a wonderful sense of invincibility.

"Get walking," she ordered in an even, childish voice.

She already knew the techniques well: never rest the weapon against the adversary's body. Taking care to not get too close to the man, to avoid unpredictable reactions, she forced him to walk in front of her clear to the classroom where Francesco's teacher was.

"I was looking a 'ttia, just for you," she said. She thought it was a good catchphrase. The gun was becoming heavy in her eleven-year-old hands, but she didn't notice, she didn't have a tremor (only afterward, her wrist hurt for a few days, as if she had punched someone).

She made a gesture with her chin, and her eyes gave an order. It was their turn now.

Her two companions undid their pants, calmly settled in their places, and pissed on the teacher's desk. When they finished, they treated themselves to a beautiful sigh of satisfaction. Once they zipped up their pants, they grabbed the grade book. The class didn't say a word; only one little girl couldn't hold back a nervous little laugh, caused more by the exhibition than fear, and covered her mouth with her hands right away. They took the grade book and rubbed it really well, page after page, in the puddle and slow rivulets of piss.

"A childish act of bravado. But I should have thought of her, about Tina. I should have taken an interest later, when people started saying it had been her. Rumors, nothing but rumors, there was never anything certain in the matter. But that act of defacement, so determined, so well organized. The severity of the intentions was already clear."

Ignazio was really racking himself over about it, torturing himself for his presumed responsibility, his lack of attention.

A soft but constant ringing of cell phones reaches us from the other restaurant tables. Everyone, lawyers, judges, bodyguards, with their cell phones always working, always turned on. Real background music.

"But how do these people live?" Ignazio's mind suddenly strays, with the intimate murmur of a friend. And yet it doesn't come spontaneously to me—not even now that contact has been reestablished—to think of him as a friend I've really found again. An instinctive caution remains, a distrust that I sense with every fiber beneath my skin, always ready to resurface. "Sure, when you get used to it . . . It comes naturally to adapt to life's turning points, follow their curves. All considered, I've adapted too," he says. And his voice turns rough with bitterness. I assume a questioning look.

"Just thinking about the mortgage for our home," he clarifies with a grimace that spreads up from his lips to wrinkle his head. "About the mortgage, my work schedule, parents who are getting older, living like this, without ever going outside of family relations, outside of a closed world that seems so protective. Then it happens that they kill someone or someone else demands money from you or your wife or your father-in-law, and then suddenly you discover that you're alone and defenseless."

"What is this," I intimate, "nostalgia for politics?"

"No. I wasn't cut out for politics, not me. Social commitment is something else. And in my own way . . . I've remained faithful to it. However . . ."

"Tina never adapted," I murmur. She didn't adapt to poverty and contempt. To anything that fate held for her. Not even her breasts that grew too fast and needed to be hidden under the tightest bindings because they amounted to a sign of odious vulnerability.

I have a flash of intuition. I seem to have reached the point of touching the secret cipher, the impulse pushing me to get into Tina's story.

It's this inability to adapt—total, absolute—that attracts me. This excess of negation—of her own destiny and her own body—that ultimately becomes a dangerous strength, unknown and exorbitant. This attracts me. But is it on this indefinable and slippery ground that our confrontation will play out? Because it's clear that, sooner or later, a confrontation will have to take place. That's the reason I came back here, for a face-to-face encounter that I can't even imagine. I still have to figure out how to unlock her life. And in the meanwhile, invent a language. Gestures, words, that can be a bridge between me and her.

"It's hard, you know, to talk with Tina. She starts laughing. It's her way of communicating. They'd arrest her, take her to the station, and from her, nothing, she wouldn't answer. She'd burst out laughing and keep on that way, with that teasing laugh. She would wait for them to put their hands on her and when they realized . . . then she really laughed with satisfaction. She liked that moment, when they became aware of the misunderstanding and discovered they had a little girl, a woman, on their hands, and they found themselves in a fix, they didn't know what to do anymore. Her sex became a weapon to play against the cops."

THAT'S HOW THE NEWSPAPERS discovered her. The police had thrown her in a cell with three boys, an entire night in a holding cell with those three males, and the morning after, when the scandal came out in front of the lawyer, she triumphed. She was literally triumphant in the face of the shock, embarrassment, and confusion of her jailers. That moment—that moment of the discovery—gave her a strong taste for a euphoria that harbored something terrible.

The newspapers had dedicated a lot of space to that event, and from there they went back to build her story. A little fourteen-year-old girl, the daughter of a murdered boss, now the head of a band of very young boys, manual laborers in crime, at the service of one of the city's mafia clans. A piece of news that was worth the honors of the national news and some women's magazines.

I scrupulously searched for and read all of the articles written in that period. They certainly don't offer the key to Tina's dark world, but some features of her personality come through in these first rushed portraits.

To begin with, her attitude toward journalists reveals an unusual ambivalence: unusual for her environment and for the typical mafia "discretion." In front of photographers, she'd run off in a frenzy and refuse interviews, then let herself become involved anyway. She feigned scorn and indifference, but then she'd throw out some joke, become curious, and get caught up in the relationship with the interviewer.

In one case, to refuse the interview, she explained with unexpected, disconcerting shyness, "My social worker doesn't want me to," referring to the assistant at the juvenile prison in Caltanisetta who was following her case at that time. Good. That sad notoriety wasn't good for her; it fed her exhibitionism, her excessive, impossible thirst for affirmation.

But at the end of every interview, conceded or torn up, carried out to the very end or sharply interrupted, she always asked, like a good obedient little girl, "Now can I go?"

The boys, her friends, her presumed followers in the gang, were more reticent. The journalists tried to provoke them. "Is it true Tina is the boss? She's the one who gives the orders?"

"What do we know about this stuff," the little boys rallied in defense. So impassive that you felt like grabbing them by their bony, adolescent shoulders and shaking them. But at times, they added, with hard, surly faces, "No one takes orders from a girl."

But what was Tina like, at fourteen years old? Who was she, really?

"A MALE, TO PERFECTION."

Ignazio doesn't have any doubts. Not only for the way she dressed, like a man. Not only for that maniacal, morbid attachment to symbols of masculinity.

"She drove like a maniac, first the motor scooter and then powerful motorcycles and big cars."

And not even for the constraints that she submitted her body to. Rather, it was precisely for her obsession with commanding others and respect. Not the respect a woman can expect from a man—that's tradition—but respect like men mean it. And that means fear.

"Tina grew up with her brother, with her cousins, with boys her age or a little younger. But little girls grow up before little boys. They're already adults before the boys have left childhood. In a very natural, casual way, Tina found herself ruling over the kids she had grown up with. She brought her little gang along with her into the adult world. And this fact gave her power over older kids too, sixteen- and seventeen-year-olds, already introduced to organized crime."

It's a simple explanation, a convincing one. I think about Tina's laughing eyes, in the photo, eyes that open up to us and then escape, that make fun of us and all our certainties.

CHAPTER 4

"One of the first things we did, as soon as we arrived, was the school census, in order to document truancy. Sky-high."

The captain is wearing civilian clothes, sitting behind his desk, and seems more like an ambitious young manager than a carabiniere. His voice has the dry and precise, measured and eloquent tone that entrenched, commonplace ideas attribute to people who are used to expounding strategies and numbers to a company's board of directors.

When I'd arrived at the station, I'd crossed the inner courtyard and gone down a dusty, shabby corridor, just like one imagines the corridors in carabinieri stations and, in general, all of the places only men inhabit. As I was stepping through the office doorway I caught sight of a quick flick of the wrist, a glance at his watch. Perhaps an involuntary gesture, but it immediately made me deeply aware of my error. Putting my trust in quite approximate Southern Italian timing, I arrived late for the appointment. And this efficient, professional behavior of his now starts me off on the wrong foot, puts me irremediably in the wrong.

"It's the truant children, really young boys—little children the schools have lost—recruited for the younger criminal generation," the captain explains. For me, his imperturbable courtesy is the most effective reproach. "The census, filing complaints against negligent parents, can be useful as an act of prevention. It's a necessary action. And it gets some results. Recently there's been a slight, very slight drop."

I don't need to press him, or to devise who knows what kind of tricky questions in order to get an answer. The captain likes talking about his work, his way of operating. He does it methodically, in a direct yet balanced manner typical of people who know the importance of words and reciprocal understanding, people who, based on experience, know which difficult but essential steps must be taken in order to make themselves understood by their listener.

"Truancy . . . It's a cultural problem, in the sense of common social values. What use is it to study, if studying doesn't give you any prospects or money?" He stares at me as if checking my ability to understand his reasoning.

"The huge change was in the seventies. It happened with the important contracts and drugs, and for the first time, the concrete, immediate possibility of becoming rich, immensely rich." A pause. "If you're skillful and determined and ruth-less enough," he clarifies. "And money is the measure of your abilities. The measure of everything. The value par excellence—money. But it's also the game that attracts kids, the passage into the adult world. It's this more than anything, I believe, for the really young boys: the exciting sensation of entering the world of adults."

This young captain who talks as if he had a clear picture, a perfectly legible reality in front of him, piques my curi-osity. His voice, lacking any recognizable accent, and the cold, restrained passion in his eyes, unequivocally Southern Italian, make me curious, and I tell him so.

"I was born in Sicily," he confirms. But he lived and studied in the north. Like me, like so many.

"To be born in Sicily is a fact . . . of strategic importance," he asserts, joking. "I catalogued—you know, we have this sort of mania of documenting, recording, cataloguing, an occupational hazard—as I was saying, I catalogued Sicilians into three classes." He stops for a moment to organize his remarks, and then launches in:

"First, there are the Sicilians of Sicily. The ones who don't move even in an earthquake. Or, if they're really forced to move—and God knows how many of them have been forced—they dream only of returning to their 'homeland' to finish their lives. Perhaps only in our times Sicilians of Sicily really exist, the indigenous survivors, the ones who man-aged to escape a destiny of emigration. Then there are the

Sicilians abroad. They're the ones who adapt immediately to any place they're cast into. Or rather, they try to get inside the host society, to integrate. With the curious pretension of maintaining, of course, their own traditions. These people don't forget, but they don't have regrets. And finally there are the Sicilians in exile. The eternal nostalgics. Always fleeing from their very own nostalgia."

A real fire of excitement, of joyful amusement, dances in his eyes. "I define myself as a Sicilian in exile. That's why I came down here willingly. I thought I could do something for Sicily. I didn't know Sicily, in fact, but it was familiar. The most familiar place for me. It was a return I desired."

I nod in a spontaneous rush of affection and understanding. I recognize in him my own feelings. The errant Sicilian. The diaspora and the promised island, the land of our respective missions. To leave and return. A perennial oscillation, our secret vice.

For what other reason would I be here digging into a story that's so desperately Sicilian? For what else if not for this unutterable fantasy, for this perverse, romantic obstinacy of mine to consider myself in a land of exile wherever I am? A heartfelt myth that only the "exiled" can recognize, unknown to the "Sicilians of Sicily" as the captain says. For those who escaped the diaspora, belonging is a given, not a choice.

I tell myself, these aren't the days of emigration but of

mobility; the memory and feelings of exile lie only in the restlessness of people who live elsewhere.

"You thought you could do something for Sicily . . ." Sitting in my caned chair, I lean forward on the desk, as if to lessen the distance. And I slowly return to his words. "Why are you talking about it in the past tense? You 'thought.' Don't you think that anymore now?"

"I lost," he sharply pronounces, while his dark eyes again assume their habitual seriousness. "I know I have lost. To the bureaucracy, to . . ." He hesitates, for the first time, leaving his words hanging in the air. Then, curtly, "I consider myself defeated."

Yet he doesn't say it in the tone of someone who's defeated, but with a lucid, determined anger.

"But we've achieved some successes. The heads of the clans are in jail or relocated in other parts of the country. The adults are all in prison. That's why the recruiting happens among the really young kids. In Gela there's certainly no lack of them, thirty-five thousand minors out of eighty thousand inhabitants, more or less. Living in conditions of extreme poverty."

From his expression I realize that the subject is deeply important to him.

"The dire poverty that exists, we see it, we touch it, you could say. In our work conducting searches, we see how they live, what they eat. Then maybe in a basement apartment downtown, under an armoire, inside an old purse, we find one hundred million lire. Wrapped up in handkerchiefs knotted together at the corners, like the peasants used to do in the old days. Family savings, they're capable of maintaining. What nerve! Truly enviable!"

The shutters on the big window facing the station's inner courtyard are closed. The room is lit by electric lights, even though outside the hot sun of the early afternoon is beating down. But not even a wisp of heat reaches inside. The cold light of the lamp even makes me shiver.

"There's one thing that troubles me," confesses the captain. "These children's awareness that their lives are marked. They become hardened, deadened, turn into statues of salt. It's not resignation. It's something worse. Something that makes giving and getting violence seem as if it were a normal event, expected, foreseen. At eighteen, even younger, they're already set on this path, with resigned determination . . ."

The telephone sitting on the laminated surface of the desk rings. The captain lifts the receiver and listens, and while listening his body visibly stiffens, a veiled, scarcely restrained irritation seeming to invade him little by little, becoming palpable in the room's suddenly tense, bristling atmosphere.

"It's not just me saying that. That's the law, Major. The law." But he immediately turns silent, listens again, and in the end: "At your orders." He has the brusque tone of someone forced to give in. It must be clear to everyone; he's not surrendering, he's retreating only in the face of the inevitable. The conversation is over.

He looks at me with a faraway air. He suddenly picks up the phone again and pushes a button.

"Don't put anyone through anymore. Say I'm busy, say I'm not here, that you can't find me, say . . ."

Someone knocks, a shadow silhouetted behind the glass door. The captain ignores it and turns toward me again. But for a moment his repressed rage overflows and he reproaches me sharply:

"And you . . . You could have come earlier, you could have been punctual."

The shadow wavers behind the glass, trembles, and disappears. The captain takes a deep breath. His tight fist resting on the desk loosens, and relaxes. Courtesy, a trait that appears natural to him, again prevails. His dark-skinned face, with regular, fine features, is naturally courteous, his voice polite. A courteousness that the habit of self-control probably reinforces and governs.

The captain smiles to put the flare-up into perspective and starts talking again as if nothing had happened.

"Just recently we arrested a minor who was hiding almost half a kilo of pure heroin in his bedroom. Pure heroin, do you realize? The storage place for a big operation. And if minors are also in the big operations now . . ."

This is what's really new in the last few years. The spread of common criminality, of "street thugs with no rules and no honor," as they're disdainfully defined by the mafiosi. Not amateurs, but professionals who frighten even Cosa

Nostra. The competition is becoming too fierce and too widespread.

Over time, the bosses of Cosa Nostra have always alternated between two strategies for dealing with the common gangs: cooptation or repression. But in recent years repression has become extermination. The men drop dead and boys take their place at ever younger ages. A state of affairs that has its advantages, naturally. The really young boys cost little, they'll work for a few lire. And they're loyal. The loyalty of the really young ones is amazing. But now that they've gotten involved, strange things never seen before have started happening in the gangs. Destabilizing.

It's Cosa Nostra's rule to officially affiliate only men as sworn in members. We know this. It's in the factual evidence. Belonging to the male sex is one of the necessary requisites for being admitted into the organization. The statements of *pentiti*, mafiosi who turn state's evidence, weren't necessary for knowing that the mafia system is a men's system, though they did confirm it. In contrast, in the growing number of gangs that are outside Cosa Nostra, in this dusting of petty criminals, it happens that even some women make their way, and assume the importance and role of a boss. It's a shocking fact. A subversion of principles and rules that risks overflowing, even touching the impregnable fortress of Cosa Nostra.

"Very rare cases," the captain informs me. "But they're already the sign of a change, of a troubling evolution. Tina, for example. Tina *'a masculidda*, the little tomboy." His eyes shine with renewed interest. "She lived here nearby, downtown."

DEEP SHADOWS, HOUSES MADE from white stone that hide inner courtyards and crooked alleys. This is downtown Gela. Moist city walls that curve into arched doors or windows, and still harbor a veiled torpor, an entirely southern charm, despite the decay, the dilapidated buildings, the filth. Slightly elevated above the street, encircled by the light-colored cordon that marks its perimeter, sits the old fish shop, with its smooth marble counters and solid grates that separate and expose it at the same time, seeming almost like an aviary.

In a small street off to the side of the fish shop, a massive portal conceals a vast cement courtyard, with the carabiniere station standing at the very end.

Tina *'a masculidda* was always at odds with the carabinieri most of all. They were her natural adversaries because of the proximity of their respective spaces, more than anything else. This was *her* territory. Her grandmother's basement apartment opened onto one of those blind alleys, in an open space you entered by passing under an arch, the real door to the home. In those streets it came easy to her to invent a skill, organize her first jobs, carry out her first robberies. She specialized in traveling salespeople. She got them in her sights, followed them, identified their car, and during the lunch hour, while they entertained their clients in some restaurant, or stuffed themselves to keep the melancholy of the job at bay, she broke their car windows and seized their collection of samples. Francesco *'u maccarruni* acted as lookout.

The station didn't represent a threat, but an obstacle, an annoying blemish on the landscape. More than a danger, a personal challenge. They were disagreeable, those carabinieri, right there a stone's throw away. Nevertheless, they gave her more motivation to put herself to the test, to sharpen her abilities and compete with them to see who was more agile.

By then Tina could recognize the smell of an officer a thousand miles away. She wasn't fooled by the wrinkled jeans, shirts left unbuttoned at the collar, gold necklaces and sneakers with untied laces, imposed by the latest fashion. That smell of cops bothered her, but just the same she didn't move on, didn't abandon her territory. Too risky to step outside of it. There was always the danger of straying into territories controlled by others without realizing it, or robbing someone untouchable. More than one boy had died because of offending someone, for a simple, banal purse snatching that knocked some boss's mother, wife, or granddaughter to the ground. Ignorance is not allowed. Exactly like the laws of the State. Whoever makes a mistake pays even if they're unaware they've made it.

So Tina, while waiting for a promotion or permission to move beyond the boundaries, didn't go outside her neighborhood's protected space except to show off on her motor scooter, the first one, bought from a blackmailer and repaired at a friend's shop. She actually had fun lolling on the motor scooter's seat while parked on the side of the street near the carabinieri station.

Besides, what else was there to do? Between each robbery and exhibition on the seat of her motor scooter, time dragged. Long empty hours alternated with short, intense minutes. A desert of sensations. A prolonged vigil. And then the overexcitement of hitting the target. Her body was like a weapon left loaded for too long and then emptied in just one shot. Loaded and then empty. Loaded and empty. Wasn't there a risk that in the end it might jam?

Then Tina would go to plant herself over by the carabinieri station. Just because. Simply to challenge herself more than anyone else. Now and then someone would stop to ask her: "What are you doing?"

"I'm passing the time, aren't I?" With that look of bored arrogance.

"THREE," EXPLAINS THE CAPTAIN, "there are three phases, stages, passages for moving up inside a gang. At first the little boy is used for attacks, as manual labor for acts of intimidation. In the second phase he advances to extortion. He collects the *pizzo* payments, threatens those who are reluctant to pay, and sometimes even has the power to set the prices and deadlines for payments. Finally, if he has talent—because even in this business a sort of talent is needed—he can make the leap. With the passage into this last category, he has to make himself available for any crime, including murder. But affiliation with the mafia is another thing altogether, the selection more careful."

The same identical procedure, the same mechanisms of inclusion and exclusion that operate in any company; besides professionalism, references and the right contacts are needed. Not everybody has the necessary qualifications and the right connections. It's logical that in Cosa Nostra the barriers are extremely rigid. For example, when men of honor, as mafiosi call themselves, are killed by mafia orders, their sons can't become members. The son would have the right to know the names of the father's killers, so the fear is that the temptation to carry out a vendetta might tear the organization apart.

"What about Tina?. . ."

"For Tina I don't believe the problem was ever raised. She's a woman, excluded from the start. At least from formal affiliation. In terms of her participation, though—real, concrete activity . . . Tina was already inside ever since she was little. And once they've entered, males or females, getting out of the circle is impossible. There's no way back. Those who try are killed by their own friends. The numbers of cemeteries of victims of *lupara bianca* we've discovered! The victims are murdered, but without leaving any traces of a body. Because for these deals a shocking, spectacular murder isn't worth it. Except for some particular executions it's not worth it in any case, *lupara bianca* is better, it doesn't raise social alarm."

The captain has a rushed way of presenting things. He

doesn't leave me many openings. He forces me to follow him into the inland deserts of the high plains, drags me through annihilating, monotonous moors. Unwilling, I reluctantly follow him across rocky mountain ranges, along steep paths that even the goats despise. There's nothing there, just heat and boulders and dirt that crumbles in the dry stream beds.

And nothing remains of the bodies crammed into rubber tires and burned for a long time, a very long time.

"Except, sometimes, a belt buckle, half a shoe," remarks the captain.

My thoughts fly irresistibly to Tina. How can a young girl, barely older than a child, cope with the thought of such a definitive punishment? What did she cut off inside herself? What impulses did she have to yield to in order to accept even the mere idea of such a penalty?

Despite my dry throat, I'm assailed by the irrepressible desire to take a drag of a cigarette. There aren't any ashtrays on the desk, nor on the small table beside the door. I vainly peek behind the heaps of papers, documents, and neatly stacked forms. It's clear. The captain doesn't smoke. Though my search was fruitless, I fish into my purse for a pack of Camels and take a cigarette out. My gesture produces an effect.

The captain breaks off speaking as he follows my hand, stands up, carefully picks his way behind me, and opens the window.

I squint, my eyes grazed by a ray of sunshine.

That same incinerating sun that turns the inland country-side white. Just a few out-of-the-way farmhouses sit in that desolate vast space, kept under control by clans of shepherds, animated only by the shootouts during clashes or raids led by young killers who learn to fire their weapons from moving motorcycles.

"We do nothing but shoot, in this country. Any occasion is good. In conflicts but also hunting, at parties . . . A country that loves gunfights, in war and peace."

In one of those farmhouses, Peppino *'u cicireddu*, chickpea dick, twenty-four years old, whose profession was training criminals in the craft, gave lessons out in the open on explosives and how to handle gasoline, before he was arrested. But the youngest, the little boys who haven't proved themselves yet, teach themselves on their own. The ones who survive make it in that career. Because even for the simplest attack, professionalism is required.

"They tell them to set a store on fire," explains the captain. "And they use gasoline. Pure gasoline. They don't know it has to be mixed with oil. And maybe they use twenty-liter cans, when just a one-liter bottle is more than sufficient. It's obvious that it all blows up in their hands."

IT SEEMED EASY. IN winter at eleven o'clock at night the streets are bare, the piazzas have emptied out. The city isn't alive anymore. It's not even necessary to wait until it's later.

"Twenty thousand now and thirty thousand after,"

Santino *'u pilurussu*, big red for the red hair covering his body from head to toe, had offered her as she sat still, straddling her ever-present motor scooter. He was standing on the edge of the sidewalk in the Quattro Canti, a wide spot in the main street. "My office," *'u pilurussu* called it.

"Okay."

Tina accepted, even though she earned a lot more with robberies and risked a lot less. But she would have done that service for Santino even for free, if they'd asked her to. It was an important sign. The first time someone in the right circles—a *'ntisu*, respected, well connected—had entrusted her with a task.

Tina knew how to read the signals and interpret them. For this at least her father's teachings had been useful. She knew she couldn't delegate the service to a young boy in the gang. It was something requested of her, *her* in particular. A type of baptism. Like a kiss between people in love, that binds without compromising anyone. But the customers were the ones not compromising themselves by having her do the service. While making that gesture of acceptance, she offered herself without reservations, and put herself in pawn.

Because that was the point of the test. Not a test of ability and courage, but of obedience and helpfulness. Something that, with know-how, would have brought her the future recognition of "superiors"—as she called them in a respectful, impersonal way—and entry into an important circle.

It wasn't a matter of blowing up a car; that was amateur

stuff. This business required a more complex technique. To begin with, you had to go into a store, or rather, a supermarket with its shutters and display window right on the main street. Cut the alarm system wires. Set the fire.

"Are you frightened? Are you afraid?" she asked Francesco.

He looked at her, surprised. His sister had never asked him that kind of question. He shook his head no. This time she really needed Francesco—to transport the gasoline, two big canisters. A mistake she would never make again. But it wasn't her line of work. Tina knew how to handle weapons, not gasoline.

"You really overdid it!" *'u pilurussu* laughed the next day. "The entire building almost blew up. A beauty of a light show." He glanced at her. "What'd you do to yourself?"

"Nothing. What should I have done to myself? Nothing," she answered cockily. She certainly wasn't going to tell him how she ended up with her hair all full of bits of plaster, her head spinning, her sweater stinking of ashes. And Francesco, bleeding from a glass shard stuck in one of his legs. A miracle they got out in time unhurt, without any burns, while the fuses, too short for the task, let loose an inferno.

She wouldn't even have told him how they stuck around tightly together, at the end of the alley, the flames reflected in their eyes, to listen to the fire that leapt into the air, exploding, hissing. They stayed there for a long time, crouching down in the dark and sweating. A hot, dazed, pleasing sweat. They could already hear the first sirens down at the end of the street and still they didn't move, intoxicated by the excitement. The bloodstain on Francesco's pants dissolved under a small stream of urine.

They slipped inside their house only when they heard the voice of the supermarket owner amidst the brakes screeching on the sidewalk and slamming of car doors. That voice put out the reflection in their eyes. The sweat on the nape of their necks turned into cold drops running down under their shirt collars.

SHE'D GIVEN TEN THOUSAND lire to Francesco. "Go have some fun," she'd told him in a rush. She intended to celebrate in a different way. It seemed as if it were her own party and everyone should know.

"Ma," she called from below. Since no one answered, she pushed the door. It was open. A whiff of mold greeted her, like a memento of rain kept in the wall. No trace of the small van. The garage was empty.

Good, she thought. *He's not here.*

A naked light bulb dangled in front of the flight of stairs at the back. She climbed to the first floor and went into the bedroom without knocking first.

"Ma, look what I brought you."

But her excitement had already dissolved in front of the messy bed sheets, and the shapeless figure hidden beneath them. The breath of illness, neglect, and depression filled the room. Coming face to face with it, Tina shrank back, awkward and impotent. A stale odor, rancid and unhealthy, enveloped her mother, enclosed her in an impenetrable aura, pushed her into a remote, strange place of sinister melancholy, making it impossible for anyone to reach her.

The woman opened her eyes, raising her hand to her forehead as if she wanted to block the light. A strange, useless gesture, since the light in the room was dim.

"I brought you a present," announced Tina, suddenly sensing the weight of the tray in her arms. She lightly dropped onto the edge of the bed, overcome by the infectious tiredness, and set the package on the blanket.

"Why are you here?" said the woman, sheltering herself with the sheet as she pulled it up over her shoulders. "What do you want," she said again.

"*Sciantillà* pastries. With custard . . . *sciantillà*," Tina repeated, faltering, not trusting her pronunciation. "Really fresh, bought at Capo Soprano pastry shop. Do you want some, Ma?"

The woman raised herself up with effort, exploring the room with the alarmed look of someone caught out.

"He's not here. He hasn't arrived yet, Ma."

The woman threw herself back against the pillow again, relieved.

"I'll get up now," she promised. Then her eyes lit on her daughter. "You know he doesn't want to see you dressed in that getup around here."

Tina automatically tightened her hand around the fastening of her leather jacket and didn't answer. Those reproaches, though made in an apathetic voice lacking conviction, always upset her. A terrifying sense of loss assailed her, as if her body might have to abandon her all of a sudden, disintegrating at a distressing speed. In order to defend herself, she'd learned not to respond.

She felt betrayed. Hadn't her dressing and acting like a boy been a game for everyone, for her mother too? An easy game, so long as she was a little girl. But with her first menstrual blood, things had changed. And the game got rough.

Everyone took it for granted up until then that she was only a fake. An act and nothing else. Everyone expected that she would change, just like that, from one day to the next. But her body refused to abandon the shelter in which it had grown.

"You know he doesn't want you to," repeated the woman.

Tina was aware of the fact that her mother would never have had the courage to say: *I don't want you to.* She always had to put a stronger authority's shield in front of her own desires. Her mother didn't approve of her. But her weakness made her defenseless in front of Tina. A small, sad vendetta.

"It's early, he's not here yet. Let's eat a pastry, Ma."

THE CIGARETTE IS FINISHED. I put out the butt on the windowsill, utter an embarrassed apology, and throw it in the waste basket. A silence full of resigned disapproval follows, underscoring my awkward handling of things. Besides, my time is over. Giving a sign of goodbye, the captain gets up. He accompanies me to the door, but taking his time, as if he wanted to find a way to give me one last piece of information, the final touch.

"I won't remain in Sicily much longer," he says, "I've already received my transfer papers." He thinks again and declares, "Or rather, to be precise, I've been transferred."

I catch an unmistakable note of melancholy in his resentment. A soft shadow rushes over the young captain's face and dissolves. So it's not just a question of work, of being clearly checkmated, of a thwarted passion. His tone of voice reveals something more. He's fallen in love, I think, and not only with Sicily.

"And where will you go?" I ask.

He shrugs. "To Arezzo, in Tuscany." As if to say: to the moon.

"Great. From the mafia to P2", Propaganda Due, a scandal that rocked the nation after a list was discovered in Arezzo, naming over nine hundred members of a secret Masonic Lodge who included corrupt politicians, bankers and business leaders, military personnel, judges and journalists, who had brokered their power for years. "At least you won't be bored," I try to console him. He doesn't reply.

CHAPTER 5

An incomprehensible loathing, but stubborn and perse-cuting, like old people's loathing often is.

"You have to leave him."

Their grandmother, when she found out that Saveria had become engaged to Nele, had gone crazy. She stuck to her day and night, obsessively.

"You have to leave him."

Saveria, who was by nature so accommodating and faint-hearted, or rather, eaten up by fears—they called her *scantulina*, little scaredy cat, at home—showed she was pigheaded for her part.

"But why *him* of all people? Why do you want to have *him*?" her grandmother kept pressing.

And so she patiently put forth the virtues of her Nele. "First of all, he finished the eighth grade in school."

Tina snorted at this point too. Saveria was really fixated on school.

"And also, he's a hard worker."

But what she might mean by that word wasn't clear. Because it was true that for a few months Nele showed up at a commercial farm where they put him on the payroll because of the sharp insistence of "friends of friends," but he'd already left long before. He sure had ambitions. And he had trafficking deals. And money.

Money and ambitions. Things that could move Tina, not Saveria. Who nevertheless would die of shame if she had to confess Nele's true virtues: a strong head of light brown hair that had blond streaks in the summer; his lanky, slender body like a beanpole.

"And also, he's respected."

Everyone knew. He was a fledgling mafioso, a boy who had good promise. To tell the truth though, he had more than promise by then. He had moved up a rank from a part-time mafioso with a cover job. Saveria was right. Nele had worked hard to earn the promotion that made him a full-time mafioso. But that was precisely what their grandmother couldn't swallow.

It wasn't a matter of principle. The old woman had the utmost regard for men of honor. Her son—the father of those children who for her were more than grandchildren: her flesh, a visceral laceration deep inside her own body—he too had been a man of honor. So it wasn't a matter of principle. And also, everybody does whatever they possibly can to get by, and where ways of getting by were concerned she was better than everyone. But she couldn't tear the memory of her son's dying that way out of her mind. "*Sciatu meu,*" my life's breath, she moaned. "Is that any way to kill a human being?" For Saveria, who was beautiful and calm, who knows what she had wished.

She looked at her, taking stock of her long black hair, her short, straight nose. Beautiful, without a doubt. A modern girl who watched her figure. Maybe if she were a bit plumper . . . "Too much into the fashion," she sighed, looking at Saveria's narrow hips. "Why do you want him, since you aren't able to enjoy him?" she kept on asking.

But Saveria would laugh, warding off any ill omens. "Do you want to bring me bad luck?"

"You aren't enjoying him," the old woman stubbornly repeated. "With his kind of life you can't enjoy him."

She held out her hand with its stiff, crooked fingers that could no longer grip objects, pointing at Tina.

"She's enough in the family," she judgmentally pronounced.

Words that violently struck the little girl. She felt them on her cheeks, two blows that cruelly turned her face red. For the first time in her young life, she had the impression of being tightly inside a sentence without appeal.

HER GRANDMOTHER HAD HOUNDED Saveria so much that the girl went off to live at her mother's where she wouldn't hear any more out of her.

So Tina acquired more space in the basement home with no windows. In the bed, where her grandmother, Saveria, and Tina had slept before—Francesco had his own cot in a corner next to the oil cloth curtain that hid the toilet behind its red and blue flowers—now the two of them could generously spread out.

There was so much space in the bed, too much by then. Over the years her grandmother's body had shrunken to the point it didn't even give off any warmth. Tina missed that rich warmth that had enveloped her like a fever, luxurious, deep, and welcoming like a fur coat. She'd lost the raft on which she floated through the hours of darkness.

Saveria had gone away, but there were still three pillows beneath the folded-over sheet. Tina was uncomfortable in the cold, white clearing that she didn't recognize. Dimensions that no longer made sense, borders that had to be readjusted directly on her skin. She was used to such a limited space that even the conquest of a few centimeters excessively enlarged her perception of objects, of the very air she breathed.

And yet, Tina didn't remember—up until that moment at least—ever feeling cramped or crushed by the home's lack of space. It was ugly, it was uncomfortable, it was a hole. A lair where it was difficult to turn around. But there, inside, Tina had found a way to build a place all her own. Intimate and limitless.

With her ever-present Walkman in her pants pocket, the band of the headphones disappearing amidst her cropped hair, Tina could withdraw into her refuge at any moment. The light wires, small plugs that softly pressed against the inside walls of her ear enclosed a music all her own within herself, which never filtered through to the outside. No one could get anything out of her. She didn't come out of her body, which was her den. Home and the entire building enclosing it. That was her private space. What the music erected around her.

She was capable of staying in there until noon—in the morning there was little to get up to on the streets—lying on the bed to listen to Neapolitan songs, the sentimental melodies of Merola or Nino D'Angelo. They sang about small children all alone, icy cold eyes, impossible wars and the desire to change, "changing in order to fight." They sang about fathers faraway, fathers waiting for kids coming out of school, fathers and sons.

I have a thousand memories of where I was born
that break my heart when I have to go away,
my home, my neighbor's voice
and my father, more and more a little boy.

In the easy beat of the rhythm, the enveloping, drawled tempo of the musical phrases, she rediscovered the atmosphere of those distant Sundays when everyone was still there, sitting around the table. After their mid-afternoon meal, her father gave the signal, and the family began singing. It was their pastime, their way to stay united, to feel close together.

I have a thousand memories . . .

In the isolation of the music, in the song's words, her father returned to be her model to follow. Tina had forgotten the blood, the crumpled body on the ground, blocking her home's front door, heavy as a rock, defenseless, defeated. She didn't remember the defeat. She remembered instead the man who'd been honored, sought out by everyone, whom everyone greeted and recognized in bars, on the street, in the piazza. More famous than a TV star. Her father wasn't a thief, a swindler, a common criminal, a "useless good for nothing." He wasn't a nobody who managed to live by taking whatever happened along. A lot of people bowed their heads in front of him. To see those heads bowed, to read the respect in the men's eyes—*that* was why her father was on the go, not for love of money or profit. Respect has no price.

Tina also wanted respect and consideration for herself. She already seemed to be well underway, despite only having just turned fifteen. But in her line of work the selection took place early, as for soccer players, in fact, even earlier. A hard selection. Very often, being rejected necessarily meant dying, killed at the hands of competitors the same age or by the decision of superiors.

Tina was fully aware of the difficulties of the task. Besides, even if she had wanted to, she couldn't have ignored the countless kids her own age who had been stopped forever at some stage of the race, at any deviation in the path they were traveling together. She knew him, Giovanni '*u tignusu*, mangy scoundrel, tortured and hanged at exactly fifteen years old, and Nardo, killed in the Femminamorta district, and still another, the seventeen-year-old Orazio, a bartender who was gunned down in the street with a machine gun by two killers, their faces hidden under their helmets.

Yes, it was a hard job that didn't let you enjoy love. Her grandmother was right. But Tina was happy that Saveria had gotten herself engaged to Nele. It was an advantage for Tina too.

The advantage, to tell the truth, was reciprocal. The young man needed the little boys that Tina organized and deployed: her "gang," according to the newspapers. And she needed the protection, advice, and support of Nele among their superiors.

Because Tina had a great ambition. A secret dream. She didn't like street gangs, common gangs. Thugs, *scassapagghiara*, small-time gangsters of no importance and little power. Tina, the daughter of a mafioso, wanted to be in the organization. With all of the duties and all of the rights. Being female couldn't be an obstacle, not for her. After all, Cosa Nostra's rules were like the State's rules: equal for *almost* all. An exception could always be made.

She gave the orders now, and would willingly adapt to

taking them, to step down from being the boss to being a soldier to acquire recognized, adult prestige. Cosa Nostra soldier: the lowest rank but also the first indispensable step for a career inside the organization. Nele had understood her craving to reach that inaccessible threshold. He enjoyed making fun of her. At the bar in the main street, in the little back room, he put on his pool cue glove and headed toward the pool table challenging her: "Step up, sister-in-law."

Tina was good, with all the training she'd done when she was a little girl in her father's retinue. She played with flair. She shot the balls in the holes, and Nele didn't get upset. But when he won, he pointed the cue in the middle of her chest, teasing: "Today you seem like a real girl. The spitting image."

LIKE TINA IN HER house in the alley, I'm also searching for a stop-off, a private space in this hotel that once seemed elegant to me. I line up the tools of my trade on the desk—paper, pen—along with my memories. My first job. Some boy's long hair. How could I have believed I was sheltered from the nostalgias of the past? Where did all my scatterbrained certainty come from? How did I dare to go back again?

I avoid trying to force open the dusty curtains, which don't move along the rods, and resign myself to the electric light and regrets. Even though what I'd need instead is a free zone, liberated from these cumbersome feelings. I would like some neutral time from which I could conduct with impunity my incursions into a present that barely lets the signs of the past emerge.

I go back to the desk. Financing deals pouring from the skies, money and business that don't cure the economic crisis and don't solve the problem of unemployment. There, I write, the new Gela, fifth largest city in Sicily.

Corruption, common crime, and war between the age-old clan of the shepherds and today's emerging mafia clans. A bloody war fought between the counters in butcher shops, on building sites, where a school, a sewer main, or a dam should stand. The Disueri dam cost seventy-five lives in two years, in the clash between the band of shepherds and the "Catanesi" tied to Madonia, the mafia boss. Everything became an opportunity for profit and an object of speculation. For every necessity, for everything needed in daily life, people have to enter an open battlefield.

A precarious life, in Gela. Harder now than in the past. Even though the mafia—the mafia of Cosa Nostra—is losing its air of mystery. It's not an invincible army anymore, ever since everything about its soldiers' loves and deaths, habits and weaknesses became known. Ever since everyone could see a mafia boss's eyes or hear the voice of an ex-mafioso turned state's evidence on the television.

The Stidda crime organization is more impenetrable. It put down strong roots in the Gela plain with its integralism and call to the age-old values, which Cosa Nostra betrayed. That island name that tangles foreigners' tongues already indicates a choice, a different mentality. The *stiddari*, members of Stidda, are loose cannons, the anarchists of the mafia. People say they have five points—a rudimentary star—tattooed between their index and middle fingers, like the jailbirds of long ago.

I open a bottle of Campari and turn on the TV. They're broadcasting a documentary on the Allied landing. The 9th of July, 1943. In Gela. More or less erudite interviews and period photos alternate on the screen. The coast, the jetty, the old neighborhoods near the sea—Orto Bugè, Chianu surfaredda—the plain and the fields of grain. Photos of another world. All you can recognize are the bunkers that have withstood time and at night turn white like moons lost in the countryside, facing the sea. The interviews continue. Not even a mention, naturally, of little Carmelu *trigghia*, the phantom, or Ninu and Peppi, the sons of the *tremolante*, flicker, who systematically emptied the military's jeeps after the occupation. Today's baby-gangs haven't done anything other than develop the abilities inherited from the little boys of that time.

I turn off the TV and start working again. Tina's childhood, her adolescence. Each interview is a small step forward. But there's something, an obstacle that continues to sidetrack me. I can't manage to get close enough to cross into her reality. Inside her way of attacking life. I can only see her from the outside, in her attempt to hold onto the survivors of a family nucleus over which she was losing power little by little. A power that she had received by anomalous paternal investiture, and still held. But Saveria had gotten engaged. And Francesco was looking for work.

"CANNIZZARO. FRANCESCO CANNIZZARO . . ." repeats Father Lillo. "How old is he?"

A quick calculation: when was it that little Francesco submitted his application to the Salesians' vocational school? While I do my complicated mental calculations, we walk alongside the parish courtyard toward Father Lillo's office.

The playground is partly broken up, but the boys who are kicking the soccer ball back and forth and running after each other in quick pivots don't seem to notice. The walls could use a touch of paint, but they compensate for it by holding up a well modelled building that's a lot more solid and resistant than any other one around here. No more than four or five boys are stretched out in the shade of the porticos, yawning. But it's the middle of summer, and there's competition with the beach. Otherwise, every day four hundred, even five hundred, young people spend their time from five o'clock in the evening until about eight or half past eight, in the Salesian parish. It's the only youth center in Gela and it works, despite the plain appearance that smells of old stuff, sleepiness, and dust.

"Boys and girls come here, with no distinctions. But the girls help me more. They're stronger," maintains Father Lillo.

I have to believe him. He speaks from experience, this

small, fat priest, whose belly jiggles in his shapeless pants and short neck struggles to emerge from a shabby, short-sleeved knit shirt. He's dressed in civilian clothes too, like the carabinieri captain. It must be a sign of the times, no more uniforms worn twenty-four hours a day. No more external emblems of authority, uniforms worn to divide and distinguish. There are other signs of command. It's necessary to look for them elsewhere.

"The boys are more introverted, they lack initiative. In short, they don't become leaders. And they get into drugs more easily."

The reception center for drug addicts isn't in this building complex, but a little further away, outside the city.

Don Lillo speaks sparingly, and with the resigned detachment of a country parish priest who renounced distant visions and exciting hopes a long time ago. Every day his battle consists of catching reluctant boys perennially on the run by the lapels of their jacket or their shirt tails.

"It's the same old refrain. They tell me: everybody's doing it, there's nothing wrong with it, I can stop as easily as I started."

He mentions a report by the police union that talks of three thousand drug addicts in Gela. An exclamation of surprise escapes me.

"So many. Too many."

"The drug traffic has enormously expanded," Father Lillo's flat voice reminds me.

In just a short time it became organized crime's most important business. Not without conflicts. In fact, only after a bloody war in which an entire generation of mafiosi in Cosa Nostra—like Tina's father, who comes to mind—was defeated and killed. A generation that condemned drugs, hated the dealers, and disdained the addicts.

"Drugs, prostitution . . . The refusal to be involved in 'dirty' trafficking is typical of an old mafia tradition. For more or less 'noble' motives. Most of all, the fear of their own children becoming involved."

Or the fear, rather, of losing ground, of being defeated— as happened—by the war over control of a business that required new skills, new abilities. New men. In fact, drugs enabled the new men of the mafia to accumulate riches and powers that would have been unthinkable twenty years ago.

"Even the parish isn't immune to this contagion, the sharks come around here too. They even set fire to the main door. But that's water under the bridge." A brief pause. "Let's hope."

In Father Lillo's office—high ceilings, dark windows facing the courtyard—the trophies won by the soccer, volleyball, and even basketball teams are on display. At the Salesian Center the young people don't only participate in socio-cultural activities, but also work out in the gym and train for sports. Good kids, from good families, on average coming from families of clerks and office workers, profes- sors, shopkeepers. These are the young people who come to the parish. Not the deprived. Not the young kids from the illegally built neighborhoods.

Father Lillo is a bit proud of who frequents the center, and a bit sorry.

"The children in the ghettos have a god of their own," he complains. "An entirely particular god, tolerant and permissive. He protects them during robberies . . . and perhaps helps them hit their target. Here they find prayers and an entirely different kind of activity."

Certainly the parish prayers and activities weren't what attracted Francesco, making him park his motor scooter against a tree in front of the Center's main entrance. A different mirage had guided him there: the famous vocational courses, his hope to enroll in the school of industrial pipe welding, the true jewel of the entire Salesian community. An important school, the only one of its kind. The specialized labor force that comes out of its classrooms finds work throughout Italy and first and foremost in Gela's chemical plant, Petrolchimico, obviously.

But Francesco's application wasn't accepted. Why?

"Unfortunately, we have to be very selective. We can't accept more than two hundred applications. We aren't able to support a higher number of students. There are so many requests . . ." Father Lillo looks up toward the sky with a mild expression of regret. "Cannizzaro . . . But had he at least finished elementary school? In any case, it's useless." He firmly closes the subject. "I don't know anything, I can't know, I don't take care of these matters. You'd have to check in the office and look through the enrollment applications. But it's not open now."

The school is closed this time of year, but visitors can tour the classrooms. As we stand up, Father Lillo puts a brochure in my hand. Out-of-focus images, horrible graphics. The photograph of a girls' soccer team. A slogan beside the calendar of initiatives: *Here we make holiness consist of joy.*

But I don't see a lot of joy spread around, in truth. Father Lillo carries along the life of the parish with the same lolling indolence with which he carries around his belly. His face is sad too, constitutionally sad, I'd say, with heavy eyelids that cast down his gaze. I can't envision him fighting, preaching against mafia culture like that parish priest whose embarrassing passion for such sermons prompted an emergency procedure to transfer him to a nearby town. Father Lillo certainly doesn't have the kind of initiative or entrepreneurial lack of principles that other priests do. And not even the erudition, the refined knowledge, the icy doctrine of Monsignor Tumeo, who teaches theology and discusses doctoral dissertations with implacable rigor. "Like everywhere," argues Monsignor Tumeo, "in the Church there are conservatives and revolutionaries. And those who watch." Asking him about his own position is an absolutely superfluous question. His icy rigor pronounces him the enemy of any change, with no possibility of misunderstanding.

Father Lillo is touched by none of these merits and none

of these defects. But at least he knows the boys and girls well. We run into two young scouts on the stairs of the school building. The young girl has an unruly ponytail that swings over her light-colored uniform. He has a shaved, shiny head. They're kissing each other. Her mouth sinks into his, breaks away, sinks inside again. But with little conviction and even less rapture. They both have the bored look of people who don't know how to kill the time. They interrupt what they're doing to look at us go by, indifferent to Father Lillo's presence, and return to their half-hearted kisses, showing the same enthusiasm with which they'd return to a homework assignment left half done.

The classrooms are well organized inside, shiny, their spaces rationally distributed. The labs have long, well equipped tables. Efficiency. Seriousness. The initiative's success is palpable. You understand it immediately from the order that reigns among the empty desks, in the deserted hallways that nevertheless hold a breath of life's presence. Everything is suspended but pulsates and waits in trepidation for the flow of young people to resume again.

Young boys. No girls attend the vocational Center.

"But in the parish . . . They help me more," insists Father Lillo. "The boys almost want to stand aside. They offer to help with the heavy jobs, but refuse guidance, advice. And they're more fickle."

I don't comment. I wouldn't know what to say. Why do the girls keep themselves far away from these classrooms?

Why instead do the boys flock into these same desks? Where do strength and weakness come from, I wonder? What makes the girls more determined and involved (to hear Father Lillo) and the boys more moody and elusive? Is it perhaps the updated legend of the Sicilian matriarchy? On the one hand, the men's clear yet faint-hearted strength, and on the other, the women's hidden yet victorious strength. Or is it simply a difference between their dreams which misleads Father Lillo?

I look at the fully equipped tables. The electrical outlets, the precision instruments. Opportunities, jobs, male dreams.

"Cannizzaro . . ." murmurs Father Lillo, lost in thought. Then, in a loud voice, "I'm sorry. If I knew where to look . . ."

"Never mind," I say.

In reality, I think: *what a shame*. But I don't even know exactly when Francesco submitted his application. I can only roughly reconstruct this period of his life. A period in which he tries to enter the world of work in a crazy, disconnected way. There's a really true frenzy in his avidly throwing himself into any possibility at all, going after any glimmer of a chance with the urgency of someone searching for shelter, a bulwark.

He works as a carpenter, a bricklayer, a barista, a mechanic, a waiter. He even sells detergents. Never for more than a week, fifteen days, a month at the most.

When does he get the idea of the Salesian courses?

Knowing exactly *when* is important for deciphering the reason he applied. A vocational school is still a school, with schedules and classes and teachers and classrooms; a world that had already rejected Francesco, a world that was hostile toward his unruly freedoms. So why return, why apply? In order to escape an increasingly binding grip? In order to get out from under an increasingly strict dependency on Tina's presence? Or was the return to school a victory—short and risky—for his other sister, Saveria?

What's certain is that the defeat served to make his confused adolescence more fragile. Another barrier, a wound that gave rise to new infections and never healed even in the very end.

After these disorganized attempts to become part of the normality he'd fantasized about, he was arrested—four times in three months—for car theft.

Surprised while he was attaching the ignition wires. "It's raining," he said, with a calm, childlike face. "It's about to rain," he announced, looking up at the sky, which actually was cloudy. "That's why I wanted to drive the car."

CHAPTER 6

"They don't feel like children, but they are children. They're insecure. They need to rely on the boss's name, on his authority. They come inside acting like God Almighty, heading straight to the owner of the store. They make some gesture or other and say the classic: Do you remember me?"

I'm eating some swordfish *al salmoriglio*, lightly seasoned with olive oil, lemon, parsley and oregano, in the Motel AGIP restaurant with Signor Licata, the owner of a furrier's shop, with its display windows on the main street of Gela.

"Furs? But do you sell any?" I'm amazed, remembering my winters in Gela, spent invariably without wearing a coat.

"Absolutely. Cash sales and installment plans. We sell them."

Signor Licata reported the extortion racket to the police

and now lives in the motel. Alone. He closed up the beautiful condominium he'd recently purchased, a penthouse in Capo Soprano, the "good" neighborhood where professional people live, and sent his family away. Far away from Gela, from retaliations, from fear. Sent away. Far away. Who knows where.

"Where it's safe." He cuts the topic short in a definitive tone, to prevent any inopportune curiosity. He's very skinny, the sharp features of his face immediately bringing to mind the image of a stone marten. Sadness isn't a very credible expression on his lips, even when he says, "I haven't seen them for a long time! Perhaps I will at Christmas. It depends on the trial, on a lot of things. Maybe for the holidays I can let them come back."

He wears a gold Rolex on his wrist and his cell phone sits on the table next to the napkin.

"Did a young boy come to collect the money at your shop too?" I ask.

Signor Licata's fingers start fiddling nervously with the strap of his bag. I'm convinced that he won't answer. The conversation hangs in the air, and right when I stop looking at him expectantly and concentrate instead on my swordfish steak, in the exact fraction of a second when I shift from paying attention to him to satisfying my hunger, Signor Licata answers me. A precise story. But impersonal.

"They come to collect the money in order to create their image. They need to be known, identified, so that people will say he's the one who 'walks' alongside boss so and so. To walk with the boss is already a promotion, they feel like they've made it. The older boys get involved only when there's an important acquisition. They come by and say, 'You behaved really well.' They never make threats, the older ones. They ask politely, nicely." He lowers his voice and unexpectedly assumes a confidential bearing. "They even asked me for favors and discounts for the youngest boys. 'See what you can do, because we care about this boy.'"

He breaks off, staring at the waiter coming toward us with a bottle of mineral water. Signor Licata is tense, in a constant state of overexcitement, with flashes of cunning that alter his features at times.

"He feels like a hero," Mimmo had warned me.

But Signor Licata decided to report the extortion only when he was cornered. During a police operation when mafia payrolls were discovered in a hideout, listing their expenses and income, with the names and surnames of business owners who were paying the *pizzo* extortion money.

"A real hero," Mimmo scornfully commented.

Nevertheless, silence—*this* silence—doesn't coincide with *omertà*, the mafia's unwritten law of silence. It is, quite simply, fear. Out of fear one pays a toll that is as inevitable as it is useless, because it doesn't guarantee anything anymore— not protection or anything else—in the great disorder of the war between the clans. So what right does Mimmo have to pass judgment? What does he do (what do I do) to erase the fear and make *omertà* useless? Could it perhaps be Signor Licata's unpleasant appearance that motivates my cousin's harsh judgment, suddenly revealing him as an intransigent critic of other people's behavior?

The fact remains that in the face of those payrolls, kept in scrupulous order and updated, Signor Licata admitted he paid and is now collaborating. A real hero. But not everyone gave in that time, even with the evidence slapped in front of their faces. On the contrary, most of the people shaken down preferred to be reported to the police rather than report the extortion to the police themselves. And not only because, all considered, it costs less, with not as much upheaval in your daily life, and fewer dangers.

"As long as you're a victim you have everyone's solidarity," Signor Licata complains. "When you decide to collaborate . . ."

In fact, there's a void around him. He's alone at lunch, alone at dinner, never a friend who eats at his table, except for the young men of some police bodyguard squad or another, who sometimes relax, wearing tracksuits and tennis shoes. A difficult isolation.

And yet . . . And yet I have the feeling that he likes this adventure. Maybe that's why he alone, among so many, has been able to bear it. The motel, being far away from his family, even the constant surveillance to which he is subjected make his eyes shine with hidden euphoria. As if all of this actually represented unprecedented, remarkable freedom for him.

With his stone marten face bent over his plate, Signor Licata greedily devours the inevitable *peperonata*, with its sweet bell peppers, onions, and garlic seasoning.

"Historically in Gela there isn't a mafia system, and there never has been," he tells me vehemently, while he wipes his mouth and fingers on the napkin. "Some disturbing individuals, for sure, but not a real mafia system. The war broke out precisely after an attempt to get a foothold . . . Even Narduzzo said so." He glances at me out of the corner of his eye to see if I know who he's talking about. "Narduzzo," he repeats.

I smile. Is this a way to test the accuracy of my information, my knowledge about the mafia? "Leonardo Messina," he explains. I nod in agreement. One of the important mafia *pentiti* who turned state's evidence.

What did Narduzzo say? That the people of Gela were used in the war between the clans precisely because they didn't have historical roots in Cosa Nostra. "The Gela people," he said, "were used for murders committed according to the books" (that's to say "officially" approved by the superiors, in Tina's words) "and for murders off the books, without explaining why to the boys. And the young kids didn't ask too many questions."

They would strike without asking. They obeyed without posing too many questions to themselves or anyone else because they were anxious to get into the criminal circle and compete in the game. With the excessive zeal of novices. With an impatience to stand out from the other boys that caused real slaughters and transformed little children living in backstreet alleys into so many apprentices-in-crime.

"They broke everything it was possible to break in my store," declares Signor Licata, who has almost entirely loosened up now. "To get inside, they drilled a hole in the glass. A little hole. Only a small child could get through it."

OUR PLATES ARE EMPTY. Signor Licata stands up and heads toward the self-service counter.

"Can I get you something?" he asks.

While waiting I look around me. Three young women sitting a little further away are eating and chatting loudly. They're teachers who have come from other cities for the state exams, as is the woman who took the seat at the table facing mine. Alone, with arms like a longshoreman's, she's diving into her double serving of spaghetti with tomato sauce. But for her main course I hear her order a diet dish, grilled chicken breasts with no oil.

My eyes move from her table to the other one, feeling something akin to gratitude. Women! I'm filled with joy. I'm not the only woman in the entire restaurant anymore. I'm not the only female guest in the entire motel anymore.

And yet their company doesn't reassure me. Sequences from old films keep reappearing in my memory. The impression of being a foreigner dropped off by the stagecoach in front of the saloon, among courageous schoolteachers, fearless cowboys, and lone sheriffs doesn't abandon me, and in fact grows stronger. Ignazio would hate me for the banality of this film. I detest myself too. But it's impossible to stop the procession of images that flashes in front of my eyes independent of my own will.

And Tina? What role, what part does she play in this performance?

Signor Licata has returned with a second helping of *peperonata*. How does he stay so skinny? He must burn all the calories by being constantly on the alert, giving way to moments of neurasthenia. With his fork poised to harpoon some pieces of the yellow, green, and red peppers, he suddenly comes out with a remarkable assertion that differs from everything I've heard so far, and from every interpretation of the facts.

"The little boys in the gangs . . . They're the children of post-industrialization. Anything but children in poverty! They come from the Villaggio," asserts Signor Licata.

"From the Villaggio?"

"Yes, from the Villaggio. They're the children of office workers and the like. Little kids without principles, cynical. Their only problem is to avoid being arrested. And they're not isolated. They have the approval of the other kids their age."

"Not everyone's, I think," I protest. Now I'm the one to

stand up to defend and champion the "good" island. It's my turn. A Sicilian woman in exile against a Sicilian man of Sicily. "Mobilizations, marches, public denunciations, taking a stand . . . People can't say that there's not a collective consciousness among young people who would like to take action, put things right."

Signor Licata's thin nose dives into his plate again, and he doesn't answer.

"And children from the Villaggio, really?" I prod him. "What confirmation can you give me? It's not evident to me. Tina, for example, comes from the Bronx and backstreet alleys. And her father was anything but rich."

"That's true. She was just a little small-time mafioso. A lot of prestige but short on cash." His eyes twinkle with satisfaction. "But it's also true that ten, fifteen, twenty years ago, opportunities to make money were meager. There wasn't any money, not even among the mafiosi. But the rules mattered."

What would Cosa Nostra be, he persists, without rules to respect? Without prohibitions intended to discipline, to construct embankments and barriers sheltering their invention of a way to live? Obedience and respect for the hierarchy. Renouncing the most traditional male vices: women and gambling. Or better yet, he laughs, renouncing ostentatiously showing off those vices.

Rules. Commandments. Passed down from one to another like the Decalogue. Tablets of an austere law. To observe and at the same time, inescapably, to transgress. And in order to give power and truth to the rules, there are the rites of affiliation that sanction membership. The silver hatpins that prick the finger, the drop of blood that stains the holy card, setting it afire, the wording of the oath. A real liturgical ceremony for young men.

"Do you remember what Falcone said?" Signor Licata challenges me.

"Falcone? He said a lot of things . . ."

"That the mafia has the strength of a church. That's what he said," he quickly retorts.

But in the cracks of every church, sooner or later heresies inevitably flourish. An association of ideas. Something clicks and slowly an image, a small figure that is still indistinct comes alive inside me.

"Tina the heretic," I exclaim while Signor Licata looks at me without understanding.

WHEN THE WIND KICKED up, another sound joined the loud beating of the surf. Short, faint. A fluttering. A pattering rustle of a hundred little wings hitting against the walls of the bunker that still stood intact among the dunes on the beach. The sounds of the surf and the wind throwing the sand up against the last ghost of a war fought half a century earlier, mingled together, and fused in musical movement. A rhythm that accompanied Tina's fantasies.

It was the right night. The light of the full moon lit the road through the valleys of sand. The place possessed a mysterious, nocturnal solemnity that smelled of blood and exhaustion, waiting and cruel emotions, solitary death and unheard pain. Many men had been killed on that beach, among the gentle slopes of the dunes. Many agonies had been inflicted in the crypt of the bunker. Friends and enemies, Americans and Germans and Italians. And also Mario 'u tripulinu, the Tripolian, a customs officer who turned up by chance on the wrong night.

Francesco never went inside first. He let the others get lost down there, the increasingly thick darkness blinding them. Slipping into the dark cavity of that sepulcher gave all of them a strange pleasure. Just like the one you experience chewing on clover, so bitter it makes your eyes water. An irritating and irresistible taste.

Tina had discovered the bunker. And it was like going directly inside those special comic-strip tales published in the *Giornale di Sicilia* newspaper.

It was February of 1986. In Palermo, the Maxi Trial—the first trial that didn't end with the mafiosi applauding—against four hundred and seventy-four men of Cosa Nostra. Falcone's victory. The first defeat of Totò Riina, the boss of bosses, still without a face and without a voice. In conjunction with the trial, the *Giornale di Sicilia* had brought out in comic-strip form the story of the Blessed Paulists, the so-called Bible of the old mafia, the book that all mafiosi are familiar with. The only book, for many of them. So below the news from the trial, the adventures of the Blessed

Paulists, men who presumed to be above common laws and even above fate, flowed in filigree. Catacombs. Tunnels running through a secret subterranean Palermo. Strong shades of chiaroscuro for an arbitrary, romantic idea of justice.

Nele had brought her the newspaper. He was smiling. But something about his smile had caused her to follow those stories closely day after day, as their historiated arabesques split open reality. They processed tales of death, thereby opening onto the noble tradition, and the legitimation of her own dream.

The bunker was a place that would have beautifully fit into those illustrations. It was suited to occult baptisms and initiation ceremonies, and to nocturnal expeditions more thrilling than taking a hundred carnival rides, that filled the intolerable shifts between reality and desire. Between the absence of a future and the affirmation of her own single, irrepressible life.

Tina had selected the site as her private shooting range. She trained with various types of targets, at close range and long, in different shooting positions, lying down, kneeling, sitting, leaning to her right side or the left. She spent entire days that way. Night would fall. And Mario *'u tripulinu*'s spirit hit against the walls along with the wind.

Intense, solitary preparation. Then she had brought Francesco there. And later, a few other friends. Inadvertently, the bunker had naturally become a mysterious space, a sumptuous backdrop for the celebration of her command.

The young boys sat on the ground in a semicircle. The slits in the walls let in light, diffuse specks of dust, which gathered thickly in vivid waves around the flame of a candle sitting on a large slab. In the dim light, fifteen-year-old Tina's soldiers were silent white masks. Minicu *spasciamaronni*, the guttermouth, who bullied and swore worse than a dock worker, Ninu *'u studenti*, the student, and Peppe *ianninedda*, the little hen, waited and kept silent. Also silent was Pietro, called "Filippo mai mori," Filippo never die, an *ingiuria*, a nickname, inherited from his father, who, at the landing of the Americans on that very beach in July 1943, had started trafficking in cigarettes stolen from the trailers of military vehicles. The Philip Morrises were in great demand, and promptly re-baptized "Filippo never die."

The dim light faded their bodies, lips, and the outlines of their noses, and gave their hair the same color, softening their differences. Only their nicknames, their *ingiurie*, remained stuck to each of them like bright labels, identification tags. Indelible distinguishing marks born from other people's caprice.

At least, Tina *'a masculidda* thought proudly, *I gave myself my own name*. She had chosen it. Tina: Short, hard, a bit foreign, or so it seemed to her—and she'd imposed it on her friends and relatives.

A few days earlier a reporter who had managed to track her down in the alley asked, "Is Tina the diminutive of Conc-etta?" On impulse she denied it. "What does that have to do with anything? . . . They're two separate names. Different in every way." She explained: "Cettina comes from Concetta." But the arrogance of her own statement didn't manage to reassure her. For the first time, she seemed to hear an echo, a note that clashed in the name she'd donned like second skin. Was there something wrong about her choice? Then she added, "My superiors also call me that."

The reporter, who came from the continent, didn't give it a thought. He was lost in the italianized Sicilian dialect, the transpositions and turns of phrase. So he didn't wonder— and he didn't ask her—who her "superiors" might be.

After the interview, Santino *'u pilurussu* had attacked her. "Shut your mouth. Those people are *fitusa*, scum. If you keep saying stupid shit we'll call you *'a buccarusa*. Tina *'a buccarusa*." Tina the blabbermouth. Who would ever have respected her again? *Tina 'a buccarusa*. Vile. Vile reporter, vile Santino.

Tina shook off the aggravation brought on by her memory of that warning and started the ceremony. She slipped her nine-caliber Beretta out of her belt and passed it to Francesco. Francesco held it in his hands a short while and passed it to the boy beside him. As Tina's Beretta passed from hand to hand, the boys touched it, tried out the grip, and slowly ran the tips of their fingers over it, until the pistol finally came back to her. Then Tina got to her feet. The moment had arrived to demonstrate her abilities, reassert her aptitudes, affirm her talents, which indisputably made her a boss.

She raised the Beretta with both her hands. In the dim light she aimed at the candle flame. She wasn't afraid of missing. The idea of failing didn't even cross her mind. Not only because she'd been intimately familiar with that weapon since she was eight years old. Looking down the shiny gun barrel she saw easy targets, figures of icy hate slipping down the thread. She fired. As always, her body absorbed the shot. She didn't hear the bullet crash against the wall. But a faint crackling joined the beating of the wind and the sea, a final jolt.

THE RESTAURANT HAS EMPTIED out. But Signor Licata doesn't let me leave. He seems fond of my company, which fills a long solitary afternoon. He and I are the only ones left, staying to drink coffee and smoke. I don't even see his bodyguards anymore.

"The strength of a church," the fur salesman retorts, critical and bitter. An accusatory finger disapprovingly taps the napkin. "But a business's way of thinking. Everything that serves to make money is permissible. Today Cosa Nostra is money. It's business. It's on the move for money only."

CHAPTER 7

Already in May, back when I would return from Riesi after teaching three or four hours, at a certain point, instead of going straight I'd take the detour for Falconara, toward the sea. In May, along the southern coast of Sicily the sand is warm and the sun bronzes your skin.

On my way out of town, I would pass by a well-paved path on my right that led through heady scented, tall mimosa trees at the Waldensian Center, which was composed of tidy homes fenced in by a stone wall, a form of modern architecture that harmoniously fit into the natural environment. A large construction sat in the middle with small, functional buildings radiating out like a sunburst. Lodgings conceived to encourage community life while respecting individual needs. Ample space for the communal cafeteria. A tiny kitchen in each room, which became a mini-apartment, a small personal island.

An avant-garde experiment in the ancient district of Riesi, clinging to the slopes of Mount Stornello. Riesi is a district that has always existed. It existed when the Arabs ventured up to the high plains of the inland, between sulfurous valleys and gypsum rocks, between floods of saltwater and seething mud, and there they stopped.

Innovation and invariability. That's how people live in Riesi. The pendulum swings, never arriving at a decision between bold utopias and everyday violence, between ancient wisdom and everyday destitution. It swings, and doesn't stop, between the proclamation of the Socialist Republic of Riesi after the war, which ended in great defeat along with the great peasant gamble, and the expansion of the Di Cristina empire, a seat of mafia command that was transmitted for at least three generations. Between the solemn funeral of the old boss of Cosa Nostra and the marriage of the young Christian Democrat mayor to the daughter of the Communist ex-mayor.

It was May. Springtime. I was leaving the town of the *alcarrazas*, the clay pots that keep water pure and cool—the same water rationed out by the extortion racket to the people and the parched land—and descending along hairpin turns down toward the Falconara beach. A dazzling crescent of sand, bordered by wild vegetation and an incredibly dense forest of prickly pears. At the extreme point of the crescent rose a rocky spur overlooking the bay, topped by a fourteenth-century turreted castle that was still intact.

At Falconara I would see the limpid sea that no longer existed in Gela, whose waters had already been polluted by industrial waste and the expansion of the suburbs. All cloudy and yellow, the great gulf opened onto the sea of Africa. The air stung. The sea stung. The waves stung. Invisible mosquitos, minute tormenting needles, scratched and pricked reckless swimmers' skin, burning their legs, stomach, and chest, while a sour smell drove away the salty air. Day after day the beach became a distressing garbage dump.

THE VIEW TODAY HAS radically changed. For the better. It happens. Even in Sicily, even in Gela, it's possible for something to change for the better.

"They're coming back to take a swim here."

A small victory for my Communist friend, for his party that has now changed its name and appearance. His two extremely brief experiences on the city council were of use if only for completing the work to equip ten kilometers of beach with everything people need to enjoy it. A stubborn determination to support Gela citizens' customary pastimes, a kind of attention that shouldn't be underestimated.

"At least we've reclaimed the shore on the environmental level," he proudly told me about at least one battle that was won, while we were trying to slice a rubbery pizza at a table on the waterfront. The entire place was turning red with lights, busy with cars, evening chats, and soccer games being played on the beach under bright floodlights. This too was a new liveliness.

"All that life," I commented, joking. "Better than at Rimini."

"Yes, it's livable," he replied, pointing at the shoreline disappearing in darkness, beyond the streetlights, beyond the low wall that borders the sidewalk.

The pollution from sewer drainage has been eliminated and the waste treatment system for domestic sewage and industrial waste managed by Petrolchimico seems to work. And the sand that is famous for its therapeutic virtues—virtues that even prompted a prince to venture out of his faraway, undisclosed Nordic town on the tip of Europe every summer—is clean.

But now it's morning. Thursday morning. I walk along the deserted waterfront with a vacationer's gait; the signs are turned off, the sidewalk empty, the doors barred shut. Even though it's the end of June, everything is closed on weekday mornings. The hordes of vacationers don't arrive down here in Gela. The cafés and pizzerias, standing in line one after the other as on any old waterfront of any old seaside town, are open only in the evening. An unusual sight. The tangible sign of a way of life that even conquered the south of the south. Because this is Gela, the extreme southern edge of Italy, facing the African coasts. It's not possible to go further south than this.

I finally find a café that's open, a little blue shanty with a small terrace facing the beach. Wood floors and a roof made of reeds. A sense of isolation, as if in a stilt house lost in a sea of sand.

A little boy, eleven or twelve years old at most, is taking the orders. Skinny, with a small rag tied around his neck and worn with superstitious faith. More of a talisman than a remedy against a sore throat. He's hardly able to whisper, his voice surely left in some humid basement home without any windows. He sets down a glass of lemon granita in front of me. His hands are scrawny, wrinkled like a small monkey's. Old.

I dip the teaspoon into the soft white foam. And it's a surprise. I had forgotten the flavor, the inimitable taste of the Sicilian granita. I'm equally surprised at myself, for having been able to forget it.

Someone spies my surprise. I look up. Through the rush matting that hangs down from the reed roof to block the light, my eyes meet the little boy's: black, wide-open, bright eyes.

"Have you been bewitched? Come over here. There's washing to do." A woman leans inside to check what's going on, big bare arms resting on the small shanty window that faces the terrace made of beams and reeds. "This son of mine, he was born sitting down." She laughs, revealing her bad teeth. "Really. I'm not just saying that. That's how I have my children, sitting on a chair."

She stares at me. She looks over at the newspapers that

I set down next to the glass, on the rotting wood table. She stares back at me again. "Do you have any children?"

"No. No children."

A compassionate look. But being kind, to console me, she says, "Lucky you." She turns around to see if her little boy is working. Then faces me again. "I have nine pups weighing on my shoulders."

I go back outside to continue my walk along the deserted waterfront; the wind makes it pleasant, tempering the hot June air. But I remember the African winds too, full of sand, devastating. I pass by oleanders and bougainvillea, bushes of sweet, juicy blackberries and black mulberries. An intense, wild perfume of summer. But the light of day beats down on torrents of garbage that still rage between the homes. When the wind shifts, the scent of rotten eggs returns, enveloping me, and traces of filthy wastewater slow my steps. Dusty sprigs of grass grow in the cracks of the uneven sidewalk, which the night disguises and conceals.

The city has given itself a light touch of makeup. A bit of painting, I think, to confuse the march of time and reshuffle the cards.

The Conchiglia, a charming beach resort built on the water, with huts and the main building that widens in the shape of a shell, continues to sink deeper into the advancing shore. Right in front of it, anchored directly into the asphalt street, stands a garish, outlandish bus-bar with two stories, painted red, with little yellow curtains that are flapping hard against the name: *The Arena—London.*

I arrive at the carnival rides on the seashore. A small amusement park where one of the men killed in the most spectacular massacre in Gela, the one on November 27th, 1990, used to work. Eight left dead, the majority of them extremely young, seven wounded, three, maybe four groups of shooters that carried out an equal number of ambushes in the dirt alleys of illegally built neighborhoods and in the crowded downtown avenue, beneath the brightly lit Christmas decorations. For years in Gela all of the major holidays have ended in a blaze of gunfire and blood: one Christmas after another, and then Easter and then the city's patron saint's day. On those days the wolves come out of their dens. They're days of solemn church masses, processions. Behind the biers of the saints, behind the municipal insignias are all of the men who count filing by. They're days filled with distracted crowds. They're days when it's easy to kill.

I sit down on the platform at the end of the bumper car track, and I wait. This is the place Tina's uncle chose for us to meet.

TINA'S FATHER HAD CATEGORICALLY prohibited it. No one in his family was supposed to see Zio Michele anymore.

"Him, he's a stranger to me," he said disdainfully, exerting rigid control over his tone of voice. "For me, he doesn't exist. And he doesn't for you either. He doesn't exist at all."

Their mother hadn't risked saying even one word to defend her brother, who was guilty of an unmentionable crime. Zio Michele had abandoned his wife and five children to go live in a dilapidated house in the middle of the sand dunes, on the outskirts of the city, with his young male lover.

A queer for a brother-in-law was a disgrace, an intolerable source of shame. Almost like finding yourself with a cop in the family: a weak spot, an opening for enemies, a disgusting stain that already had people talking.

"That guy. You've all got to forget him."

But this time Tina hadn't obeyed. She had fun with Zio Michele and she liked the boy with the highlighted hair, always fresh from the hairdresser. He had the mysterious power of a dangerous influence. But with the oblivious, natural sagacity of a little girl, Tina understood that the lure of a dangerous influence could frighten just as it could enchant. Those smooth eyelids that lifted with a calculated, heavy slowness to expose blue irises exerted a disturbing attraction.

Her uncle would say, "As for being beautiful, he's beautiful. If only he didn't always have his feelers out . . ."

The boy would blush, his eyes dissolving into a tearful sweetness, and her uncle would laugh, and he'd laugh, too, his laughter fresh and young. As if he had suddenly lost every care. Besides, though the family's reaction hadn't been kind, business wasn't going badly at the wrecking yard. And there wasn't anybody as skillful as he was at handling stolen cars or documents. People who despised him needed his experience and services sooner or later.

Her father's death freed Tina of all her fear. He had gotten himself killed. He'd abandoned her. He was the one who'd betrayed her. Stunned by an unforeseen freedom that broke the bonds of obedience, she wasn't upset by her own betrayal. She could indulge freely in the magic of a dangerous influence.

So every Sunday during summer Tina's motor scooter would stop in front of the house in the middle of the dunes. It was a habit she could no longer give up. She'd arrive at noon, the customary time for a swim. All three of them would go down to the beach, the slender, glabrous boy, Zio Michele, corpulent and hairy, and Tina, her body still boyish and flat-chested, wearing a pair of boy's bikini underwear that bulged over a clump of rags. She gave up taking a dip in the sea. All for the haughtiness of that mound that rose precariously on her groin and for her love of showing off, she denied herself a dip in the sea to cool off. She preferred to lie sweating on the beach, peeping through her shuttered eyelashes down at the fabric as it curved over an imaginary swelling. It weighed on her pubis, as if it wanted to put down roots, to cling, actually grow, making her flesh blossom.

A crazy old lady who lived with the two lovers stayed at home. They called her Milli, and she still saw a few clients: the four north African immigrants who lived in the area, and the young boys with a little money in their pockets.

"Only under eighteen years old," she specified. "I only take the ones under eighteen years old. They're suited for me, all in all. There's no lost time with them. Always ready. As soon as you touch them, they're off."

One time they arrived in a group and seemed like too many for her—"Too many at my age," she decided. She convinced them to stand in line, one next to the other, and organized a beautiful masturbating contest.

Tina would return from the beach with dazed eyes, her sweat like a warm oil that subtly crept inside the briefs, soaked the rags and made the cotton collapse into a small, pitiful bump. The excitement spilled over, transformed into a painful awkwardness that drained her strength.

Rays of light filtered through the broken slats of the French door, but the shade of the living room was refreshing for anyone coming inside. Partly reclining on a wicker armchair, Tina waited for Milli to bring her something to drink and dispel the girl's acute pang of disquiet with her presence. The old woman was chasing the sweat on her breasts and stomach with a towel. Her dark cotton dress gave off the reassuring scent of fresh laundry. Then, playing around, Milli's hands slipped inside the briefs and fixed up the cotton, fluffing the fabric, inventing a shape that assumed life and warm consistency at her careful, precise caresses. Until Tina again felt the same swelling that rose, that started from her flesh, that became flesh while old Milli's fingers searched around with a slow, exasperating touch and the tension built, built up until it finally exploded.

"HOW MUCH WILL YOU give me for the interview?"

"What interview?"

Zio Michele, wearing mechanic's overalls, the sleeves of his plaid shirt rolled up on his forearms, strong like a farmworker's, looked me up and down with a mix of avid curiosity and skepticism. He's exactly like I had imagined him. Except for one detail: the white hair on his furry chest. I struggle to pull my eyes away from the white clump coming out of his unbuttoned shirt, practically under his Adam's apple. This detail upsets me, as if it revealed a weakness, a fragile spot. It makes this thickset, ungainly man who is asking me for money pathetic in my eyes.

"Don't you want an interview?"

"I want to talk with you, that's all."

"And it's not an interview?"

"No, I'm not interested in an interview," I explain, trying to be—and seem— as straightforward and simple as possible. "I'm not here from a newspaper or a radio station. I don't have any money to give you."

His face becomes set in a suspicious, perplexed expression. But after a moment of hesitation, he sits down too, next to me on the bumper car platform.

At this point I don't know exactly what to do. I'm unsure about whether to stay on these uncomfortable boards or invite him to a café and offer him a cup of coffee or whatever else you can drink at this time of the morning. I look at the clump of white hair again and decide it's better to forget about it. I don't know what the right moves are, the degree of amiability I'm allowed, the limit I must not cross. I don't want to raise his expectations. The possibility of negotiating, of my giving in on the question of money mustn't even remotely flash through his mind.

Now we look each other over close up, his light brown eyes, nearly yellow, a short distance from mine. "If it's not an interview, why do you want to talk to me?"

I note his Italian is precise, even though spoken with a strong accent. He doesn't use dialect, but his voice possesses all of the deep resonance of people who use Sicilian every day. By now everyone is bilingual, I come to think. The merit—or fault—of immigration (Zio Michele surely spent a few years in the north) and television. It's not like it used to be anymore, when my colleague and friend Mariarita, a tenured middle-school teacher, would say three words and then slip punctually into dialect, no matter whom she might be speaking to. The habit has weakened, and now people use one language or the other depending on who they're talking with. If it's a stranger, Italian is called for. Not so much as a sign of respect or for the love of communication, but in order to keep their distance.

"So, why do you want to talk to me?"

"I'm writing a book." Nothing else comes to mind. Just this dry statement.

"About my niece?" He's amazed, but not excessively.

"Well, the thing is, not exactly. I need your niece as . . . a model, let's say. The places, situations, are all true. But everything else is an invention, a fictional story."

"A book . . ." he says.

"Yes, a book. A novel."

A sophisticated pursuit, I realize, in a city with over eighty thousand inhabitants where there isn't a single bookstore. Not even one.

I look at him and ask, just for the sake of it, "Novels . . . Do you read them?"

The question sounds a bit like a challenge. It goes without saying that the territory in which we're moving is mine. I'm the ruler of the game.

He looks right back at me and starts laughing.

"And what are novels? Do *piccioli* come out of them, does money come out of these novels?" he insists mockingly, defeating all my vain, albeit vague, ambitions to intimidate him.

"Money? Unlikely," I admit. "Very unlikely."

"Then why do you go around everywhere doing *curtigghiu*, talking here and there? What use is this novel to you?"

I shrug. I look at him again, he looks at me again, and we both break out laughing at the same moment. Together we laugh at my folly.

"I'm not an idiot," Michele says. But I hit the right key; my position is so eccentric, my pretension to talk without offering anything in exchange and without having surefire earnings for myself is so strange, all of this is so outlandish that it arouses sympathy. It earns a gesture of spontaneous collaboration.

"I'm not an idiot," he repeats. "No money, no interview. But I do want to give you a gift."

He fishes around with two fingers in the small pocket of his overalls. Then he offers me a snapshot.

The wind drags paper wrappers along the wide-open beach in front of us. The waves push swollen flows of foam that leave black outlines behind on the shore. It's the least exciting stretch of seashore. It's decidedly dirty. But all the same, there's a beach umbrella planted in the sand, between belts of algae and fans of tar.

I brush the hair back from my forehead, as the wind keeps blowing it in front of my face. I turn the photo this way and that without understanding it. Then and there I don't recognize the girl wearing a miniskirt, high heels, and lipstick. But then, beneath the heavy makeup, I encounter Tina's by now familiar gaze.

"A masquerade," says Zio Michele, delighted, it seems, at my surprise. "That's how my niece thinks of it. The skirt, the heels, all a masquerade."

In fact, I think, that clothing, that makeup, transforms Tina's mischievous face into an austere Greek mask. Her even features, high cheekbones, full lips, lowered eyelids that let an oblique, dazed look filter through, her whole face acquires a dramatic immobility. And the skirt doesn't suit her, though her legs are beautiful and slender; on her it's an authentic artifice.

"A girlfriend did her all up like that for fun. She has a shop . . . She's a hairdresser and likes to shake up my niece's look a bit. Tina is wild, but she lets Giovanna preen over her. She played along with the joke of the photo! Tina takes her jokes, and reproaches. Caresses and slaps. Giovanna's the only one who can smooth Tina's rough edges. The only one."

One of his shirt sleeves slides down to his wrist and he rolls it back up with his fingers, darkly stained by mechanic's oils. He murmurs, "But they don't know that I took the photo."

"A masquerade. Your niece is right," I say, clicking shut the fastening on my purse in order to put away the precious find; an unpredictable Tina who opens up an unedited chapter, a new page in my dossier.

Michele blocks my gesture, stopping my hand with his. His palm is rough and calloused.

"No, the photo stays with me."

"Wasn't it a gift?"

"I let you see it. That was the gift."

CHAPTER 8

"They say they'll come at night, like bandits."

The woman is very young. Her home in Sette-farine is one of five homes designated to be razed to the ground, as stipulated by the final judgment on an ordinance. Apparently, it will be the army that does it, because not even one company answered the call for bids on the public contract for the demolition work. Nobody is crazy enough to brave the people's fury.

A light-complexioned face framed by a huge mass of copper blond hair. The woman doesn't even look thirty years old. She speaks in a shrill, strained voice, that's no longer able to bend to a normal conversation. The tone of someone used to shouting from one end of the street to the other. And that's how she got hold of me, yelling from the opposite side of the street:

"Who are you looking for? Giovanna, the hairdresser?"

I couldn't see her, hidden partly behind the door as she was, so I got closer.

"She went down to town." Slightly cracking the door open a few centimeters more, she added, "She's my cousin." But evidently the subject didn't seem sufficient enough to justify her interest, her own intrusive courtesy. So she started explaining it to me:

"I always get frightened . . . At every sound down in the street, at each new face, I think: okay, this is it, they're arriving. They're coming to destroy my home. Most of all, I get frightened at night. Because they'll come at night, like bandits."

The door continues to crack open slowly. But not wide enough to reveal the inside of the house. I vainly try to get a glimpse behind the woman's shoulders. On the inside, the houses are beautiful, I've been told.

Settefarine is the sad imitation of a nondescript suburb, if such a thing is ever possible. The dirt streets don't have names. No municipal map includes them or recognizes them. And yet they form a perfect square network of cross streets and parallel ones in an effort to resemble an urban plan. Everything in Settefarine seems barely roughed in, waiting for the work to start. Everything is temporary. The water and electricity hook-ups, the garbage left behind the houses, and the sewage discharged in front of them are all temporary—and illegal.

And yet, inside, the homes are beautiful. That's what I've been told. Inside, the homes are sacred. Untouchable. People don't wash up in order to keep the bathroom clean, they live on top of each other in the space for the garage; after all, they're used to tight spaces, to rooms that have to be used by everyone. The residents of Settefarine are peasants; it's possessing something itself that matters, and since they're not able to possess land anymore they try to possess a house.

"Giovanna is my cousin," the woman intentionally repeats. But she doesn't dare to openly ask the reason for my visit. I pretend not to catch the allusion to the unspoken question, and she doesn't insist.

But remark after remark, one sentence after another, one smile following another, a question and an answer, the door finally swings wide open and the woman invites me to come inside.

"If you want to wait here inside, make yourself comfortable."

"Thank you. It's a great pleasure."

The ground floor is a large room with no windows and no plaster on the walls, and the floor is rough and grainy. A car and a Vespa are parked in a corner. On the other side of the room stand a couch, a few chairs, a battered table, and the television. And a very old, very used gas stove. The telephone is attached to an extension cord that hangs down from the stairwell. The woman points at it.

"Every time it rings . . . I live in fear. Every time I imagine that they're calling to warn us: They're arriving. I'm not afraid of anything else." She proudly straightens herself up. "My husband is a truck driver, an honest job. And I don't have broken kids."

"Broken?"

"You know, delinquents."

Her children are there, beside her. Two little girls gazing at me with their mouths open, and a cute boy, younger than them. Taking advantage of the unusual confusion, he has reached the door and is trying to slip outside unobserved.

"I lost my head over this business with the house. For a while I didn't even send the little girls to school." She tugs at her top that keeps riding up over her large, maternal breasts. "School is really important to me. I wanted to study. But then, as always happens, my father snatched my books away from me. And even my mother, when I became a young lady, said that was enough. I'd sneak out of the house to go to school. Then in the evening my father would beat me with a belt." She heaves a resigned sigh. "Now I have the house. Only the house, in my life. Nothing else. Only the house."

Her impulsive, genuine sharing of a confidence touches me. Her frustration must have been really strong for her to vent this way to a stranger. And at this point it's inevitable that it should happen; I can't escape a "guided tour" of the house, nor do I want to. My curiosity is about to have free rein.

We go up the stairs to the first floor and a large open

combined living and dining room with a kitchen. Brand new kitchen cabinets made of wood, and a glass dining table. Everything is shiny, impeccable. To the side are three bedrooms and a bathroom, perfectly tidy. The stairs continue up to a second floor. But the wall is painted up to eye level, then sharply becomes just coarse naked bricks.

"We still have to finish it. But there's time. The second floor is for our daughters, when they get married." She moves a chair, inviting me. "Here's a seat."

All of us, her, me and the two little girls, find a place in the living room, sitting in a circle near the table, facing the kitchen. The woman clasps her hands on the crochet-bordered tablecloth, which protects the sheet of glass and continues to pour out words expressing her nagging worry.

"We made a mistake, it's true. I recognize that. But we built this house to *live* in, not for property speculation. We paid for the land and in order to keep the construction work going we deprived ourselves of everything. When I signed the documents for the lot, wasn't it the notary's job to make inquiries about what the situation was and warn us? And the politicians who kept telling us 'go ahead and build, we'll regularize the construction.' Then they wanted to put us in the same category as the illegal villas, those second homes on the beach . . . Amnesty for everyone. But we only have this house. Where do I go if they knock it down? It's different for us. For us, it's a necessity."

She looks at me questioningly, her eyes confused, almost

sounding me out or asking for an opinion. I nod. How could anyone not recognize her necessity?

"I know, there was a swindle involved," I agree.

An unbridled housing development. And everyone declares they're innocent. But I'm certainly not going to be the one to condemn this woman, suffering real, authentic anguish.

On the other side of the street, a car brakes, and stops. The woman turns toward the window. "It's not Giovanna," she says, and looks at her watch. It's noon. "If you still want to wait a bit longer."

"Thank you, since I'm already here . . ."

It wasn't easy to get my bearings in these streets, designated in the best of cases by a letter of the alphabet followed by a number. B4, C6, V9 . . . It wasn't easy to find the house, without a number on it. And the shop, with no sign.

"How is it that you know Giovanna?" asks the woman, then suddenly, remembering her duties as host, "I have some cold coffee." She gets up. "Do you want some?"

I hate cold coffee, but say, "Gladly."

While she pours the dense liquid, a corrosive concentrate that I already feel churning in the pit of my stomach, into a glass, I find myself struggling with quite a dilemma. Up to now, I haven't lied, but I played on a misunderstanding. Ultimately I decide to tell the truth.

"I don't know Giovanna."

The woman stops stock still, alarmed, and her beautiful, creamy face turns red with anger.

I immediately try to reassure her. "A friend gave me her name. I have to talk with her. For something that I'm writing . . . A book. Yes, a book." I hurry to clarify, "I'm not a journalist."

Who knows what she had imagined. Hearing my explanation, the woman visibly relaxes, and smiles. "You think I'm afraid of journalists? Before this business with the house, I didn't understand anything. I didn't even watch the news on TV. Now I understand everything. Everything." She loosens the hair clip gripping the great luminous mass of her hair and asks, "But what do you want to talk to Giovanna about?"

"About a friend of hers. A girl."

"And what's this girl's name?"

"Tina," I say. "Her name is Tina."

"Ah." Another wave of red inflames her skin. "That girl."

"You don't like her?"

The woman lifts her hands again to fix her hair, which is too billowy for just one hair clip, as locks slip loose and escape, curling down her neck, above her ears.

"Giovanna is everyone's friend." She enunciates the words slowly. "Everyone's."

She puts the glass on a saucer, places it in front of me, and sits down.

"She was good to me when I couldn't sleep because of

this house business. She helped me, even though her house wasn't in danger. She always finds ways to fix things, she has someone who fixes things for her . . . Instead, I fight my own battles."

Her excitement erupts again, the desire to tell her story. Nearly shouting, hands and head moving, she plays out the events. "When I organized the march, all the women spread the word: *pe' case, curremo*, we run for houses. All of them were behind the effort. All of these women walking in the rain, and the children who came running from school. We were in Palermo nine times. And nine times at City Hall. An usher said to us, 'Do you think a few women can stop an ordinance?' But there were at least fifty of us, and we were angry. Even though at times . . . There are some people who are ashamed to come out of their house. Because people point at us and say, 'Look, those are the women who live in Settefarine.'"

The older girl turns sullen, and frowns. The younger one continues to stare at me adoringly without saying a word. Both of them glance admiringly at my colorful Swatch watch, at my purse with its wealth of straps and studs, a souvenir from a trip to America.

"I even tormented my husband. We don't eat around here anymore, nothing gets done anymore with all this worrying, he'd say. But now I've calmed down a bit, I'm buying a baby."

For an instant I stare at her, disconcerted. In all of the

years living on the "continent" I've lost the habit of the Sicilian vocabulary. Then it clicks. "Sure," I confirm to myself. Here you aren't expecting a baby, that's too simple, too direct. Here they say babies are bought.

"I'm happy about this child. He helps me. It was a true desire for me. Don't you think so? Come with me," she urges me, changing unconsciously to the informal manner of address. "I'll show you something. You two stay here," she orders her daughters.

The double bed is covered with a shocking pink synthetic satin quilt. High on the wall above the head of that satin, perfectly in the center, hangs a faded pastel painting of the Madonna, her hands clasping a pearl rosary. The woman gets on her knees on the bed and takes down the painting. She turns it over. A packet of birth control pills is stuck into the frame.

"You see? I know how to look out for myself. You know what they say: men get all the pleasure, women get all the problems. My husband, poor sweet guy, respects me. He's not like so many men who don't care. But in order to stay safe, I . . ."

She puts the painting back in place and quickly makes the sign of the cross. "You see?" It's really my desire to have this child." And she tells me, "You know, Giovanna is also buying a baby."

"And is she happy as well?"

She takes a while to answer this time.

"Giovanna isn't married yet," she replies, avoiding my gaze. Embarrassment for that improper motherhood? It doesn't seem likely. It's a fairly common situation, accepted in spite of the stereotype that always and forever, across the centuries, has invariably portrayed the Sicilian woman as a virgin, shut away alone somewhere.

"He had to go away. To the north," my hostess says, remaining vague and generic, as if she wanted to get around an obstacle.

"Why?"

"What do I know? Maybe it was Giovanna's mother-in-law. She doesn't want her son to marry her. She's too jealous. Yes," she says, relieved as if she had finally found the right argument to make, "she's too jealous."

It's clear she's lying. But I don't understand why and what she wants to hide. I realize she's glancing furtively at her watch. She can't wait to get out of her bind.

"It's late," I hasten to say. "I can't wait anymore. I'll come back another time."

"I'll tell Giovanna. I'll tell her to look for you."

We go down the stairs and cross through the large, windowless room on the ground floor, part garage and part living room.

I go outside. In an open space of bumpy dirt, the little boy is playing all alone, going in and out of the carcasses of burned-out cars. Orange peels roll up around the clotheslines, drying under the sun, smelling fragrant.

"JESUS, HOW BEAUTIFUL."

Giovanna and Saveria appeared at the window to admire the Alfa Romeo 164 that Tina had borrowed from Nino, the mechanic.

"A spin to check the engine," she had proposed while the boys in the shop were checking the car's tuning. She couldn't resist when she saw it looking so new, shining, the chrome recently redone. The smell of dirty, burnt oil, stronger than usual, was stagnating in the narrow space of the auto shop and putting everyone in an intoxicated daze. The boys seemed like a bunch of cats ready to slip under the cars to get drunk on rancid traces of oils and fumes.

"Just a short spin," Tina insisted impatiently.

And Nino agreed to it with a magnanimous wink: "Bring her back to me tomorrow."

"Jesus, Jesus," Giovanna and Saveria kept on exclaiming. A customer with her wet hair wrapped in a towel was wedged between them, pushing against them with her legs, so big they swallowed her ankles, in order to look out the window too. She wasn't a regular customer. Tina didn't remember ever seeing her before.

"Is it yours?" the woman asked, clearly torn between envy and suspicion. "But do you have a driver's license?"

Tina stiffened. Nobody risked treating her that way, like a little girl, anymore. Anger flashed in her eyes, then was quickly held in check; the woman was one of Giovanna's customers. And Tina loved and respected Giovanna.

She shrugged, tossed the keys on a shelf between bottles of shampoo and hairspray, combs and containers of soft, delicately colored creams, and sullenly began to wait for Giovanna to finish setting the meddlesome old woman's hair.

"You're too much of a troublemaker," the old woman insisted, getting settled under the hairdryer.

Tina put on her headphones and turned on her Walkman.

The roots of her bad mood sank down into embedded realities that were different and deeper than dissatisfaction or unfulfilled needs. She would have liked to make a spectacular entrance that day. She dreamed of the splendor of an entrance worthy of her. The Alfa 164 and black leather jacket. An exceptional combination. The right occasion for enhancing her image, for trying out the role the newspapers had invented for her. A public personality, they wrote. But what did that mean? And each time Santino *'u pilurussu* sneered: "Did you all see her? Rambo." Constraining her to give tough answers, always poised on a razor's edge. But if it hadn't been for the threat that seeped out of Santino's jokes, she would have liked a beautiful photo of herself on the front page, fully decked out.

The Alfa and the black leather jacket. She could already feel Giovanna's disapproving but admiring eyes on her. But when she'd gone to get the jacket out of the closet, she discovered it was green with mold.

"Damned house."

Tina tightened her fists to repress a rash desire to scream.

The newspapers wrote that she was a boss, that she commanded and was obeyed, feared, and respected. The journalists came down from the north to interview her. Who knows what they imagined: what profits, what money, what kind of life. Her life, ha! Forced to rot in that awful place. And her house! An ugly room, mold seeping through its walls, an old motor scooter, a borrowed car. That's all she earned from being a boss.

"Would I live here if I were a boss? A real boss?" Tina had said exasperatedly to a reporter. But all he did was stare at her with a fake look of understanding, hiding his excitement at managing to pry a few words out of her mouth.

Finally the customer left. Her fine, thinning hair hung in waves around her cheeks. The lipstick she had retouched on her wrinkled lips stained her teeth. Tina shuddered with disgust. Red on her lips, red on her fingernails, red on her cheeks. Not to speak of all the prostheses that women put on: high heels and garter belts and bras. An illness, a dark evil among women, young or old. What else could that fixation with hiding, correcting, inventing heights and measurements and colors be? Her own vanity was different. Her vanity was that unmentionable fantasy of seeing herself in the newspaper with the Alfa and black leather jacket.

Her fingers suddenly froze while she was running them through her hair, her eyes fixed on the mirror in the hairdresser's shop. With the tip of her index finger she slowly examined the blood red stain, right at her hairline. For some time, round, annoying blotches like burns had been appearing on the skin near her hair. They'd appear, then disappear after a short while, leaving a ring-shaped scar. Tina thought they were the screams that she kept inside.

She rubbed her hands on her jeans. Then she pulled the envelope with the money out of her pocket. She gave it to Giovanna. "It's an extra payment from the jeweler."

Since the moment when Nele and Antonino *'u niuru*, big black, Giovanna's fiancé, had gone into hiding, the money was never enough. It was up to Tina to fatten the bank accounts registered in Saveria and Giovanna's names, which served to pay the two fugitives' expenses.

"Two elusive super-killers," the newspapers called them. But without Tina's money and the two women's bank accounts, how long could those two have stayed on the run? Antonino, twenty-three years old, and Nele, twenty-four, were both wanted by the police because they were responsible for some ten homicides, according to the investigators.

The money in the envelope, collected by Tina's little soldiers, belonged to the organization, which, however, authorized the deposit for the fugitives. A kind of salary. A pitiful sum, thought Tina. A few crumbs of charity, with all of the real money that was going around. There wasn't any justice.

"In a few days I'll send them on another round."

"You're crazy." Saveria was nearly yelling at her. "You come here to bring money in that car? And if they had stopped you? If they had arrested you for driving without a license?"

Tina brusquely shut up her sister. "I know what I have to do." In retrospect, the fear over her carelessness gnawed at her stomach.

Meanwhile Giovanna had lifted up a pile of towels and pulled a photo out of the rudimentary hiding place, holding it out to Tina.

"Look at this."

The two elusive fugitives were smiling, with their hands in the pockets of light-colored, elegant coats, surrounded by a host of pigeons. The wind had ruffled the tufts of Nele's hair, which had grown too long, whereas Antonino was lowering his eyes to hold back the smile playing around the crease in his firm, sensual lips.

Antonino was the more worldly of the two. Working as a ragman with the cart hooked onto his car, he had traveled to the markets in all of Sicily and Calabria, pushing onward toward northern Italy. A job that he liked. It gave him the freedom to drive in perfect solitude from one town or piazza to another. And to exert the charm of his smile, which revealed white, hungry teeth shining from the gloomy, dark face that had earned him the nickname *niuru*. But the trade in rags wasn't as profitable as the heroin trade. Leaving one for the other was inescapable, at the first opportunity. To get into the right circle, though—the serious circle that made wealth possible—took time. The apprenticeship for people who started from scratch could be long. And useless. And deadly.

In the background, behind the bodies of the two friends who'd become even more united by being on the run, you could make out the blurry portal of a church.

"It's Piazza Duomo," exclaimed Tina, happy to recognize the place. She had arrived right in Milan during her only trip beyond Sicily. Nele had had to meet someone and had chosen her as his escort because she was an expert at using a gun and had an innocuous appearance, looking like a slim, timid little boy, despite those flashes of provocative mischievousness that would light up her face.

They were traveling armed, and so had taken the train, to Tina's great relief, since she'd never have confessed her superstitious fear of flying in an airplane.

"And you two tell me *I'm* crazy. You keep this photo here?"

Giovanna ripped it out of Tina's hand, as if she were afraid to see it disappear.

"What good is the photo? After all, they're coming back now. They have to conclude a job."

"Does his mother know?" Tina maliciously probed. She didn't like Antonino and his man of the world pomposity. She preferred him far away from there, far from Giovanna.

"She told me," her friend confessed, in defeat. And she started to get busy cleaning up the shop.

Seeing her compliance, Tina filled with regret. Regret

about her question's veiled aggressiveness, and about her own ill-concealed aversion.

"Wash my hair, come on."

She planted herself under the faucet. Her head was clean, but she'd suddenly had the desire to feel Giovanna's hands in her hair. With Giovanna, and only with her, she instinctively sought out physical contact when she was troubled by something she couldn't explain.

"A job," she said, turning it over in her mind. "They have to finish a job."

The stream of cold water poured onto that thought, which made her involuntarily shiver. Giovanna's fingers began moving slowly, persistently kneading her temples, descending down her neck.

"More," sighed Tina. "More."

CHAPTER 9

Twenty years ago, one only had to go a little farther on the abandoned plain, between piles of debris never removed from the sides of the road, beyond the mouth of the polluted Gela River, beyond the embankment where empty drums were sinking into the mud and the foam from industrial waste was dying. One only had to go a little farther, around the barbed wire that replaced the boundary wall, beyond the charred remains of some bonfires, beyond the manure heap of the escarpment where rats raced through. One only had to go a few meters farther in the direction of Petrolchimico's iron and cement structure, amidst the waste, piles of crushed stone and brushwood, to run into packs of stray dogs.

I used to stop, shut inside the Fiat 500, to observe the huge garbage dump to which the dense brush of oleaster, holm oak, and mastic trees had been reduced. And I would ask myself if all of this might be the sign of promised wealth or the revenge of an impregnable poverty. Everything was polluted. And not only along the Gela River.

Those were the times when people were talking about nerve gas in Comiso and atomic fallout shelters at the American military base in Sigonella. The newspapers reported stories of mysterious containers abandoned in the countryside. An oil tanker had sunk, and its gashed sides poured a sticky slime onto the pink beaches of Scicli. In Augusta and Melilli, the dirty smoke from the refinery made holes in the clothing hung out to dry that no mending could limit or hide. In Sicily, the great garden, everything was contaminated, ruined, corrupted, infested, dirty.

Not all in the same way. There still existed the filth of the rich and the filth of the poor. The former possessed the levity of a child's game, seeming to not leave any traces, not have any consequences. In contrast, the latter set off epidemics and infections. It filled the hospitals in Gela with vomit and diarrhea.

But on the other side of the Fiat 500's windshield, the world—the world of the rich and the poor, of the Villaggio and the first illegal settlements—already vaguely appeared like a poisonous nightmare.

The trees in the grove, laid bare by the smokestacks' breath, exposed their skeletal branches and, like pitiful cemetery ghosts, cast a sickly white light on the oily water of the river. At times a yellow cloud billowed out from the Petrolchimico towers. Up there in the air, poised between those lunar volcanoes, it swelled up and then fell, rolling vertiginously down onto the city, spraying black lightning.

Driving in low gear, I would go deeper into a landscape that looked bombed out, ravaged by insatiable plunderers. All of a sudden, the dogs would be right there. Dull fur, hollow flanks. The head of the pack checked out the humans who violated his territory, his pupils the toxic yellow of the cloud and throat vibrating with a suppressed growl. It was a war of nerves between men and dogs.

I would immediately give up. I'd roll up the window and turn the car around, going in another direction to continue my "aimless jaunt," as I used to call my idle, solitary roaming that took me to the most unexpected places and revealed the unknown island to me. I'd get in my Fiat 500 and off I went. And yet my roaming needed a definition, a precise positioning on a scale of activity; at the time I thought that it was my instinct for exploration guiding me.

A little further on, my "aimless jaunts" took me to cross over the mighty arch launched toward nothingness, part of a highway that didn't go anywhere. It was a good idea, in the beginning: to build an escape route from Petrolchimico, a highway link road for the trucks that drove through the city, a direct juncture between the plant and the highway to Catania. The link road was built. The entrance ramps arched their powerful spans. The exit still had to be constructed.

After the overpass, I'd sometimes go back again, out of an unexpected taste for a challenge. The road seemed like a track prepared in anticipation of fortune's landing. And the dogs were still there. So many of them, hungry, menacing.

I still feel like an explorer now, even though my "jaunts" always have an aim, now that life has become shorter. So I should avoid the useless search for an exit that has never been built. The trucks continue to drive through the city and all that remains of the original idea are a few kilometers of highway, cleanly truncated over the void.

And yet here I am, again traveling over lost roads. Sitting still in the Fiat Uno rented at the Catania airport, beneath a grandiose, superfluous overpass. A monument to the impossibility of escape, to the barrier to all development. A triumphal arch that celebrates the fracture, the leap into nothingness. The leap of young lives wasted in the streets of Gela.

But the dogs aren't there anymore. Garbage, cars, the desolation of dismantled industrial buildings, of faint, evaporating streams of smoke. But no dogs. In the end, they were defeated by men. The hunger for land, speculation, illegal construction reconquered the territory inch by inch. And now the dogs only fight in closed breeding pens.

FRANCESCO DIDN'T LIKE THE dog fights. Nonetheless, he stayed. With his eyes clouded over and back held rigid, he tried to isolate himself from the other boys' excitement, while at the same time not moving away from them. Francesco 'u maccarruni: a monotonous, obsessive refrain that numbed his heart and wounded his mind. So he went on and on searching for approval, a sign of agreement, a friendly touch in the heat of the dog fight. He couldn't walk off, carrying the weight of voluntarily excluding himself on his shoulders. He had stayed there, trembling with the same insane tremble of the beasts hurling themselves one against the other.

The boys' shirts were soaked with sweat that flowed from an inner magma, from bodies self-combusting. The material became light and transparent, glued to strong, mature shoulders or to adolescent backs, to the knots of their spinal cords. It gave off a wild odor.

An entire day had gone by. Nevertheless, the stench of the sweaty shirts, the slobber and blood of the animals, and too many glasses of red wine, sludgy like petroleum and bitter, still churned in Francesco's stomach. Sitting in the back seat of the Lancia Thema, at every curve in the road he felt a wave of nausea rising inside.

"Stop."

Tina braked, pulling over. The boy barely made it in time to get out before a stream of vomit shook his entire body.

In the front seat, "Filippo mai mori" grumbled in disgust, "Great way to go to a robbery." On his right hand, which was drumming impatiently on his thigh, the shiny, celluloid-like skin of a large scar stood out. A souvenir of the boiling water he'd spilled on himself when he was a little boy playing in his basement home.

Tina was staring straight ahead, gripping the wheel tightly. Careful to divert any suspicion of shame by erasing it with impassivity. The world imagined people like them having total and continual control. They even expected, yes, expected, perfectly orchestrated executions, as if they were marionettes, puppets made out of wood. People couldn't imagine how normal it was in their work for the body to fail, to have muscles unexpectedly and uncontrollably contract, cramps, painful spasms in the pit of the stomach. In their work, pretending was fundamental. Precisely that, pretending.

A good actor must know how to get into the part at the right time. She had seen a film being shot once, in a piazza in a nearby town. She was impressed. The clapperboard strike, and action. Nothing else exists beyond the actor's gestures, movements, expressions. Taking off the mask for an instant is all it takes to blow the whole performance. It's all in appearance.

The same ability, she'd said to herself, surprised. Actors were required to have the same ability that was necessary in their work. To change skins on command, from one moment to the next. Francesco didn't have that, she thought, he had never been able to do the necessary quick change. He didn't possess the talent to become a great actor.

"I'm fine." The boy wiped off his face with a tissue.

He balled it up and threw it on the side of the road. "I'm fine now."

But a sense of discomfort and premonition of misfortune still quivered in his throat. It wasn't a lucky day. Until he was touched by the air coming from the hills, carrying away the smells and tastes that were suffocating him. He took a deep breath, finally free. A burst of euphoria. His legs and his chest felt at ease. Now he was ready.

On the right appeared the homes in Giarratana, a village with under fifty thousand residents and just one jewelry store: their objective. A modest, small-town jewelry store, without any showy splendor in the display window or in the safe. But on the other hand, it had no security doors, just a doorbell—not always working—to allow a superficial and superfluous once-over of the customers. Everyone knew everyone in Giarratana, and the townspeople went inside to chat, sometimes forgetting to close the door behind them. The location of the shop was perfect too. It was downtown, but practically at the end of the main street, near a widening in the road where the Lancia Thema could park without any problems and immediately get onto the highway. A really easy robbery. The "superiors" had given the okay, a necessity for any job outside their area. Nothing to it, routine business.

It was a calm afternoon that was drawing peacefully into evening. The piazze, streets, and shops were empty; the evening stroll hadn't begun yet. The situation could be considered under control. The Lancia Thema pulled over to the sidewalk, on the opposite side of the street, right at the entrance to the widening. Looking out of the window, they saw the jewelry store owner who was reading a newspaper spread out on the counter. Alone. It was time.

Tina stayed inside the car, at the wheel. Before getting out, "Filippo mai mori" made the sign of the cross. "Amen," he whispered when he was done, raising his fingers to his lips for a kiss of devotion. He got out. He crossed the street and rang the bell to ask for the lock to be opened. A well-dressed boy, blue linen jacket and white shirt. The man in the jewelry store lazily reached out his hand and pushed a button. The door opened. The boy hesitated for an instant in the doorway. The instant Francesco needed to reach him, go in front of him and plant himself at the counter, with a pistol pointed at the man's forehead.

During the few steps from the car to the shop, Francesco had pulled the balaclava down over his face. An excessive, absolutely unnecessary gesture, especially for a piece of action outside their habitual field, outside their territory. "Filippo mai mori" was there fully at ease with his face uncovered. But Francesco preferred as always to conceal himself behind the balaclava.

Prudence didn't have anything to do with his ritualized, propitiatory gesture. It was the contact between the cotton and his skin. It was a screen that suddenly separated Francesco from himself even before separating him from others. It didn't serve to hide, but to invent. It was a rebirth. There was also the expression of the people who couldn't find anything to grab onto, and didn't dare enter the bare light of his gaze. That was where a hidden power was concentrated, and emerged. That was where Francesco *'u maccarruni* no longer existed.

The jewelry store owner was a strong man. Forty years old, perhaps. His face contorted, one of his eyelids began flapping like the wing of an entrapped bird. But he didn't put up a fuss. He opened the safe that was on the wall facing the counter, his eyes constantly glued to the barrel of the Beretta that Francesco aimed with his outstretched arm. "Filippo mai mori" swept necklaces, rings, and watches into a modest dark plastic bag.

"Now the cash."

The man went back behind the counter to hand over the money he kept in the cash register. That was all. In a few minutes they had finished. "Filippo mai mori" had already gone outside, holding the bag, and Francesco was also about to leave when he picked up on a movement.

Incredulous, he saw the man's right arm slide across the wood counter, slip down below its edge, and almost imperceptibly move around blindly, searching. His eyes continued to follow the barrel of the Beretta, but with a different kind of determination. As if they wanted to keep it at bay with the simple strength of their gaze. It was an absurd, insane challenge. For a long moment, in a paralyzing stupor, Francesco watched that careless hand moving automatically, independently from the man's conscious will. Driven by a dangerous, irrepressible impulse.

Without hesitating, Francesco's index finger tightened on the trigger until it clicked. The weapon rose up in his hand while the man fell over on the counter and his head bounced with a crash that resounded more loudly than the shot itself.

The first sensation he had was relief. It had been easy. Simple. The breath held in during the mechanical concentration on the act of shooting had dilated his chest. He didn't dwell on thinking about whether the man lying on the counter was dead or only wounded. Then, anxiety about escaping overrode every other sensation.

He rushed out while his breath of relief still lingered behind him. He checked the street, looking to the right and the left. He dove into the car.

Easy. It had been easy. His index finger had closed around the trigger. The target had fallen. But in the instant that had elapsed between the two movements, in that infinitesimal fraction of a second, Francesco had had the time to see the man's hair, which was starting to thin, the first signs of baldness. And his left hand had started to slide along on the edge of the wood counter. His fingers kept on moving, closing in the act of grasping, of grabbing onto something that slipped away. A fraction of a second. But that was all it took for Francesco to have the feeling of seeing the real target for the first time.

They went all the way to Licata to have dinner in a

pizzeria. They'd gotten rid of the Lancia Thema and were traveling on two high powered motorcycles. Twenty-three kilometers there and twenty-three back. Nele was there too, even though he was a fugitive, and had gone on ahead of them in a car.

Four tables on the sidewalk and a long, striped curtain that went clear to the ground. On the side, a plastic plant blocked the way for pedestrians, forcing them to step into the street. Beside them, a large table with boys and girls who had the nice appearance of students on vacation. They kept their voices low, they laughed politely. Louder than them, the mosquitos and moths sizzled as they hit the blue light of a mortal trap.

"Will you make up your mind?"

Tina had almost ripped the menu out of Francesco's hands.

"I'll have a pizza napoletana."

She was irritated, nervous. Not because of what had happened, but because it had happened to Francesco. She was keeping an eye on him, evaluating every little movement, sign, every piece of evidence conveying an emotional reaction. There was an involuntary respect in her nervousness, but also an ambiguous agitation, as if the boy had wrongfully invaded her space in some way. And her voice had a new distant tone that masked a nebulous will for revenge.

For his part, Francesco was chewing listlessly. Even in his plate or the rippling wine in his glass, he continued to see those fingers closing, groping around in the effort to grab onto an invisible hold.

Nele filled the boy's glass again. He showed understanding.

"You learn," he said. "Take it easy. You learn to not let it bother your appetite. Or your sleep."

After all, Francesco was only sixteen years old. If everything went well, if fate shined on him, he had time to learn.

CHAPTER 10

July is the official vacation season. In July, not any earlier, the little summer homes of Manfria are opened up. Years ago, you almost couldn't see them, scattered along the shoreline, hidden by the dunes, long Mediterranean dunes held by tufts of vegetation that stubbornly crept up to the shore, green umbilical cords at the foot of sandy knolls. The solitary sixteenth-century watchtower rose high, with its one little window looking out toward the sea.

Located seven kilometers away from Gela, Manfria was the traditional vacation spot of the nobles, followed closely by the new money, the beneficiaries of land speculation and illegal construction.

Now the rolling landscape looks as if it is stretched out, flattened, the beach leveled by the growing density of small summer homes. Vacationing in Manfria is fashionable, the recognition of social status. A new kind of trafficking was born around the villas and small homes, rented out to the tune of millions. Already in the month of June, finding a basement apartment, even in the neighboring areas as far as Licata, is a real stroke of luck.

Besides, trips, the large summer migrations for vacations, never conquered Gela.

All of southern Italy, to tell the truth, is reluctant to give itself up to the modern tourist frenzy. For far too long, ships and trains left from stations and ports of the south for an entirely different kind of trip, day after day, year after year, digging the furrows of emigration. Along the same furrows of summer, people came down to find family, share talk and food. And desire is still attracted by the return, not the departure.

I'm not surprised to know that tourist agencies are having a hard time getting off the ground. People flee, run away from the alleys of Gela, pursued by mafia vendettas or arrest warrants (and in that case tourist agencies certainly aren't needed). But people in Gela don't go on vacation. If they go anywhere at all, it's a few kilometers away, in order to repeat the usual rituals: afternoon naps, friends paying visits to each other, Sunday lunches.

From my uncle's summer home, the sea isn't visible. Through the shoots of climbing plants that shield the large, tiled terrace, I only get a glimpse of shiny light bouncing off the naked countryside. The whole family is reunited in my honor: my uncle and aunt, Mimmo, his wife, and their fourteen-year-old, Rosalba, who hastily calls me aunt in turn. There are guests and others who will come in the late afternoon, to have some ice cream or fresh fruit.

"The mafia, the mafia . . ." mocks my uncle, motionless in his chaise lounge. In his old age, his body tends to expand. His asthma makes him exhausted, and even standing up leaves him short of breath. "What is this 'mafia'? The mafia doesn't exist. Criminals exist. Criminals, that's it!"

Mimmo and I exchange a knowing look. At his age, what can you do? My uncle is one of the few people left (sometimes though I have doubts about the actual small size of these "few") to defend a thesis that had illustrious supporters in the past, but is by now dead and buried. Nevertheless, in contrast to them, my uncle's sarcasm isn't aimed at negating the existence of a mafia organization. He only wants to remove the mysterious secrecy from the word "mafia," the age-old patina that shields it against the vulgar banality of common crime.

"In the days of Federico II, Gela was a penal colony. What can you expect from the descendants of thieves and murderers?"

"The mafiosi also agree with you." Mimmo is making fun of him. "The mafia doesn't exist. That's the first piece of information that the little boys get at the moment they are inducted, or more precisely, as they say, 'made.' The name is Cosa Nostra, our thing. Mafia is a word invented by the press, by politicians."

The shiny reflections of light fray into sparks of pure incandescence, but nobody seems to notice, neither the young people nor the old. My brain is pierced by flashes of sleepiness that I try to resist, devising a thousand little tricks: I stand up, sit down again, straighten my back. Sitting on chairs and benches, the others indulge in quiet chatter. Isn't the afternoon nap, the noon siesta, customary anymore?

"Men of respect," spits out my uncle, loosening some phlegm that isn't at all metaphoric. "Thanks to drugs, they've gotten their villas and designer clothes and chandeliers worth millions of lire, just so they can be admired by the relatives who come to visit. Who else do they receive in their homes, those arrogant louts? Just to be envied by a cousin or brother-in-law, they buy marble bathtubs and tile floors."

Mimmo doesn't stop drinking. He has this habit of pouring a finger of wine and watering it down with sparkling water.

"There's hardly any left," he notes with plaintive regret, lifting the little bottle crowned with small bubbles that fizz on the glass rim. "Do you want to finish it?"

I quickly push my glass away. "How disgusting."

"Isn't it customary on the mainland?" he jokes. Then he points at his father. "It's not the mafia at all! It's you he's angry with, if you haven't understood yet."

"With me?"

Ill at ease again, I turn toward the patriarch of my family. The old man squeezes his swollen eyelids and wheezes a bit.

"Precisely with you," he confirms bitterly, narrowing his eyes again. "You never bother to maintain relations. Doesn't family mean anything to you? You've become worse than a mainlander. You disappear. Then you suddenly reappear only because you've become fixated, started fantasizing about that little girl, what's her name?"

"Tina," I say automatically. I'm always surprised by the scornful, hasty way others say the name of the girl who has become the object of my greatest worries.

"Who's Tina?" intervenes Rosalba, clearly letting us know it won't be easy for us adults to keep her out of the conversation much longer.

From the kitchen doorway where she's watching over the baking of a cake intended for our afternoon snack: "A girl with a gun," declares Mariangela, Rosalba's mother. "Do you all remember Monica Vitti? She was so beautiful with that poufy hair. But this girl, this Tina, doesn't need a gun to kill her seducer. Those guys, who kills them any more?"

Rosalba wrinkles her thin, light eyebrows. It's clear the reference to the film means nothing to her. It's logical. What can an old film say about honor and a shotgun wedding to a fourteen-year-old girl? And why should she be familiar with it? By now it's a code that only my generation or older can decipher.

"Sicilian women, they've changed," Mariangela suggests for my exclusive benefit. Her friend Pina, who works in market research, always traveling alone at the wheel of her car between Niscemi, Butera, and Ragusa, nods in agreement.

"In a few short years, a radical change."

Both of them vigorously work at convincing me, in the attempt to demonstrate that by now, even if you looked for them, differences between Sicilian and mainland women can't be found anymore. They're showing off an uncommon art of speaking. As if it were important for them to make a good impression on a foreign guest. And I'm still there searching for the connection, putting forth my credentials while they throw me back to the margins.

Will it happen like that with Tina? But there's an additional obstacle between her and me. An obstacle that requires special tactics for approaching her.

"We've changed, that's right," I say, my voice accentuating the "we."

Actually, something must have changed if a little girl can get it into her head to become a mafia soldier, to enter the most violent men's universe of all as a protagonist, to make the ruthless law of her father her own. A great subject for those who might maintain that the roads of emancipation lead directly to hell.

"Naturally," Mariangela admits, "when it's about ensnaring a husband, the games are always the same. When it comes to that, there's never been a difference between the island and the mainland."

"Sicilian women, maybe. But Sicily hasn't changed."

Mimmo breaks in with his knowing grin. "The front step of the house. Everything stops there. What lies beyond the front step of the house isn't of interest. That's why they leave the exterior walls without any plaster; what does the outside matter, you don't invest, spend money, wear yourself out for the outside. It's not 'our thing.'"

"Tina . . ." Rosalba interrupts us, all excited. "I saw her, Tina."

Mimmo abruptly turns toward his daughter. Mariangela stares at her, squinting her eyes, a vertical wrinkle of worry running down the middle of her forehead.

"On Telecittà. I saw her. They were asking her things . . . But I don't remember that well, it was at least a year ago. Maybe more. I was little."

Mimmo lets out a nervous burst of laughter, relieved.

"By the way, Papa. Are we going to pick up the award tomorrow?"

In the one month since school closed, Rosalba has won five awards playing all of the games and quizzes on private television channels all across the board.

"I passed all my classes. I have the right to have fun, don't I?" She spreads her arms in an expression of comic resignation. "Having fun . . . Well, I have to pass the time somehow." But on her little face there's a flash of authentic sadness.

Time. The eternal problem of adolescence. Boredom is different for adults, too busy living, and for old people, too busy surviving to count the time. It's the young people who struggle, caught in the rarefied suspension of fragile, useless days like soap bubbles.

"Let's go get the figs. Come on," she invites me, jumping to her feet with impatience for the game she's finally hit upon.

Stony and barren, the garden behind the house has the stark order of a suburban courtyard. Just a few trees, one standing at a distance from the other. In the middle of a rectangle of dry soil, a fig tree loaded with mature, overripe, and extremely sweet figs. We pick them carefully to put in a small basket. Rosalba is tall, I realize only just now, astonished. She's almost as tall as I am. She has full cheeks, the lines of her figure uncertain, chubby, belonging to the little girl who hasn't yet made up her mind to become a woman. She proudly wears a pair of pants that are the latest rage, the legs flared at the bottom. Exactly the same as the ones that were in fashion during my adolescent years.

"Listen. What kind of impression did Tina make on you?" I ask.

She glances at me sideways, her lips tightly set. She hesitates, as if she doesn't want to bring herself to disappoint me.

"Um," she lets out in one breath. "She liked that terrible music. Those Neapolitan songs, you know, that make you cry."

I smile. "You don't like them?"

Little by little, through Rosalba's eyes, I get closer to Tina.

It's not an easy maneuver, even if Rosalba helps me through the obstacle course. I push ahead. I approach cautiously. Until I succeed at going inside the empty times of that other adolescence, Tina's.

IT WAS THE LAST "crazy escapade," as she would say afterward. The last action taken recklessly, with no aim other than the affirmation of her existence. For some crazy fun, capricious exhibitionism.

The intention was that the gathering was supposed to be a kind of party. Like all parties, a lush meal was planned. In the countryside, on a Sunday. Nele had assured them he'd participate. He would come with a guest of respect, a mafioso. A promise that had electrified the boys, determined to show off, to do cartwheels in front of the two men. Fast on their motorcycles, experts with knives and guns; there were a lot of them and they were talented. Their skills had to be displayed. A competition in order to get themselves noticed by the two adults.

Ultimately though, neither one nor the other showed up.

The farmstead belonged to a family of shepherds who were connected to the man of honor. Tina knew that for months, two armored cars had been hidden in the stable.

"A hundred million lire each." Nele had spelled it out, rubbing together his thumb and index finger to mean in cash. But in that moment the stable was empty and the farmstead unused. The boys had the all-clear.

There were forty of them, perhaps more, all male. They ate roast chicken and pizzas bought in town, because they were used to delis and fast food. They were boys, not men like Nele and his friends who wouldn't give up eating roasted mutton and prepared it with their own hands, during those meetings where they didn't want even one woman under foot. They were boys. And they'd go even a hundred kilometers there and a hundred kilometers back for a dinner at McDonald's or any other fast-food restaurant that was in fashion at the moment.

The farmstead was sunken in the basin of a valley. Pastures in front of it, pastures behind. On the sloping hills the deep, dull green of the almond trees mingled with the shining gray of the olive trees.

The boys were eating and taking turns playing chicken on the dirt path. They took off at full speed on their souped-up motorbikes, from opposite ends, hurling themselves one against the other and dodging away at the last second. The tires raised the dust, veiling the path in an artificial haze that made it more difficult to calculate distance and when to dodge. And it made the final impact still more natural and more probable.

This game bored Tina. She would never have wasted her beautiful Yamaha with its rounded sides and flawless chrome plating on an empty thrill.

Miserable, like a poisoned beast! Nele not showing up wounded Tina's pride. It was a source of anguish, of apprehension, revealed by the red blotches that broke out on her face at every appointment he missed. She knew how risky it was to relax or simply let one's guard down now that the relations between clans and even between men in the same mafia family had become a continual war. She knew how to measure the exact level of danger, the point at which the game of "you kill one of mine and I kill two of yours" had arrived. She knew. She wasn't like those nobodies who shot at empty Coca-Cola bottles, busted wheels and engines spraying dust on a country path, and threw their life away in a crappy show.

She checked where Francesco might have gone off to. Lately it seemed that he was getting mixed up too much with a little blond kid, a small boy eaten up by drugs. He'd meet a bad end soon, if he continued that way. She'd warned the kid, he had to quit. She didn't want junkies around her. He should take her example. She only drank Coca-Cola and orange soda, and she didn't smoke even cigarettes anymore, a habit she'd given up, girlish nonsense. A toke was understandable in certain moments, when your heart was bursting and your hand couldn't grip the handle of a weapon any longer. But letting yourself get hooked on that stuff was something else. A weakness like that couldn't be tolerated. A junkie is capable of ratting anyone out.

If at least he had only done coke. But she suspected he had passed over to the needle. And he used certain new stuff, an American invention, that caused terrible diarrhea.

"A bullshit job," the crazy kid had exclaimed, shrugging. "Who turns down happiness for a bullshit job?"

"You've gotten skinny as a candle."

And what does it take to put out a candle? Nothing. A puff of air, and she'd breathed out threateningly in his face.

But meanwhile Francesco and the little blond guy were deep in conversation, laughing, and punching each other's arms playfully. Despite the hot weather, the boy was wearing a canvas jacket buttoned up at the wrists, over a black cotton turtleneck. Francesco was oddly animated. His complexion had an even color, and his cheeks weren't blushing the way they did when his tongue got twisted up in the effort to transform sounds into words.

Tina suddenly felt all alone. And bored. Boredom was a cold shadow. A dark stain that spread, swallowing her heart. Melancholy took hold of her like a shot of pain, while the cold shadow transformed into a fire that burned in her stomach and made her legs twitch. It was a feeling that took up more and more space, and overwhelmed her time. It no longer limited itself to seeping into the gap produced when she careened from the excitement of dangerous games, from the peaks where the rushes of adrenaline propelled her, to the empty mornings laying on her bed, listening to Nino D'Angelo and Merola. Now, even in the middle of a game, in the midst of others, the emptiness would suddenly spread wide open.

The boys had stopped. The air had become clear again.

Then it clouded right back up again while groups of boys swarmed, stirring up the dust on the road back home as they sat on their motorbikes, leaving greasy paper, plastic bags, dented cans, and empty shell casings in the clearing in front of the farmhouse. It was already nighttime when they realized that a power outage had left the town in total darkness. The Villaggio was totally dark too. The sky was illuminated only by Petrolchimico, which shone like a beacon in all that darkness.

Fascinated, Tina stopped. She liked the refinery plant. She liked skirting that desert of cement and iron, listening to its subterranean vibrations. She even liked the smoke's pungent odor. She looked at the dark road, the dark outlines of the homes in the distance. Only the monster's gasps kept the night awake and alive.

At that moment the idea came to her. She yelled out excitedly and called the others to gather round. When she saw they had all joined her, she started her motorcycle again. The Yamaha gained speed, quickly pulling away from the others. She slowed down. In a compact group they descended on the Villaggio. A swarm of grasshoppers, a flock of locusts, a wind tightening into the spiral of a tornado.

Sitting in twos on their motorcycles, they held each other tightly. They put on the brakes, then sped up, braked on a dime, then sped up. One of them would get off his bike and destroy the parked cars, smashing them with a crowbar. Turning around, in one leap he shattered the store windows.

He jumped back on the seat, put his arms around his partner, and off they went again. They sped through a flower bed. They blocked each other doing wheelies. Then they went back through the flower bed again, skidding in a spray of dirt.

It was an explosion, fireworks, a *masculiata*, a climactic burst that launched them up high, and higher still, where there was no anxiety anymore and everything burned, but painlessly. Their bodies and minds were ashes that drifted upward, lighter than the blue flames at the top of Petrolchimico's towers.

"A real circus," Tina commented a year later, her lips curling in disgust. "A stupid night. Over and done with. The Villaggio kids weren't even sitting on the low walls. What satisfaction could there be?"

TO ERROR IS HUMAN, *to get revenge is divine.*

"Don't rush, let me read this," I protest in front of the graffiti in the piazza in the Villaggio, the chosen hangout of Gela's young people. Rosalba, who nominated herself to be my nighttime guide, stops patiently. My memories don't extend beyond late afternoon walks up and down the main street. All this is truly new for me.

"Which one do you like best?"

I point to a column that's completely historiated. There are ample possibilities to choose from: declarations of love, political slogans (*We're beyond Europe in a deep sleep:*

goodnight Gela!), existential ravings. She frowns, as if working on a hard assignment. But in the end, she's certain about her preference.

"This one," she says.

It's a conversation more than a slogan:

If he doesn't love you, why don't you leave him?

But would you ever leave your sky?

"Isn't it a bit sentimental?" I hazard to say.

But Rosalba isn't listening to me, busy instead saying hi to this boy or that, thrown headlong into young nighttime worldliness. It's midnight and the little piazza is animated by clusters of kids slowly gathering and scattering. The short portico gushes with young people, sitting on the low walls, standing next to their motorbikes and the latest bicycles, masterpieces of fluorescent colors. The tepid air is awash with streaks of red, green, and blue lights that seem to shine from a dance club but come from a spinning globe of a café instead.

"You know there aren't any dance clubs here," says Rosalba, slightly annoyed this time. Her role is starting to weigh on her.

It's true. I don't need anyone to confirm it. There aren't any dance clubs where you can drink yourself into a stupor until the wee hours of the night and then crash the car on the way home. The "Saturday night massacres" are a specialty of northern Italy among young people who live in another world and die not because they're killed as a vendetta against some mafioso or in mafia wars, but in their own cars, racing at the speed of disco music. No dance clubs in these parts, I know. It's useless to ask Rosalba and divert her from her demanding involvement in a group's chatter.

I also know that of the three movie theaters there once were, one of them now shows pornographic films from Monday through Friday, and another one left, its space now occupied by an evangelical church. The third theater, which operated now and then twenty years ago, is frequented only by rats. Also closed is the Municipal villa, Gela's only green oasis, with its shaded avenues, lush vegetation, and ancient trees. On the other hand, new churches, new religions, are appearing. In the Margi district, I passed in front of a very recent billboard: Jehovah's Witnesses.

And then there are the low walls of the Villaggio.

"I'd really like to go to a dance school. I could even lose weight," sighs Rosalba, wrapping her chubby hand around my arm. This act of intimacy means she regrets dismissing me too briskly and peremptorily a moment ago. She looks at me with the eyes of a little lamb. In a gesture of peace, I offer to treat her to a Coca-Cola.

Disco music blares out of the café's wide-open door, its shutter held in place by a giant sign, a bottle of Corona Extra, the *cerveza mas fina*. The room is striking for how empty it is. Only three really young boys at the counter, a brown-haired boy standing between two tall blond ones who seem like twins. Staring blankly into space, they silently bite into three hot dogs. Hanging on the wall is an announcement for a donor drive, authorized by police headquarters, to buy a new wheelchair to replace the one stolen from a handicapped man on December 29th. Meager proceeds, diligently noted: seven thousand lire, two thousand, ten thousand at the most.

Outside the crowd explodes again, the same fauna one sees sitting on the low walls of towns throughout Italy. I try to imagine Tina wandering about in the middle of these boys in Hawaiian shirts, long hair pulled back in a ponytail or cut really short as dictated by the latest Caribbean style. All wearing the inevitable gold earring. I try to imagine her with these girls, dressed more soberly than the boys, some in leggings, some in miniskirts. I see her hanging around ill at ease amidst the chatter of students and amorous intrigues. Her stride, accent, everything is out of key. Even her jeans, even her shirt, however identical to the shirts the others wear. This isn't her place. It's easier to imagine her in an arcade.

But the uneasiness I feel as I move around, despite Rosalba's protective presence, is mine, not Tina's, I suddenly realize. I'm the only adult passing through this area. A voyeur. That is the sensation, hardly pleasant, I have as I peek at the young faces intermittently struck by the lights. These are the faces of good kids. Kids who go to school and study, and get bored in the evening. Kids who still bear a trace of childish naivete in certain expressions, in certain slightly awkward movements.

The same trace that makes "Filippo mai mori"'s eyes pop out in the black and white photos in the local newspapers weighing down my shoulder bag. Not even twenty years old and he's charged with numerous murders, the latest as of today. But he too has a small diamond in his left earlobe, and the childish awkwardness of his gaze is no different.

Where is the dividing line for risks young people run? Where is the line crossed and the difference between them produced?

Perhaps, for now, in knowing how to read and write. But Emanuele the poet, a student killed in a clash between gangs in the Nissena province, wrote verses and *cunti*, stories, for them as well, and for the admiration of his illiterate companions. And graffiti like this, black on the white columns.

Tre le cose importanti della vita:
donne, droga, morte.
Io ho scelto le prime due,
la terza ha scelto me.

The important things in life are three:
women, drugs, death.
I chose the first two,
the third chose me.

CHAPTER 11

Reconstructing the events involved in the ambush was extremely easy, both for the investigators and for the journalists. The ambush followed a fixed pattern, a technique tried and tested many times on many occasions, with few variations that were for the most part absolutely by chance.

Even the choice of the day could have been by chance. But someone underscored the inclination of Sicilians toward rituals, symbols, the search for hidden meanings, coded messages. An inclination that in Cosa Nostra becomes a method and takes the form of a real passion, obsessively pursued. Maybe because falsehood, the unavoidable human weakness that resolves so many problems of great importance and small, isn't part of the mafia's code of honor. Therefore, almost as compensation, every word and gesture in mafia environments goes beyond its immediate literal meaning, always tending to transcend it. Communication becomes a complex network of signs to decrypt, in which deception and betrayal nestle with greater ease.

In any case, whether it was by choice or by chance, the execution unquestionably happened on a special day. It was November 2nd. A day not of mourning in Sicily, but for celebrating the dead. Now habits have changed, they tend to conform to the customs observed on the other side of the Strait. But back then it wasn't baby Jesus or the Befana who left gifts at the foot of the bed. It was the dead who brought sweets and gifts to the little children of the island. Because value lies in death, not in life.

It was November 2nd. It was getting close to lunchtime but the streets downtown were still crowded. Francesco was walking on the sidewalk on a side street off Gela's main street together with Liborio, a cousin the same age as him. He was carrying a tray of sweets in his hand, just purchased and wrapped up in shiny green paper in the pastry shop behind him, by now a few meters away.

They were sixteen years old. It was their turn to buy the sweets for their youngest little cousins. They were big boys now, Francesco and Liborio. On the morning of November 2nd they no longer found dried fruit, walnuts, and baked sugar puppets on the table. Francesco's grandmother no longer scratched his feet at night and then later asked him, "Did you feel the dead people?"

The two cousins were walking along distracted and silent, all dressed up for the holiday lunch. Liborio was wearing his new watch, gold-plated with a large face and luminous hands that even glowed in the dark. Francesco was wearing a black motorcycle jacket, softer and warmer than Tina's, which he had always envied. Wearing that jacket, he'd gotten on the bus behind Sara and had finally found the way to declare his feelings to her. She started to laugh, revealing her sugary teeth, like almond paste, but then had told him: "This is the bus I always take." As if he didn't know.

No cars were going down the small street. And even the voices of the crowd were muffled. Then from the distant noise of the traffic in the background a stronger rasping of a motor scooter broke off. Francesco automatically registered the change. He looked up. A white Vespa was at the end of the street, coming toward him. At an even speed, though slow, very slow. And yet, its appearance, that swaying, measured advance, emanated an indefinable threat. There were two people on the seat, their faces completely hidden by helmets.

That was enough for Francesco. A jolt, perhaps a chill, sent goosebumps up his arms, making the fine, adolescent hairs stand on end. He turned around. A Piaggio moped stood crossways down the street, blocking the way out. The driver kept both hands on the handlebars and his face was uncovered. Long hair, stiff with gel and tied back behind his neck.

I don't know him. He's from somewhere else. They brought him in from somewhere else, Francesco thought as his instincts suddenly kicked in. He ran toward the stranger blocking the escape route and hurled the tray of sweets in his face. That move gave him a few seconds' advantage. He flung himself headlong in the direction of the main street, hugging the wall, and dove yearningly toward the voices of the crowd still off in the distance. As fast as his young legs could carry him. With all the bursting strength of his madly beating heart. Behind him, the gunfire broke out.

A machine gun. The shots were hitting the walls of homes, the closed doors. A corner of his mind was working away, pulled by the inertia of habit. Francesco found himself assessing the caliber of the cartridges. The force of penetration. The stopping power. His mind kept working. His legs were running. They continued to run even though they knew, as one knows in dreams, the uselessness of running.

A thud behind him, in the little street.

The image of Liborio falling flashed before Francesco's mind's eye—an impossible and sharp vision, a jolt inside his brain—and he felt the impact on the pavement directly on his own body, on his own flesh. To his amazement, he realized that his body was falling forward. *I'm the one falling, I'm falling down,* he thought, while a sudden pain struck the small of his back and his legs stopped short.

He fell sharply against the tree, on the sidewalk a few steps from the main street.

Fourteen little circles drawn in chalk, eight in the small street and six around the oleander that was dropping its pink flowers and fragrant petals; that was what remained on the asphalt the day after. Fourteen little circles drawn in chalk to indicate the exact places where the shower of shell casings landed. To mark the last border of Francesco's life. And the beginning of a new phase in Tina's.

AT A DISTANCE OF almost two years since the execution, it's not difficult for me to recognize the spot. In place of the oleander, there's a stump of rotten wood crumbling in the curve of the flowerbed.

"They sawed it down one night," explains the owner of the pastry shop, who has the soft body of a mature woman, left free beneath a light house coat buttoned up in front. "That old woman, the boy's grandmother, brought flowers every day. They sawed it off with her in mind. The mean woman, she hasn't been back since."

The woman opens up a Chinese-style fan and begins fanning herself, more out of habit than necessity. The shop is small but well-ventilated, and the wind carries the scents of sugar and sweets with cream fillings onto the street.

"It was November second, I remember it clearly. People were buying sweets for the little children."

Instinctively I run my tongue over my lips, filled with nostalgia brought on by the memory. For me, cookies and vanilla were the flavor of surprise. The thrill of macabre pleasure, munching on figures covered in white shrouds, stretched out on a flattened oval that was rigid and dark, simulating the bottom of a coffin. Some were flat on their backs, others were in the act of getting up, leaning on an elbow. Cookies you had to gnaw at, really hard, even for our teeth as little children. Not for nothing were they called "bones of the dead" in our area.

"Bones of the dead? No, the custom around here is only sugar puppets," says the woman. Curious but slightly annoyed, she adds, "I'm amazed by the name."

She has a wart at the corner of her mouth and another at the beginning of her neckline, in the cleavage between her breasts. Minute fatty, pinkish growths like miniature pastries, temptations for a sweet tooth on her moist skin. I'm distracted as I follow the journey of a drop of sweat that breaks on the tiny rock of bright flesh.

I struggle to let go of my confectionery reminiscences and indiscreet reflections in order to concentrate on the fact at hand.

"The shots . . ." I begin.

"Further up," she interrupts me. "He was further up, *'u sicarru*, the killer. Here the street was clear."

"But the shots, you heard them," I reply. "What did you do at that point?"

"We put the shutters down. And we started praying to the most Holy Mother of Graces."

"So you didn't see anything."

"We're buried alive, we are." She pushes back a sweaty lock of hair using the tip of the fan. "The buried alive don't have eyes. And then . . . What was there to see? Was it a show or something? There were people here inside, mammas with their *picciriddi*, their little children. We closed up."

She distractedly moves the fan more slowly, suddenly closes up the delicate sticks of wood, and leans forward on the counter so far that her face almost brushes against mine.

"But the other boy, the cousin of that Francesco, managed to drag himself, all torn up as he was, up to the door of my shop. So I discovered him, when we dared to lift up . . . The poor soul! He still had his eyes open." She starts fanning herself again with tender resignation. "I closed them."

"And Francesco ended up dying under a tree in the main street."

"God wanted him to end that way."

In truth, it doesn't seem like God has much to do with this story. But I prefer to say nothing and pretend to be amazed instead. "But why? Why cut down a tree, then, why go to the bother?"

The pity on the woman's face is only a bland variation of disdain, and she can't conceal the question I clearly read in her thoughts: *do I have to explain everything to this woman?* But she patiently says: "They didn't want him to be remembered as a human being. Shot dead like an animal, like a mangy dog, that's how they wanted him."

"Who? Who wanted him shot dead?"

She taps the closed fan on the palm of her hand. "You're asking me?" But then her chin and breasts tremble as she heaves a sigh of sincere maternal grief. "Beasts. He was light as a feather, that's all his sixteen years weighed. Beasts. Why kill him?"

It's true, he wasn't a killer, Francesco *'u maccarruni*, and even less a boss. He was only a small-time criminal with no weight and no prestige. But he was a little cog in a mechanism that someone had an interest in stopping.

"At the time," I say, "the newspapers presented several theories."

I list them, so she knows that I've done extensive research. "Some of them spoke of 'loose cannons' . . ."

According to this hypothesis, it was a lesson for those minors—loose cannons in the warring mafia clans—who had dared to touch a shopkeeper that wasn't supposed to be "bothered." The man was in good standing, paid the *pizzo* and enjoyed the protection of one of the two mafia families that were competing for control over the illegal activities in the area. A lesson. Just a lesson for young boys who had crossed the limit by touching an untouchable. One of them had to pay for the offense with his life.

"Others talked about a third clan growing in strength . . ."

This hypothesis put forward a more complicated background: a real mafia war.

In any case, the ambush was a warning, a way of reaffirming the rules that had been broken and re-establishing contested powers. Gangs that were too strong had consolidated, growing dangerously on the borders of Cosa Nostra. It was necessary to reduce their size, give a signal.

The woman slowly sways her head, expressing something I fail to grasp.

"What do you do when a tree grows too fast? You prune it," she then says sadly.

"Francesco?"

"No, of course not."

She walks tiredly over to sit down on the only stool in the shop, behind the cash register.

"I'm talking about his sister, Tina. A plant that had grown roots, branches and leaves. It took up too much space. It had to be pruned."

A FEW STEPS—THE FEW steps that Francesco hadn't had the time to take—and I'm in Piazza Umberto I, the heart of Gela.

Twenty years ago, it was still the meeting place, the outdoor living room of middle-class people, students, the "upstanding" people. Further ahead, on the other side of the street, behind the poor neighborhoods, is the bare facade of the Church of San Giacomo. There, in the churchyard, young people once sat around to sing *canzuni* and tell *cunta*, while dark coppola caps crowded the piazza; that was the place where the free market for hiring day laborers took place.

Now their children stagger between one church and the other, one piazza and the other, looking for drugs and opportunities.

I don't have anything to do until lunchtime, and I don't

feel like going back and shutting myself in the dusty motel room. So I stroll along too, whiling away the time by going up and down one side of Piazza Umberto and the other, up to the tall steps where the beautiful neoclassical facade of the Chiesa Matrice towers above. Inside, I'm horrified by the restorations: touches of pale blue and naive lines suited to votive holy pictures on the paintings newly hung in the archways and vaults.

It's late morning and there's a wedding going on. Astonishing hairdos, fantastic braids of ribbons and hairpieces, chlorophyll-green veils, long dresses with golden fringes. I have the impression that I've landed smack in the middle of an American film about Little Italy. In the corner of the churchyard, three small bridesmaids dressed in white are stuffing themselves with potato chips.

I go back down the high flight of stairs, toward the crowd that is holding out despite the hot time of day. In the shade of a tree, an old man is selling oranges, lemons, and citrons of Sicily in small plastic bags.

In the middle of the piazza, standing high on her pedestal, the *nude woman*, the statue of Ceres, continues to reign. Heavy buttocks and strong thighs, the generous belly typical of a Mediterranean goddess. But among the people of Gela she is more arcanely known as the *nude woman*.

I move closer, pushing through the crowd and crossing to the other side of the piazza, which is a men's place. A place of males. Men absorbed in their business deals. A crowd of busy *masculi*. Here negotiations and meetings are held, men are hired, approached—as they say in mafia jargon—and recruited.

When she slipped between one man and another, between a broker and a mediator, between a negotiation and an argument, Tina, with her hands in her pants pockets and denim shirt or leather jacket closed clear up to her chin, sensed the indulgent gaze of the nude woman on the back of her neck. Time had turned her round shoulders, arms, and breasts green, the same shade that it had given to old Milli's flesh. It made her fantasize about going up to her to breathe in her smell, to see if she had the same odor.

But, alone and silent, she continued to slip between the male voices. *Masculi* dominated by the nude woman's green flesh.

Then processions would come down from the Mother Church and the time of religious holidays arrived: Holy week or, in September, the Triumph of the Patroness. And the oblivious, powerful body of Ceres would be covered in a dress made of red, yellow, and blue lights. For the holidays, everyone got dressed up and everyone got undressed. They put clothes on and they took them off. Long habits and bare feet, naked chests and heavy veils. Behind the canopy of Our Lady of Grace, every July 2nd, little children were stripped of their clothes at each station of the procession. Their clothes, exhibited in church, were bought back by their own mothers. Undressing and dressing again: a ritual that possessed a secret empire.

Tina kept her arms straight down along the sides of her hips, her shirt tightly pulled around her, and hunched her shoulders at the weight of her small yet growing breasts. Even without looking at her, she felt the soft, ambiguous presence of the nude woman. At the same time, she felt her own body taking on new extraneous shapes and escaping her. More violently and rapidly since Francesco was no longer there. And also her friends, her "soldiers," who were losing themselves one by one in their own particular destinies. A heroic epoch of life had come to a close.

Then Tina looked up toward the nude woman. And she remembered that Cosa Nostra is a man's thing.

The sun is high in the sky. I walk along, keeping to the edge of the piazza. I'm also under Ceres's ancient gaze. Following in Tina's elusive footsteps.

But a little ways off in the distance the scene changes. The fantasy's spell is broken, swallowed in the muzzles of the rifles. Soldiers pass by and come back again in armored cars, and in open jeeps fitted with machine guns on top. Soldiers are also standing in glass sentry boxes at the sidewalk corners, stock-still, their eyes staring into space. It seems as if they're not looking at anyone, as if they don't see the people going by, and are also lost in some taxing dream from whose depths the enemy might suddenly emerge. But would they know how to recognize him, if necessary? The metal ring of the rifle barrel glints like flames as it pops out of the narrow crack that cuts the sentry box in two.

Thirty years ago, Petrolchimico. Today soldiers. There has to be something wrong, somewhere. But where?

CHAPTER 12

Eight kilometers more or less from downtown, in the direction of the industrial area—that's how far the new cemetery is from Gela. The road runs alongside the plant's entrance, so as I pass by I manage to catch a glimpse of the murals, eye-catching colors, tangled letters on Petrolchimico's long walled enclosure.

I slow down, softly braking and letting the Fiat Uno slide onto the edge of the road so I can look closely at the ribbon of images that runs continuously across the wall. From my observation point, the profile of a woman with a thick headful of unruly hair leaps to view. A sentence flows from her lips, enclosed in a balloon: *This is only the beginning.*

I don't doubt the intentions were good. The idea came from the Enichem company executives and the municipal administration, who were overcome by a desire that was positive, yet rather confused and ultimately eccentric, to soften the harsh features of Gela's landscape. And here is the result: murals at Petrolchimico, murals scattered across a few buildings in the city. But graffiti is usually born from stealing space. It represents the eruption of creative disorder in the bureaucratic order of cities. In Gela, the exact opposite happened.

Fantasies of a mythic past, Greek columns with bunches of agave springing up behind them, knights with athletic builds holding harmless swords. The soft colors and paintings entirely contained in orderly squares framed nicely in white paint serve as a counterpoint to the disorderly violence of the landscape. An unreal order. Timid. Engulfed by an overwhelming barbarity. Inert, without any life and without any conviction, the murals disappear, flattened like anonymous postage stamps on the desolation of the houses, on walls shedding plaster, corroded by dampness.

This is only the beginning. It was meant to be a declaration of hope, I imagine.

A QUADRILATERAL AREA OF prefabricated buildings in cement and glass. I've arrived. The atmosphere is very different from the one that reigns over Gela's main "monumental" cemetery, a garden of green, smelling of lifeblood and earth, that opens onto the main street.

In front of me there is a narrow building with three floors, and long terraced corridors with a view of the industrial zone and the immense, deserted plain: light-colored cisterns like the domes of mosques, gleams of silver that cross through yellow land, artichoke fields, rows of prickly pear trees, the highway overpass that was never finished and disappears into nothingness, uselessly leaping toward the sky.

Below, in an alleyway that's bustling like a construction site with the incessant sounds of saws, drills and jackhammers, they're building a row of pretentious chapels in pure "illegal building style." Plastic instead of wood, imitation marble inserts. Materials that mimic precious luxury. The friezes, the lettering of the inscriptions, and the decorations don't have even the spark of imagination that poverty sometimes manages to ignite. This isn't the Sicily of November 2nd. The dead are no longer the ghosts celebrated on that holiday, here in Sicily.

I walk slowly down the corridor under the portico, trying to locate the name I'm looking for. Here lies, here lies, here lies. Only these two words flow on the endless row of tombstones. Two words that are so simple as to appear rushed, hasty. Here lies, here lies, here lies. As if every addition, each additional sentence would be a useless waste. An exaggerated essentiality. A restraint that is suddenly interrupted by the epitaph written in large letters, summarizing one man's seventy years of life: *He who lives on love dies of pain.*

My eyes go back to the search, losing their place as they follow the monotonous row of tombstones, all the very same. I have to force myself to continue exploring. I have to repeat the goal over and over again, which is precise and not at all pointless, and brought me all this way. I have to tell myself again that it's not useless morbidity.

I came to look for Francesco's tomb. That's my objective. But it's not here, or I just can't see it. I don't want to ask the cemetery watchman, who is sprawled on a woven straw chair at the entrance, looking at the rare visitors with the same light interest shown by men seated in cafés, watching people out for a stroll. I'm held back by reserve, an unexpected embarrassment, a sort of modesty. Almost a nausea brought on by all of this asking around, reawakening other people's expectations and curiosity, by my forcing open barred thresholds, demolishing shelters, even getting inside the privacy of dreams. Perhaps the Sicilians' suspiciousness about words, and more so about written words, isn't entirely unjustified. At times writing has something indecent about it, in its obstinate investigating.

By now I've arrived on the third floor, uselessly. I go back down. Behind the chapels under construction, a rectangle of brown dirt stretches out on the blind side, with turned clumps of soil as if the land were recently plowed, swollen with mounds arranged in irregular rows. They look like termite hills that have been knocked down; in place of the characteristic towers, crude crosses made of wood rise up. Black wood for the adults, white for the children.

I walk among mound after mound. Here and there, green plastic bottles, dented and crumpled, with two or three scrawny flowers drooping over shredded labels, are planted in the soil. Photographs are rare, stuck on clumsily with a thumb tack.

A man and a woman standing in front of a gravestone follow my coming and going, staring insistently at me, giving no sign of cordiality. He's wearing a black tie and she has on stockings and high heeled ankle boots. I'm watching them out of the corner of my eye too, behind the dark lenses of my glasses, while I walk up to a mound that's different from all the others. It's leveled out and covered by a slab of pink granite that a man is cleaning with a rag. He's the only other visitor, along with me and the suspicious couple, on this workday morning.

Hearing me arrive, the man looks up. "I didn't want to leave my father like this, without any cover," he comments, pointing at the adjacent little mounds of swollen earth. He starts wiping the smooth granite, still awaiting the usual engraved words "here lies." "It's an illegal gravestone," he explains sadly.

"But what is this area?" I inquire.

"Municipal land. A transition zone, free of charge. After ten years, they remove them. They put them up there." He points out the three floors of burial niches. "Or else they throw them in a common grave. Obtaining a niche isn't easy. I applied for one for my father a long long time ago."

There's no shade in the middle of the bare field. The man rolls up his shirtsleeves and, after carefully inspecting the rag, wipes the sweat off his forehead and behind his neck with a strip of it.

"They had promised me . . . At city hall they assured me . . ."

He breaks off, immediately regretting he'd confided so much. I turn my head. At the opposite side of the field, the couple is still absorbed in keeping an eye on my movements. I turn back toward the man who concludes quickly and definitively: "But for now, there's no space."

So there's a racket for burials here too? In Palermo, the racket yielded twenty million lire a year. It profited from everything, from the concessions and construction of the plots to the unattended burial niches. People who returned to Palermo to bury a relative would discover the family tomb had been sold and occupied by strangers. Even the dead down here risk turning out to be illegal.

A trace of suspicion has crept into the man's eyes, rendering him watchful like the couple that is keeping a close eye on us in the distance. The sadness that prompted him to confide in me has vanished. "But you . . ." He suddenly stops mid-sentence, looking quizzical. He doesn't continue. What need is there to finish the sentence? At this point we both know it's my turn to clarify my position. There was a confidence. Now I'm the one to be in debt. I owe him a confession.

"I'm looking for . . ."

Right, what am I looking for? What am I doing here in

this cemetery, spying on dead people who don't belong to me? And yet in some way that little boy I'd never seen or met, that little sixteen-year-old boy killed in a settling of accounts between rival clans, belongs to me. Just as his sister's proud and desperate dream belongs to me.

"I'm looking for, I was looking for . . ." I can't finish the sentence either. And then, "Well, I was looking for a photograph."

The proof, the trace of a life.

"Only a photograph."

The man abruptly interrupts the mechanical gesture that he had never ceased, that constant wiping of the rag back and forth over the slab of granite. He straightens up and slowly takes two steps back. To look me up and down all the better. Or to distance himself from my obvious insanity. I smile at him and walk away with a pathetic nod goodbye. I begin searching again.

He's here. I've finally found him. But there's no photograph on Francesco's mound. Only his name, on a black cross. *Why black?* I think. The white cross would have been more appropriate for his young years, still a child.

THE RITUAL HAD BEEN fast, officiated quickly in order to avoid the interference of enemies and undesired attentions. But fear kept people away. Fear and indifference.

"They don't go to the bother for so little. For a boss, perhaps . . . For someone who is really mobbed up and even from the grave can provide satisfactions and move things along."

It was an observation. A thought that didn't leave Tina bitter but served to find the right balance again, the exact point where suffering, anger, and anxiety intersected. The moment to change the music had arrived. No more antics, no more grandstanding, no more errands and odd jobs for a pittance.

Tina was observing her mother, who let herself fall to the ground and was immediately lifted up by Zio Michele, or "that guy," the man who had taken the place of her father. Once, twice, three times. A scream and she slumped down, becoming limp inside her black coat, which was too large for her. Again, she was lifted back up. And again she threw herself on the ground. From an extreme, impenetrable distance, Tina contemplated that representation of pain, while the words she herself had spoken to Francesco so many years earlier standing in front of their father's body returned to mind: "We don't cry here."

But Francesco had grown up. And by dint of staying in the pack he'd become a wolf too.

Tina instinctively looked over at her grandmother, her aged face enveloped by her handkerchief.

A freezing wind was blowing from the sea, lifting the ribbons on the funeral wreaths and swelling the clear cellophane wrapped around the bouquets. The men wrapped their scarves around their mouths and raised their coat collars. The cold stiffened Tina's back. She trembled. But it was a trembling that disappeared in the gusts of wind; the unreality of her body coincided with the unreality of pain.

All around them were balconies with their shutters closed, deserted doorways, empty streets. Only relatives were at Francesco and Liborio's funeral, along with a small group of young people that held the journalists at bay.

There was certainly no shortage of them. A crew from Telecittà showed up and reporters from the major island dailies were elbowing each other so they could get closer with their tape recorders running and pens poised over notebooks. Uselessly. The nucleus of young men and boys was a security cordon, a policing force, that was locked tightly together, putting up a firm, tenacious struggle. They didn't let anyone through. On the other side of the barrier, Tina remained unreachable.

One journalist resigned herself to ask the boy who seemed the youngest, and therefore the most approachable: "Were you a friend?"

Continuing to block her way, the little boy replied, "Um . . . nah."

"So what are you doing at the funeral?"

Impassive, tough: "Just watching."

A man in the back yelled: "You all have to get out of here. Do you understand, yes or no? Do you understand you have to get out of here? You're the reason everything is in ruins. You're a disgrace. All of you."

The hearse moved. Tina got into Zio Michele's Ritmo. At the first turn in the small street, she looked up. A sign was sticking out of a window, supported by a horizontal rod and stretched out like a weathervane, announcing: *The Wizard of the Nile*. She didn't need the Wizard of the Nile to know who had delivered the sentence and issued the order. A sentence with no appeal: Get rid of that little rooster without a crest. She didn't need a wizard to understand these elementary truths.

Yet all the same, she went inside the room, lit by a low light, covered by an orange silk shawl, and permeated by the sickly-sweet odor of incense that wafted up in wisps of smoke from a burner. Thick, dusty rugs. Cushions. A low metal table carved with openwork like a piece of lace. A small domed cage, empty, painted white and blue; the wizard was from the African coast. His arrival was lost back in time by then. He had done the most oddly assorted jobs on the island before deciding to practice the art of divination. Tina remembered running into him at the open market, where he sold good luck charms, little hands made of silver, wonderful bracelets. His way of speaking was a caricature, a fanciful Italian with a strong Sicilian accent. But he even knew the spell of the ancient *magare* sorceresses.

> *Metti acqua di la funtana pura,*
> *metti ogghiu di l'oliva virdi:*
> *l'acqua l'astuta e 'u focu l'adduma.*

Put in water from the pure fountain,
add oil from green olives:
with water extinguish and fire ignite.

His complexion had a greenish cast to it that the reflections of the lamp heightened, creating a strange, unpleasant patina, and his black hair was combed straight back, with a brilliant white band running over it that began at his right temple. Sitting cross-legged on a cushion, dressed in a pure white Arab tunic, he had her listen to some music that went from thunderous to cascading sound, then fits and starts.

Once she was back inside the Ritmo it sped up. Tina recalled the man's words, both a warning and promise: an opportunity, only one. But, if you knew to seize it, the vendetta would arrive, quicker than the rooster's crow, even faster than the inevitable betrayal.

A NAME, A DATE, a cross. No flowers, no photograph on Francesco's grave in the new cemetery.

But I do have a photo, as a matter of fact, in my dossier of newspaper clippings. Not of Francesco, but of his funeral. Grainy images, like all the images stamped on the spongy paper of dailies. It has the two coffins, too cumbersome for the small street, barely large enough for both of them. It has the women dressed in black, belonging to an archaic Sicily that no longer exists and survives, only for a few instants in narrow, suffocating little backstreets, and reappears in fleeting apparitions in suburbs resembling an Indian metropolis of an unknown Gela.

And it has Tina. You almost can't see her, a small dark figure that fades into the many others. But I recognize the clear, short curve of her hair on her neck. Her body's self-assertion held in check, her hand closing the shirt collar under her winter jacket.

After that, there's a gap in my dossier. No more interviews, and not even any photographs after Francesco's death, as if Tina had suddenly changed her style. A cautious silence, on her part. Oblivion on the part of the press, which records only evidence, what comes into the public eye.

A year or so goes by, and she briefly, fleetingly returns to the limelight, with the umpteenth robbery, her arrest, and the sentence. By now Tina has turned eighteen and it's no longer possible for her to avoid experiencing prison. The news is picked up by the papers. But there are only press agency newsflashes, pieces built on impressions, tableaus of her environment, rehashings of the past, journalistic inklings. Tina never lets her voice be heard, not even in the contradictory, reticent manner that has been her very own from the beginning.

A few months ago, she was granted house arrest and transferred to the old house in the alley. A piece of news that relieved me when I arrived here in the city. I no longer needed to chase her down, run after her, search for her. I could go through her life taking my time as needed, as I did, stopping a while at every stage. Tina under house arrest, a piece of news I then voluntarily ignored, until this moment. But now . . .

Now I'm slowly approaching that house with its damp, windowless walls buried in the ancient heart of Gela. Without any hurry. Step by step I come closer. In that small but familiar space, Tina is shut up inside, a prisoner. She can't escape my siege. In some way or other—with the judge's regular authorization or without, in an official manner or clandestine—I'll see her. She can't escape.

That's what I tell myself, but at the same time, beset by annoying anxiety, I wonder if I'll manage to overcome the obstacle of her hard distrust. Will she want to talk to me? With me, will she break the silence she's maintained all these years? Will she agree to come closer by yielding to her desire for a meeting? They're open questions that I've avoided up until now, but the time has arrived to solve them. Now, I have no hesitation. I can take the last step.

In the photo, it seems like Tina is shivering. Her hand on her jacket is stiff from the cold. In a few seconds it will move lower in search of a pocket's warmth.

It seems to me as if I know her to the point where I can anticipate her gestures, the simplest ones and the most unpredictable. And even her words. I know what she'll say to me when the circle I'm drawing around her is complete, and we'll meet one in front of the other, face to face. Finally at the center of reality.

CHAPTER 13

Since she's been working at Telecittà, they've torched her car two times. The accounts are right. They torched her director's car once more than hers. The hierarchies are secure.

"But Tina's story doesn't have anything to do with this business."

Graziella is a nervous brunette who's going back and forth between a printer and a video, extricating herself from snarles of wires that are hanging down and getting entangled between stools and tables, obviously hindering her movements. But more than her exuberant nature, I think it's her still very young age that makes her easily confront a job whose dangers she doesn't see, even though she knows perfectly well what they are, and complain only about the job being temporary.

"I'd like to contribute pieces to some national news-papers," she says excitedly, smoothing back her dark bobbed hair that falls back onto her forehead again. "Who knows . . . !"

She has a deep, seductive voice, to which the microphone surely does justice.

I know just a few essential things about her. That her skill has given her a certain notoriety around the city, and that she lives alone, separated from her husband. Since then, her home, a small villa at the end of the street that goes over the Capo Soprano hill, seems to be the center of complicated intrigues of a political and emotional sort, so much so that she's been saddled with a signifi-cant nickname: "Dallas." Ever since her car was torched, her ex-husband makes the rounds at her house at night. Without Graziella knowing about it, otherwise she'd be furious.

Sicilian women, either Amazons or geishas. For battle or for harems. Eumenides or Erinyes, as my uncle judgmen-tally declares. And there's no middle ground.

There are five of them, including the director, who are working in the one large, square editing room, each of them absorbedly concentrating on their own video terminal. Intermittently, when the door opens, a burst of noise and laughter sweeps through the room.

"Come take a look."

We put our heads in the doorway to the studio. A group

of little children is having the time of their life singing and playing on a live broadcast.

"A community center." Graziella's pride betrays a didactic nuance: "Isn't this also a bit of local TV stations' function?"

We return to the editing room and find everyone lined up in the same identical order, poised in front of the bright screens. I have the feeling that a gang armed with weapons ready could burst in and no one would deign to look away from the video. The only things meriting attention are running across that screen.

Graziella frees up a stool from a jumbled mountain of papers, faxes, and newspaper clippings, and offers it to me.

"It was more than a year ago," she begins. But for an instant, the memory envelopes her in a troubled silence. Graziella is the only journalist who managed to reach Tina during her prison stay.

"She had just turned eighteen and it was her first experience of a real prison," she explains, coming out of her brief reflection. "As a minor, she'd gone the entire usual route: rehab centers, the institute for minors in Caltanisetta. It was . . . logical. I really can't think of another adjective. It was . . . natural that she would enter her adult world in that way, with an internship in jail."

She tears off the edges of a sheet of printer paper and throws them in the wastebasket. She can't keep her fingers still. There are people who invent all sorts of things, even love, to fill their time, yet she evidently needs to fill space.

With little gestures, automatic movements. She has to constantly be active. A frenzy compensated by the calibrated, contrasting persuasiveness of her voice.

"Prison doesn't frighten them. On the contrary. It's a test. A fundamental stage. It can't be missing from the resume of any criminal who wants to move up in the ranks."

From the opposite side of the table, the director—a likeable, sporty forty-year-old wearing shirt sleeves and a ready smile—lets out some kind of triumphant yell. He brandishes a piece of paper, waving it in the air to get the attention of all of his writers.

"Hey, everyone, a tragic blow in the 'good' part of Gela. They discovered a ring of high-class prostitution, brothels for businessmen, right here downtown. The wives of professionals, irreproachable housewives . . ." He slaps the paper down on the table. "Bored Housewives Turned Prostitutes. Great title. Right? What do you think?"

Graziella listens distractedly. She gives him a hasty nod of agreement—as if she were the director, and not him—and resumes talking right away: "I found out she was in prison by chance. I'd gotten it in my head to interview her quite a while back. We have a program where we feature people's life stories. It's a springboard, actually, a pretext for discussing social problems. So I try to call her."

Her grandmother answers. Graziella asks to speak with Tina, and the woman says, "She's not here at the moment."

"And where is she? Where can I find her?"

The grandmother confesses in an embarrassed voice, "They took her, okay."

"She's not here at the moment," laughs Graziella, imitating the grandmother. "Never ever do they say: they're in jail."

Her darting, pointy face turns serious again. "At any rate, I had to change plans. But I didn't want to give up on the idea. Tina had become a little myth, a hero. The symbol—her, a woman—of our ghettos' youths. Kids who consider life, their own and other people's, worthless. Yes, I wanted to interview her, and the fact that she was in prison . . . well, that was already news. If I'd been able to get inside, to talk with her . . . Not for the television, perhaps. For television, the piece would be difficult, probably impossible. But a great article for a newspaper . . . I contribute to a few newspapers, on and off."

"Too many different jobs." Partly hidden behind his video screen, only half-joking, the director doesn't let the chance to find fault slip by.

Graziella shrugs. "I prefer television to print media. If I had a good contract . . ." She refocuses, returning to our subject. Her hands spread open to follow the movement of her memories, then move alongside each other to collect their flow. Suddenly they close, grasping an image. "In prison, I found Tina different. Different from the little girl everyone wanted to interview a few years ago and who played around with the media."

TO GET TO HER, she had followed the simplest procedure, a meeting—productive—with her defense attorney, a phone call to the registration office of the Ragusa correctional facility, where they had taken the girl, to find out the visiting hours.

Mistaking her for a relative, the man on the other end of the line, full of understanding, had asked her: "Is it your first time?" His voice was surprising, almost tender.

Graziella explained the situation and he reassured her. Since the girl was an appellant ("Amazing the terms those people use: appellant, collaborator . . .") she needed the prison director's permission. She just had to come, even the following day, in the morning. A simple matter, too simple.

The next day, when she showed up at the entrance to the Ragusa correctional facility, she discovered that the director was on vacation and the substitute was off somewhere, in some faraway prison in the province, unreachable for the moment. Maybe later, maybe by the end of the day.

"Come back tomorrow," advised the guard.

"You had me come all the way here," Graziella rebelled. "And now what? How do we resolve this?"

They put their heads together for a while. "Wait here."

She waited sitting on a bench in the shade of a Mediterranean pine tree, in the paved courtyard inside the boundary wall, right in front of the bolted door.

Waiting along with her was a small crowd of relatives, composed exclusively of women and little children. And a boy, sixteen or seventeen years old at most, with a gaudy gold necklace hanging around his neck and a cell phone perpetually glued to his ear. They waited there calmly, as if in a park, without giving any signs of impatience or restlessness. More calmly and imperturbably than if they had been in line at the public records office. One woman was crocheting briskly, the skein of red thread unrolling in her lap, spinning.

From up in the tree's high foliage, a bird shat directly on her notebook. Graziella moved, standing out of range. Now and then a guard emerged from the dark doorway and yelled: "Does someone have to come inside? Any laundry?"

She waited for a long time out there, with tried and tested resignation, so they might untangle her case. Then, just to remind them she was there, she moved into the entrance hall. The guard in front of the gate inside was walking back and forth, back and forth. Around noon, a petite, slender woman dressed in black rushed inside, worriedly looking around, her mouth agape. The guard began explaining something to her, speaking in a whisper.

It really is the first time for her, thought Graziella.

Finally, the authorization arrived. Signed by the commander, in the director's absence. While they were searching her, before letting her go inside, they explained the real reason for the long wait: "It was the girl who couldn't decide."

After agreeing to talk with her, she regretted it and said no, and then yes again. That uncertainty didn't bode well at all.

They'd allowed her to use the lawyers' room for the meeting, which was more discreet and isolated than the visiting room. Tina was already there, standing in the doorway. Graziella almost didn't recognize her. "You've lost weight," she blurted out. "Did you go on a diet?"

"CAN YOU IMAGINE?" GRAZIELLA shakes her shiny bangs back, her lightly made-up eyes widening in a self-deriding grimace. "Can you believe the question I asked her? A girl in prison. And it was the first time I'd spoken to her! 'Did you go on a diet?' A diet . . . Clearly she was taken aback. It made an impact that was, you know, unexpected, at the very least. But maybe that was precisely why, in a certain sense, she was disarmed. After all, my attack must have confused her. I felt like an idiot, however . . . this brilliant remark paid off. It made her more willing, it somehow piqued her curiosity. She signed the consent form for the talk."

A pause. Hypnotized, I follow the jumps and starts of her nervous fingers as they fiddle with a pencil, and continue to maul sheets of printer paper. She doesn't have nail polish on her rough-edged fingernails. Tormented hands, without any rings on their fingers; they're the most unadorned part of her body, both exposed and defenseless.

"She wanted to see me," Graziella clarifies, "before signing the consent form in front of my eyes, in her shaky illiterate block letters. I don't know if that's a regular procedure. But that's what happened. And I . . . Yes, I felt like an idiot, but I burst out laughing. And the oppressive burden from the wait dissolved. I looked at her closely. She really had changed, physically changed. A different person, compared to the last photographs I'd seen. Or to the way I remembered her, in a debate about young people at Telecittà. She was still a little girl, a *masculidda*, a little tomboy, in every respect, her figure, her way of moving. Now instead . . . Now I had a woman in front of me."

A young woman, tall and slender, with petite features and a slant to her eyelids that gave her a cryptic appearance like certain ancient statuettes. Or a peasant woman from inland Sicily, thought Graziella, with that strange Saracen sweetness reflected in blue flashes on her corneas. Her skin was in poor condition, typical of people who don't have healthy nutrition and certainly don't live an orderly, regular life.

No frills, no feminine ornaments. A Lacoste T-shirt (clearly fake) and shorts, short hair pulled back in the kind of small ponytail that was really popular among boys.

"I came just to see you," Graziella immediately resumed. "I came a long way, in this heat." She wasn't able to avoid a propitiatory tone, vaguely affected. Tina was still standing up, perplexed. She let out an embarrassed laugh. But her eyes remained serious, scrutinizing.

"I don't recognize you," she replied.

But when Graziella decided to move the chair and take her place, she sat down in hers too.

Sitting face to face, separated by a shabby little table

that seemed like a school desk, they looked each other over, sizing up and evaluating. Standing in the wide-open door was a woman, with her arms folded, who kept an eye on them. Now and then Tina would fleetingly glance at her, as if asking for a suggestion or gauging a reaction. It was clear that she trusted her more than Graziella. Whatever her role was ("a social worker or guard, I wouldn't know"), Tina could understand her perfectly in her world. That woman, even though she was on the opposite side of the fence, spoke her same language. There wasn't any mystery about her for Tina.

"We already met each other once, during a discussion." Graziella refreshed her memory, specifying, "I wasn't the one hosting it."

"I don't like interviews," replied Tina, darkening. "People think: this girl does interviews, she talks. She shows off, she wants to stand out. They think bad about it."

"And yet you came to Telecittà."

With a wave of her hand, Tina brushed off the episode and pushed it back into a distant past. But she admitted, "It's true. I came." She added, "I came with all my heart. But the way you introduced me . . . What could people think with that bad introduction?"

"People . . . But what do you care what other people think?" burst out Graziella. "You're not like all the others." Equivocal, careless words of flattery.

Tina replied, anger flaring, "And what am I like? Exactly

like everybody. A normal person. Like everyone else. That's how I want to be. Normal."

"THAT SEEMED TO BE her fixation: normality. She was in prison for attempted breaking and entering. The whole business was pretty unclear, I didn't buy it. I don't remember how many months of prison she was supposed to serve, maybe a year or even more. In the sentence, the conviction was motivated, literally, by her 'known danger to society' and going out at night with known offenders 'despite her sex and young age.'"

Her lawyer had emphasized those words as she read the file to Graziella, seeking a pretext for easy ridicule and underlining the judge's bias.

"And here instead I find her obsessed by the desire to be like everybody else. She aspired to normality like other people aspire to, I don't know, a brilliant career as an actor. To reach the goal of normality would be a success for her. And she wasn't lying. She was sincere. I'd swear to it."

And yet Graziella's interest, the fact that she had searched for her, wanted to talk with her, and therefore had gone to a lot of trouble getting people and things to move along, didn't leave Tina indifferent.

"She was pleased with herself, though in a secret, contradictory way. And she wanted to be regarded as a woman 'of respect,' in the mafia sense. If this kind of figure can exist. In any case, she was very close to it. And this was not very 'normal' at all."

Graziella smooths out her bangs, pulls them down over eyes, then pushes them back. Watching her, I become nervous too. She finally folds her hands together in her lap and calms down, resuming her story.

"DO YOU KNOW I'VE collected all of the articles that talk about you? I clipped them out, one by one. Quite a nice dossier. Do you want it? I can get it to you." She realized she'd hit the mark. A smile of childish vanity crept over Tina's face, her full lips parted as in a beautiful, precise drawing. Despite everything, despite asserting a desire for the norm and anonymity, Tina continued to oscillate between fear, prudence, and vanity.

"But do you read them? Newspapers, that is," Graziella asked again, with a touch of calculated malice.

Incredibly, Tina blushed. "Yes . . . well, no. The ones that talk about me, yeah."

Graziella felt ashamed. Ashamed of her strategies and her presumptuousness, of her arrogance as a woman who knew how to handle the instruments of knowledge. And yet right at that moment, an intuition she'd had became clear, something about Tina's attitude that had always struck her, but that she had never thoroughly comprehended. In that moment she understood that the girl, that little girl, illiterate, a gangster, had her own precise, studied way of conducting an interview. She'd invented a set pattern of her own that exactly met her need to cultivate a kind of flattering notoriety, without exposing herself or throwing herself into the fray, shrewdly meting out pieces of information and remarks.

First she would test the waters, then reveal a bit of herself, throw out some bait, and immediately pull back. She'd pretend to interrupt the conversation in order to pick it back up on safer, more favorable ground. She had a way of keeping hold of the scene, like a consummate actress, that was all her own. And when she'd say, "I don't understand," it was a message she was sending. It meant: *This is a minefield. Careful, because otherwise I'm not budging.*

She was an expert in the art of communication.

Graziella was amazed it had taken her so long to understand this feature of Tina's personality, which now seemed fundamental. A key to get inside that inaccessible, immured world. A breach in the barrier of suspicion the girl had erected around herself, that separated her from others.

But betrayed by the sense of security this discovery gave her, Graziella made an error. It seemed like an innocent question, coming from a real, harmless curiosity about the other young woman's life. So without thinking, she asked, "Have you ever been outside of Sicily?"

Tina reacted with excessive harshness. "What do you want? I don't understand what you want from me," she repeated, standing up and nodding at the woman on guard just beyond the doorway. "I don't recognize you," she spelled out slowly, deliberately. She moved toward the door, then stopped, looking Graziella over from top to bottom.

"I'm not going to answer you anymore," she informed her. But she stuck her hands in the pockets of her shorts and stood there, with the air of someone who is still willing to be patient, if only for a short while. So Graziella was again taken by surprise when out of the blue she heard Tina speak in an even, reasonable voice, explaining, "I'm afraid of making a mistake." And yet again, "I'm afraid," she said.

But at this point it really seemed to Tina as if she'd given too much of herself.

"That's enough. If you want to interview me, ask my lawyer for a meeting."

"Didn't he let you know?" replied Graziella, amazed. "I spoke with him. He's the one who sent me."

"Him?" Her tone suddenly changed. "How dare he." Suddenly she became a little arrogant mafia boss. Every undercurrent of sympathy, every veiled willingness to have an exchange, every possibility of a dialogue magically disappeared.

"How dare he. I'm sending for him right away." She laid it on thick, with fierce haughtiness.

Graziella understood that any opening for communication had closed. The visit was really over. She stood up, in turn. Nevertheless, as she was getting up, it seemed as if her gesture provoked a slight bewilderment. Evidently the girl expected greater resistance, more insistent pressure. She was disappointed by Graziella's ready adherence to the decision, which in reality was a challenge, a trial of strength. But by then, it was too late for either of them to turn back, to renounce a choice.

They walked together down the corridor of the prison: Graziella, Tina, and that other woman, who placidly shuffled along with indifference in shoes that were too big for her. They walked in silence. But it wasn't a natural silence.

At the other end of the corridor, way down where the prisoners' cells started, Graziella saw a door standing wide open and a guard at the threshold, who kept it open and watched them step by step as they approached. A spider attracting its prey, moving very slowly toward the central knot, the point where all of the threads intersect. The guard was waiting for Tina in front of her cell, his hand already on the lock.

A sudden, irrational panic came over Graziella, instantly transporting her to an unknown perceptual universe. Plunging into the sensitive womb of this universe, she strongly perceived the girl's presence. And a hesitation. An imperceptible collapse. With no warning, she found herself immersed in enthralling, bodily emotion. As if Tina's mute body had transmitted her unexpressed and passionate desire for an understanding, for contact.

Graziella stopped. "Good luck," she said, lightly touching the girl's shoulder. At her touch, Tina jumped violently, her muscles tensed in an involuntary spasm. The contact seemed to continue on and on, expanding, shattering into minute, sensitive shards, waves that shuddered as they spread from the stone's point of impact with the water, and little by little they reluctantly disappeared.

Finally, Tina stared at her, and laughed. Then, taking slow steps, she started to move toward the cell while Graziella stood in front of the closed gate. Waiting for the guard to arrive and take her outside.

"IN THE PRISON COURTYARD, under the pine tree, the boy still had his ear glued to his cell phone. I got in my car again and drove back, toward Gela."

Somewhere in the room, the fax machine lets out a brief noise, then starts spitting out paper. Sounds and laughter can no longer be heard from the broadcast studio. The program must be over. The fax stops. There's a moment of silence under the stark white light cast by the lamps.

"I was very upset," says Graziella.

The director has come nearby and started to fiddle around with the photocopier, right behind us.

"Are you ready?" he asks, turning around briefly, then gets right back to the photocopying.

But she continues: "I was driving distractedly. I passed by Comiso again, by the junction for Acate . . . The town where the Columbian prostitutes are sorted out to work one place or another." She raises her voice: "Nothing like bored women turned prostitutes!" She points her chin out provokingly in the direction of the man who's working unperturbed at the machine behind our backs.

"They arrive together with drugs, then end up in inland farmhouses or the brothel neighborhoods of Catania or Palermo. *They* certainly don't do it out of boredom."

The director retrieves a piece of paper from under the machine's plate. He turns to look at us. "We know. The slavery of the future," he says with an air of infinite patience. And he repeats insistently, "Are you ready?" Winking at me, he adds, "Tonight she goes on camera. The sexiest voice in Sicily."

CHAPTER 14

Even though two years have gone by, the door to the house in the alley still has the mourning announcement on it: *For my grandson.*

I futilely ring the doorbell, which makes no sound within. I futilely knock on the door. For a long while, repeatedly, with stubborn knuckles. Enough. In order to collect myself and have a break between one attempt and another, I go to buy some cigarettes on the main street. In the store right beside the tobacconist's, a shop assistant is dressing up the display window. She's barefoot. In front of her, on the sidewalk, a pressing crowd of boys. Their eyes slyly follow her skirt lifting up when she raises her arms or bends over to position a mannequin.

I make my way through, take my Camels and go back to knock on the door again. None of the shutters open, none of the windows open, no sound of a voice, not even to protest.

The old woman won't open the door for me.

But I can't resign myself to defeat. If this turn of events, this dramatic twist, is a defeat. Mimmo's voice on the telephone comes back to mind: "Have you heard?"

"Heard what?"

"She's disappeared."

Tina disappeared a few days ago, violating her house arrest. A short blurb in the *Giornale di Sicilia* newspaper. Some anonymous reporter wrote about the news, pondering the motives for her escape. Assuming it *was* a question of escape. This is where the most disparate and troubling hypotheses open up. Did she really just go away or did someone make her disappear? And, in the former hypothesis, did she go away voluntarily, based upon her own autonomous decision, or was she forced to do so in some way? Because of some dark fear or an inability to tolerate imprisonment? In any case, the most probable hypothesis seems to be that she took off to become a fugitive and chose precarious, tough freedom.

I ring the bell another time, knock on the door, and call out, "Is anyone home?"

Up until a couple of days ago, Tina was still in this basement home, on the other side of this door that's right in front of me, shut tight. Perhaps if I had come around here and stopped a moment to listen, I would even have caught some sign of her presence, made out a voice, a call. She was here, and I would only have needed to find the right key to open the scraped-up wooden door that stands beyond the stone arch opening onto the alley, and not to force it.

Instead, I approached with excessive caution, by degrees. I imagined building the encounter little by little, preparing it the way you prepare for a difficult exam. An exam in which I would have had to perform the dual role of examiner and examined. I proceeded slowly. Distracted also by the spell of a past that returns, crowding my soul. Losing myself in the stages that I invented in order to expand and delay my own search.

I took too long, certain that I was moving from a strong position, and confident I could control the circumstances. Tina was there, trapped inside, and I would succeed at driving her out.

Instead, I lost, and Tina has vanished. I reluctantly go away from the courtyard, from the locked door in the alley. I'll let some time go by, an hour or two, before I come back to keep trying. But I'll come back.

ON MY RIGHT, THE Doric column of the Acropolis marks the boundary of the ruins. On the other side, beyond the Gela river, the towers of modernity rise into the air. I climb back up a wide stairway that takes me toward the Archeological Museum.

The guard is chatting behind the glass door, in a relaxed

position at the entrance table. Two other men are keeping him company, clearly friends who've come to visit. When I go inside, all three of them scrutinize me, immediately falling silent.

I'm the only visitor. I'm the only visitor from time immemorial, as I see when I sign and date the guest book that the guard opened up in the middle of the table.

And yet the museum is so very rich with materials, dating from the Bronze Age through the Greek and Roman eras up to the Middle Ages. The rooms are modern and well lit. A real "cathedral in the desert."

I hadn't ever been here either, when I lived near the seafront, just a short distance away. Is this an act of reparation for that? What else, I ask myself, could this pilgrimage to the only place of glory still possessed by Gela be? The only place she puts on display instead of hiding it. Otherwise, this city of hidden fugitives and trafficking swallows up everything: people, habits, its very own history. "An important archeological center, popular seaside resort, and major industrial center." Statements in an old Touring Club guide that I've lugged along with me. Words from 1963.

The guard smooths down his mustache. He contemplates my signature. He lifts his fingers from the black walrus that completely covers his lips and taps them on the guest book. "Put in where you come from too."

I again lean obediently over the empty page, where my name alone stands out in black and white. The guard's torso imperceptibly stretches forward while the other men's attention converges on my hand. With silent concentration everyone follows the pen running across the sheet of paper. I write: *Rome*. And I hear a soft but clear sigh, almost of relief, of pressure that relaxes with the clarification. Aaahh. A sigh that simultaneously escapes from all three men's parted lips.

I rather like my solitary walk through the display rooms. I can stop for as long as I want in front of the glass cases protecting fragments of a distant age. Here's the famous horse head of the fifth century B.C. and the laughing Gorgons with their full cheeks, tightly twisted curls and tongues sticking out in a screwed up ritual face (I go back to check, surprised; it's the same identical facial expression of the Maori sculptures in New Zealand, at the other end of the world). A fragment of a vase, in basic colors—white, black, ochre—showing a small, perfect erotic scene, with a symmetry of gestures, geometric correspondences.

An observation made by Graziella comes to mind: "They're very cerebral," she'd told me, staring at me from underneath her dark bobbed hair. "Passions are very cold here among us. Otherwise we wouldn't have invented honor killing. Something that's thought through. Nothing to do with jealousy."

One of the guards follows me a short distance away, up the stairs to the first floor. He turns on the lights without saying a word, and turns them off again behind me. I try in vain to strike up a conversation. On the other hand, loud voices reach me from the entrance: "Foreigners saw it, the Gela people haven't."

The initial distrust has condensed in a type of spiteful admiration, a resentful gratitude.

I've returned to my point of departure, in front of the table in the museum entrance hall. I go outside. Almost triumphant. Standing with smiles on their faces, the men shake my hand, one after the other.

THIS TIME I SIT down in a slice of shade on a step located in the small inner courtyard, facing the door to the basement home. I've decided I'm not moving from here. Sooner or later someone will have to come out, or go inside.

From my shady corner, I look at two geraniums that are trying to poke through the metal bars on a small balcony. Dark cardboard stands in the place of a broken window on the French door.

Someone is home, on the first floor. A friend, a neighbor . . . I hear muffled noises: water running from a faucet, a chair being moved. Maybe they're even coming from a room in the basement apartment. Yes, someone's there. I can only hope that this someone is the grandmother.

At this point, the closed front door doesn't discourage me anymore. It's all a question of interpretation. If I interpret the silence and refusal to open the door not as a denial— absolute, definitive, irremovable—but as a challenge, then I can meet it, stay on the field, and be patient. Patience plays in my favor; nothing else, patience alone will enable me to put all of the puzzle pieces in the right spot.

This obstinacy of mine owes more to superstition than reason. There's no rationality in the thought that forces me to wait, but rather, stubborn self-persuasion that employs the illogical procedures of superstition. If I manage to speak with the grandmother, sooner or later I'll manage to speak with Tina, somehow, any way I can.

But for now, meanwhile, I'm held in check.

I fold my hands and squeeze them between my knees. My eyes explore every corner of the courtyard.

In the widening on my left, four rows of wooden boards are standing against the wall, supported at the two ends by chairs or empty plywood crates turned upside down, that serve as sawhorses. Spread out on the boards are tomatoes, cut in two and salted, thickening in the sun and already dark red. A deep smell of tomato preserves, condensed juices. A greedy buzzing of flies and wasps that are searching for the thickest pulp, pungently fermenting.

Next to the door jambs, a horseshoe hangs from a nail, rusting.

For two interminable hours I follow the coming and going of ants, the scuttling of a cockroach against the wall. The shade has dwindled, squeezed toward the small balcony. The stench of cat urine mingles with the intense whiffs of the tomatoes and reaches my throat along with cigarette smoke. Finally the door opens.

It's the old woman. White hair in a neat, tight bun. Heavy black cotton stockings, despite the midsummer heat. Ostentatiously, but with dignified calm, the old woman ignores me. Taking short limping steps, she heads toward the boards that are exposed to the sun. Her hand half-heartedly waves at the flies, shooing them away. The old woman starts turning over the tomatoes. She clearly has a hard time stooping over to work, with one of her hands gripping the back of the chair that's holding up the wooden board. She never turns my way. Instead she's rigid, her neck bent over the level red surface, soft and buzzing. She puts effort into willfully feigning indifference.

I stand up and move closer to her, walking around the long boards. And I too begin turning over the tomatoes, standing in front of her. I don't say anything. She doesn't say anything. We continue like that for a good while, both of us leaning over that dark, viscous carpet, a warm mixture on our fingers, an overpowering essence in our noses.

I've finished one board and am about to start another one. But the old woman raises her lifeless, impenetrable eyes and stops me: "Not those ones, sweetheart. Not yet."

I walk up to another board, while emotion momentarily makes my hands fumble. Contact is established. Cautiously, my voice tentative, I comment: "This courtyard, it's useful."

She raises her head again and nods no.

"There's sun here only in the morning." She straightens up, having a painfully hard time and leveraging herself with her hand on the chair. She glances around the courtyard, as if she wanted to fully size up the situation. And she concludes: "It's not that I don't like it . . ."

Her eyes suddenly light up with a combative glint: "They say I have to leave. If they have enough courage . . ."

They'd like to evict her, I know. To get rid of the old tenants, that's the intent of the owner of the house. And then update the apartment, and afterward rent it out at a higher price. But the process isn't as simple as the owner would like. To evict a family with apparent ties to the mafia isn't a decision one might make lightheartedly. The eviction went nowhere. Purely an intention, seeing that no one dares to take legal action. And the old woman continues to eke out her life in her dark cave.

Bent over the tomatoes again, after a brief silence, she asks, "Do you work at the court? Did the court send you?"

"The court? Of all things!" I protest.

Without straightening up, she moves her scrutinizing gaze all the way up my body. "A journalist?"

"No . . . yes . . . that is, something of the sort."

"To who are you trying to find, sweetheart?," she calmly asks with authority.

"To your granddaughter Tina," I reply, spontaneously ready to adapt to this intransitive way of using Italian. We Sicilians abhor direct objects. We always need this little particle, this *to* that creates a space and distance. So on the island, I can't try to find a person. The undertaking requires a lot of stages, a lot of digressions. On the island I inevitably try to find *to* a person. And during the search I have to adapt to all of the stops, I have to make my way around all of the traps set, and even required by this oblique, intransitive forward movement, somehow accomplished in itself.

"Everyone is trying to find her, to my granddaughter Tina. The cops, journalists. Friends. Even a priest, one time. He told me: pray. To whom? To the god that finished off my son, that finished off my grandson?"

She wipes her hands, stained with dark lumps, on the apron tied around her waist. "It's all of you people's fault she had to go away. It's your fault I don't know where my granddaughter is. It's all the newspapers' fault. They talk and talk. And my granddaughter had to run away, a fugitive."

"I'm not looking for her for a newspaper."

Then why? I get mixed up, I get bogged down by the inevitable question. I can't budge at all, take one step forward. Answering becomes harder and harder. And the whole thing increasingly resembles a hunting match. But the role of hunter, not game, is certainly more suited to Tina.

"I only want to see her, to get to know her," I breathlessly whisper. A meeting that would fill in my fantasy with flesh and blood.

"My granddaughter, she has nothing to say. She's already put herself out there too far."

As if associating ideas, the old woman turns her gaze to

the mourning announcement. The white bun, streaked with gray, lowers.

"It was two years ago that they killed my grandson, Francesco."

She slowly turns the weak veil of her irises toward me. "Do you see? Do you see what great things happen in Gela?"

"Who did it?" I murmur.

"They came from out of town. They paid them and those guys did their duty. They had a good time, they amused themselves killing my grandson."

"Such a young boy . . . But why?" I ask, turning over the last tomato. I'm done. I bring my fingers to my lips, sucking the thick, tangy drops.

"All because of jealousy and revenge, sweetheart. Because of jealousy and revenge."

CHAPTER 15

At sunrise, when the smell of manure was most intense, the shepherds would arrive. There was always some human being to talk with during the day. But the nights were different. Tina counted them out one by one.

"And that makes four."

As Tina lay on the mattress that she'd dragged to the back of the room so she could keep an eye on the door and window, sleep eluded her. She drifted into fantasies. She thought about the bed in the alley home, when it was still full of everyone's breath, softened by their moods, by the little one's pee, by Saveria's uncontrollable monthly blood. She also thought about the cops' footsteps walking down the corridor in front of her cell. They had a hint of certainty and reality that was missing from the night wind's chaotic rustling in the countryside.

230 • MARIA ROSA CUTRUFELLI

There were some who spent their time as a fugitive in their own bed. And some, like her, who couldn't find a secure refuge even in some ghost house on the extreme edges of town, in the inextricable tangle of nameless streets. But it was no time to complain. She'd rushed to the countryside because Nele had ordered her to. Preparations for great things were being made.

For now, she lay restlessly on the mattress, unable to sleep and without even a TV for distraction. She sensed the fetid taste of stagnant water in her throat, and it almost made her feel like having a cigarette again, to dry out her mouth with the tobacco smoke. And to exhale, together with the smoke, the insistent memory of her friends who'd disappeared.

Her gang practically didn't exist anymore. Some of them were dead. And they were the best of them, Tina would say. Others, growing up, found a place all for themselves, assuming a different relationship to the gang, which made them less ready to follow her orders. For her own part, she was firmly tied to Nele. In the real circle, important. And yet this didn't compensate her for the loss of authority. Not yet, at least. But she wasn't short on patience. The patience of women ran inevitably in her veins. And it gave her the ability to put up with life on the run better and longer than any man, despite the contrariness and malice of the shepherds who were hiding her.

Meanwhile, great things were being prepared beyond the farmstead, great "theatrics": deceptions, performances, subversions. The rumormongers were at work, they had already started to spread their poison, to move masks and puppets. They were working for Nele. Therefore, to some extent, for her too.

So how could she complain? Even though she didn't have any money anymore, not even the little needed for a game in the arcade or soon, for a fruit soda and a Coca-Cola. But she couldn't complain, because in that farmstead she was waiting for Nele and his great opportunity.

He has an interest in me. To him, at least I'm worth something.

With the same obstinacy with which she practiced shooting for hours and hours during the day (after all, no one—no one who wasn't a friend—dared to venture into those scorched dirt roads, and she could help herself to ammunitions galore from the arsenal hidden in one of the rooms), with this same obstinacy, at night she clung to the idea of the great opportunity. The decisive test. The opportunity she'd waited for so long. The one that would let her savor the pleasure of vendetta, riches, and power. This idea alone enabled her to make it through the alien night in the country unscathed.

But then at sunrise, instead of Nele, the shepherds punctually arrived. And Ciuzzo with them.

THE GELA PLAIN IS devastated by fire. As if drought, landslides, erosion, and the desert that descends from the rocky peaks to crumble in the valley floor weren't enough.

Between Friday and Saturday, at least forty-five fires have besieged the city, one flaring up every half an hour, at a distance of ten kilometers from each other. The tongues of flames rose pointing in all directions. A party in pure mafia style. Impotent firefighters, terrorized salespeople and farmers. What's at stake is the monopoly of the grain market.

As a first move, the racket tried to eliminate a cereal crop salesman who had barricaded himself in his granary, armed with a 38-caliber gun (legally owned, the newspapers write). He had it in his hand when they shot him, aiming at his face. He risks losing his left eye.

"First attempted homicide. Now fires," Mimmo sighs.

Fires are still exploding unexpectedly in the grain fields that escaped the preceding bonfires. It's a splendid summer evening. From my uncle's top floor home, on the seventh floor that enjoys a panoramic 360 degree view, we see the sunset melt into the masses of flames on the plain, creating a single source of fire. An ephemeral sight: the sun immediately changes color in the flames of the advancing fire. The clouds of smoke are tinged with yellow and fall apart on the countryside in luminous, bluish breaths. From up here they look as if they're exhaled and come directly from cracks in the exhausted earth, breaths that come up from the bowels of ancient mines to blow sulfuric dust into the sky.

"Emperor Nero ought to be here to appreciate all this." Mimmo screws up his face in his usual ironic, bitter smirk.

"Once it was the Petrolchimico towers."

The towers would erupt and spew clouds from their swollen, hot bellies onto the city. Now the refinery's flames rise sharp like drawings. Each one with its little blue heart that throbs at intervals. The devastation comes from the flat horizon of the countryside, alive even at night.

We try to count the points of fire, the long swaths of smoke that mark a fire further away.

"And to think that the men of Gela are by tradition *strazzalenzuola*."

The double "z" is hard but hisses on Mimmo's lips. *Strazzalenzuola* means that in the evening everyone comes back to town, because the night is for wolves to roam, but for human beings, darkness marks the time to rest. The farmers have always avoided staying overnight on the country farmsteads; you sleep at home, this is customary.

Until everything was turned upside down in a new economy of life and emotions. Night has become a time to work. And the countryside hides the solitude of fugitives.

"Do you have any news?"

I look at Mimmo, dumbfounded. What does he mean? Is it possible that he's asking me for news about Tina? That's an odd reversal of roles.

And yet I've realized that these days it's an expectation many people share. As if I were a funnel through which everyone pours facts, signs, clues, dirty sand of an uncertain color. And then everyone expects that by some miraculous alchemy or some magic potion, light, clear sand will perhaps come out of the other end.

"Me? I expect news from you, from everyone."

"But . . . but you're waiting for something. Otherwise you'd have already left."

My cousin isn't wrong. I don't know if it's a matter of suggestion or something else, but I feel a strong catalyst at work inside me. My desire is a magnet capable of attracting events. And I never doubted the outcome of my research, the possibility of the meeting. Not even now. Otherwise, Mimmo is right, I would already have at least started to think about leaving. The story doesn't end here, I'm certain.

Even though for now I only know that somewhere, down there, in the dark night that covers fugitives, Tina is hiding too, sleeplessly tossing and turning on a makeshift bed. Waiting . . . I know, or I *believe* I know what Tina is waiting for, while I contemplate the siege of fire, fascinated, in spite of myself.

CIUZZO WAS A LITTLE eight-year-old boy with a sturdy body, really wiry hair, and a square face older than his years who was used to expressing himself in monosyllables.

"He doesn't even want to hear about school," and so his father, uncles and brothers took him along with them. "He's better than a grown man at battling the animals."

And he really did keep very busy working on the sheep pens, in the chicken coop, keeping an eye on the dogs.

He'd tensed up hostilely toward Tina right away. When she asked him anything at all, he'd answer bluntly, "I obey my brothers."

Tina would laugh, "You think I'm getting mixed up with you?"

The time had passed when being in command of younger boys gave her pleasure. She was almost twenty years old by then and wasn't interested in looking back. But another kind of relationship, a woman's spontaneous, familiar simplicity, was difficult for her.

"You don't know how to deal with them," Giovanna reproached her. And that's how it was. Tina didn't know how to deal with little children, and not even with girls her own age, neither before nor now that they were already married with children. She was only able to be close to Giovanna, who was a few years older.

Maybe the fact that Tina had never gotten involved in girl stuff was to blame.

"*Carrìa.*" Get out of the way, clear out, her grandmother would tell Tina when they had finished eating. The dishes were Saveria's chore. She'd taken that role upon herself, because the role of first-born male wouldn't have been hers due to sex and order of birth.

But with Giovanna it was another thing. It was a tranquil, happy way of being together. She missed the evenings spent in her friend's home watching the TV, singing karaoke while imitating the gestures of Fiorello, and envying the kids who performed on the stage in one of the town's piazzas. The pleasure of singing lingered in Tina, after all those Sundays celebrated at the kitchen table with wine and songs. More than singing, in truth, she liked the sound of her own voice, and following that slim trace of herself to recognize and find herself in the midst of other voices. In this way, it seemed like she acquired a stronger consistency, a unique value of her own.

The days went by, the nights too, and Nele didn't arrive.

For food she had what the shepherds brought from town, but one time Giovanna sent a pan of baked pasta, made just for her.

Tina settled herself outside on the stones of a crumbling low wall, far away from the smell of sheep and hens and the farmyard scattered with dog shit. Ciuzzo ate with her. They ate greedily, sucking on the silverware, stopping only to squash the ants that crawled up onto their knees and to swat away the flies.

The midday wind had a pleasant warmth that made them drowsy.

Tina stirred. She suddenly felt like forcing Ciuzzo to break his stubborn muteness, get a word out of his mouth, win over his suspicion. But unexpectedly the little boy surprised her, and confided in her.

"It was last year. The carabinieri showed up," he explained, eyes shining. "But by mistake. And they didn't get anything out of it." He hesitated as he remembered.

"There was one really fat guy." Another silence and then he reasoned: "Cops eat a lot. They have four stomachs, like cows."

Evidently the episode had made an impression on him and the food had loosened his tongue and mood, because that was the longest—and most spontaneous—statement that she had heard him make.

So she threw out a question: "Well, what do you want to do when you grow up?"

Said with the condescension of an adult toward a little child. She was the first to be surprised that the words had escaped her mouth. A strange, absurd question, that's what she'd always thought it was. Typical of teachers and journalists. When you grow up . . . Ever since she was Ciuzzo's age, she'd felt she was deep inside her life, way too deep inside to imagine a "grown up" time for herself. She hadn't had any way to carve out a space for herself where she could fantasize about a "grown up" life. And maybe all of her battles were born from that, from the desire to feel herself grow up, to have an "after" to imagine.

Ciuzzo looked down and continued to squash a long line of ants with his finger.

The question was stupid, but she couldn't take it back.

"Well? Are you scared to answer?"

Blushing, the little boy said, "Come on. Like my father."

Tina nodded. That was a dream that she recognized. Even though she had never wanted that: she didn't want to be like her father. She didn't want to end up killed by some stranger. She wanted to be more than him. And to win, at any cost. To win on her father's death. A thought that frightened her a little, as if it were a curse or a sacrilege.

AT THE MOTEL RECEPTION desk, they hand me a note, a message that someone had called me. A woman phoned me to set up an appointment. Giovanna Incardona. A moment of uncertainty. A void. Yes. The hair stylist, Tina's friend. A sign, finally. Enthusiasm, a sense of expectancy, the heat of impassioned engagement begins to flow strongly again.

Another step closer to Tina. I slip the message into my notebook. Or perhaps Tina is starting to take a few steps toward me.

CHAPTER 16

I slow down at each pothole. I move ahead in fits and starts. When I put on the brakes, the tires kick up dry dust that parches my lips and makes me thirsty, while children on both my right and left stop their games to watch the approaching car, driven by a complete stranger. An outsider. On one side of the street, the curtains made of cloth or plastic that stand in place of doors lift up, and slowly drop down again. There's no way to escape the whole neighborhood's silent attention—an alarm that's instinctive yet apathetic.

I already drove far and wide across Settefarine once before. And yet, despite the grid design of the streets, it's still hard for me to get my bearings. They're all the same, these narrow alleys made of dried dirt or cracked asphalt, these brick homes that the sun's rays turn deep red, like an open wound. Between large mounds of excavated dirt and eviscerated furniture, in the middle of all the debris, stands a spot of green: a lone palm tree.

"I'm coming right now," yells a woman in the middle of a heated argument, silhouetted by a man inside the dark recess of the window. "I'm coming right now," echoes her close woman friend.

I finally recognize the house that belongs to Giovanna's cousin, with the carcasses of automobiles that her youngest child was playing in. A little further ahead, at the other end of the street, is the building I'm looking for. A single-story house, located in a strategic position on the edge of the neighborhood. There's only one other home facing it, and just open land beyond, devastated, filthy countryside. A path of compact dirt connects it to highway 117, which runs from Gela to Catania. The walled side of the house, carpeted in moss nourished by the rains, faces the neighborhood.

The hairdresser shop occupies a room on the first floor, equipped with three hair dryers and a sink that seems like a slightly readapted kitchen sink. Two shelves covered in floral paper sag, jam-packed with bottles, combs, and brushes. A rainbow fringe door curtain separates the shop from a kitchenette. No clients. Either they're usually scarce, or perhaps it's because of my presence. An imitation wicker basket made of plastic holds a big bunch of photoromances, illustrated romantic pulp magazines. It's been ages since I've seen any.

I sit down uncomfortably in the tight space and browse through one of them—simple, flat photographs that shy away from movement. A fixity that attracts and captivates like the eyes of a snake.

The curtain fringes swish open, letting Giovanna pass inside carrying coffee all ready to drink. Two tiny cups on a brand-new silver-plated tray, heavily decorated in etched friezes and complicated scrolls. Catching the direction of my gaze, Giovanna brims with pride: "I got it by collecting reward point stickers for my laundry detergent. I use a lot of it. Piles of it, and it disappears. Mountains of it, you know, with the work I do. The cloths, towels, sponges . . ."

She immediately spoke to me with the informal "*tu*" address, as if we already knew each other. Certainly with all my asking around left and right, disturbing relatives, sowing unrest and apprehensions, raising questions, I've made myself known. At this point she likely knows more about me than I do about her.

She doesn't sit down, perhaps because she's used to working on her feet. Sitting on a stool, I casually observe her barely-showing tummy right at my eye level, a small melon under the large blue blouse that rises in front and drapes down like a train in back. Her ankles are white and swollen in her slippers. My gaze slowly sweeps upwards, toward a young, yet worn, face. A pallor heightened by two dark circles that turn bluish at her temples.

"I did this all by myself. The shop, the house. My husband paid for everything in the kitchen, because that's the custom.

The man's responsible for the kitchen. He's the one who has to pay for it."

"Your husband," I say, forcing myself to not show any surprise.

She immediately clarifies: "We ran off together, we're not officially married." She moves carefully, setting the tray on the window ledge, the only empty surface in the whole room. "On account of my mother-in-law. She only has one son. She didn't want to give him to a foreigner, it makes sense. I come from another town. Sutera. Not even. From a place near there, where the Montagna Spaccata is. Are you familiar with it?"

"No."

"It's the mountain that split open when our Lord said three things with his last breaths. That's what the ancients say." When she smiles, her face lightens up, becomes pretty. "We ran off and stayed with a relative of mine in my town for three days. When we came back, my mother-in-law went crazy . . . Then our friends jumped in as go-betweens to arrange for making peace." Her smile turns sad and etches an ever so slight crease at the corners of her mouth. "Of course I'd like to have a wedding, with flowers, a big hall, photos, everything that goes with it. But now . . ."

Now Antonino is a fugitive, even though he's evidently not too far away from here.

"But I'm satisfied with what I have. I'm satisfied with working. At least I have my own money." She pauses to reflect, as if the assertion doesn't entirely satisfy her. "It's not on account of him . . . He bought me things. My husband is loving. But I don't like to act like a sheep bleating about this or that, and so I'm satisfied working and spending my own money."

Still standing, Giovanna gulps down some coffee, and sets down the cup. Leaning toward the side of the window, she lights a cigarette.

Despite her formal, even ceremonious, courtesy, she doesn't pay much attention to me and my needs, forced as I am into an uncomfortable position, sitting on a stool with nothing to rest my back on, my neck craned so I can look her in the face.

But compared to my discomfort, my embarrassment is stronger, making me sweat and keeping me entirely still in this absurd position, as if any slight movement might make a boulder perched above our heads tumble down. It seems like I can't find all the questions I had prepared and pick them out of my confused mind, as if I'd lost them somewhere along the road, in the potholes where the tires plunged, the wheels spinning, struggling to grip onto a crumbling piece of earth. In fact, I no longer know if I'm here of my own will or Giovanna's, if I'm the one who wants to ask questions, or if she's the one who wants to ask them of me.

Giovanna taps the ashes into the sink. "There's not much work, but . . . I was hoping Tina would be my assistant. I always hoped so, but that's not her thing. Tina likes to fight too much." She raises the cigarette to her mouth, a darting little snake with a pointed tip, and says as she exhales the smoke, "She's a warrior." A reverential fear that gradually dissolves in veiled disapproval.

She suddenly falls silent. Her left hand comes to rest delicately on her tummy.

"He's moved to the side. Feel here. He moves entirely to the side, this son of mine. *Sciatu meu, scia'*, my life's breath." She fusses over him. Her thin lips parted, head bent, her light brown hair falling forward. "When he moves I'm mystified."

My body's stiff from sitting on the stool, my neck hurts from craning upward, I can't take it anymore. What masochistic impulse is keeping me in this position? I stand up, and while rising I brush against her tight belly, the wan skin of her arms, untouched by the sun this summer or any other summer. A lock of hair, moist with sweat from her forehead, falls over her eyes.

"The room's too small," Giovanna apologizes. "Sit over here." She quickly wipes a cloth over the seat in front of the sink. She pushes back her hair with the back of one hand while she puts her cigarette out under the water dripping from the faucet with the other. A studied gesture, as if she wanted to stall for time. Now that I'm not forced to look at her from the bottom up, I realize that she's also nervous, embarrassed. Having a difficult time. And out of the blue she makes a suggestion that's eccentric, to say the least: "Shall we do your hair?"

From the relief in her voice, she seems like a person who has finally found the solution to a difficult problem. I look at her in amazement, then realize what the offer means.

"Sure, yes, let's do it." If this puts her more at ease, gives her a more relaxed way of connecting, if this lets us undo the knot of embarrassment, I have no objections.

The water from the faucet is cold, as if the water heater were turned off. Maybe, I think, there isn't even a water heater. How can she work this way in the winter? But right now, with the heat that gathers in the close space of the hairdresser shop, this cool stream is even pleasant. And Giovanna's long, slender hands move slowly as if looking for the path that leads to a dialogue, to a more hidden point of contact.

She wants something from me. That's why she called me, why she had me come all the way here. It's clear that she wants something, but I don't understand, I can't imagine what expectations I might have raised in her, what she needs or has dreamed up that pushed her to seek out my cooperation.

"They overdid it with Tina."

I have my eyes closed and her voice is floating up high, above me.

"They wouldn't even give her two hours to go do the grocery shopping. You know, when she was under house arrest . . . Not even two hours. And she was there all alone with the old woman, who's sick and can hardly move. They went too far."

"I'd like to meet with Tina," I try to suggest. "Under any conditions. I'm willing to . . ." I was about to say "accept any agreement." I stop myself, barely in time.

"Can't you be satisfied by talking with me? I can tell you everything. Whatever I don't tell you, Tina can't tell you either." But she's acting without conviction, reciting a lesson that she's memorized.

She's finished rinsing my hair after the first shampoo and begins washing it another time, massaging the foam over my head.

I suddenly notice a change. Her touch has become uncertain, upset by an imperceptible tremor. In the body close to mine, in its wrists, in the fingertips themselves, I perceive mounting anxiety, worry, a strong tension. I duck away from the massage and turn to look her in the face. She drops her foam-covered hand on the sink and unexpectedly, unforeseeably, starts crying. Crying silently, her tears falling without altering the calm sadness of her features.

At this point I don't know what to do anymore, what kind of demeanor to maintain. I'm sitting there, staring at her, dumbfounded, while the shampoo is dripping down my forehead, burning my eyes.

"I'm sorry." Giovanna wipes away the tears with the back of her reddened hand, and with the other she has me lean my head under the running water again.

"It's just that I worry. I worry a lot."

I'd like to turn to look at her again, but she applies a light pressure, forcing me to stay still.

"She's consumed by living on the run. It's not right for a woman," she says. "Not even for Tina. She's too consumed by it . . . And who can talk reason into her now?"

"Reason?" I stupidly repeat.

"Maybe Tina could get out of this tight spot, if she doesn't get mixed up in things that don't concern her. And they mustn't concern her."

The stream of water has dwindled, and trickles down finer and finer, on the verge of running out.

"You're looking for her. For a book, you've been saying. What good does that do? All of your questions are upsetting the whole world. But what can you do for her?" Giovanna continues wearily, as if she were asking a rhetorical question, secretly pervaded, nevertheless, by an insane hope.

More than an impression, by now it's a certainty. Vivid, immediate. A confirmation. Giovanna wants to pull me into some impossible plan of hers: to "talk reason," she says. And she expects me to help out. My peculiar, obstinate search is nothing else for her but a sign of my willingness to help. Because to have the aim of nothing but writing is inconceivable.

"Worrying about it . . . it's obvious."

But I don't dare ask, why right now and why so much? I think of the long years of Antonino 'u niuru living on the run. Giovanna should have gotten used to it, or at least have resigned herself to his absences, the dangers of staying in hiding, that precarious way of living. But this time I sense that there's something more, different.

Perhaps she knows she has only a partial hold over Antonino. She can be his silent or reluctant accomplice, sharing in his destiny, but she can't bend him to her desires; a woman's strength isn't enough to do it. Whereas she's hoping she has a stronger, deeper sway over Tina, or deceiving herself she does.

Or perhaps there's something she still hasn't told me, that she's still hiding.

By now only long drops of water are falling from the faucet, too slowly to wash anything out. Giovanna turns off the faucet and very slowly smooths my hair, wrings out the excess water, and combs through the wet strands.

"The last time I saw Tina . . . Well, it doesn't matter when. She had things she urgently needed to buy. We went together and we stopped at a shoe store. She chose a pair and had them wrapped up right away, without trying them on."

I wait for the rest of the story, but Giovanna looks like she's finished.

"And?"

"Don't you understand? Don't you know what this means?"

"No, I don't," I say impatiently, tired of always having to play guessing games.

"It means that she didn't have to walk in those shoes.

They were shoes to wear after her death. Shoes for her funeral."

My body jumps, but Giovanna has already spread out a towel and starts wrapping it around my head. She wraps and squeezes, squeezes as if she were crushing an enemy. But I don't even have time to give out a yell before she suddenly loosens her iron grip.

"Tina thinks she has to die. And she let me know in her own way. Even with me . . . even with me she's arming the puppet show."

She unexpectedly raises her voice, overcome by a furious, desperate anger: "But what does she think, that other people like living this way? As if in a film . . . or a comic strip?"

With her wet hands she hurls herself on the bunch of photoromance magazines, pulls them out of the basket and furiously rips and tears them up, one after the other, with her slender, white fingers. Minute shreds twirl and scatter on the room's tiles in a crazy chaos.

CHAPTER 17

"We're the new tourist attraction in Gela." The man, little more than a boy, smiles joylessly.

The Las Vegas arcade, located right downtown on Corso Vittorio Emanuele, had a sad, undeserved notoriety. The episode happened a few years ago by now, but no one has forgotten the "children's massacre," as the newspaper immediately dubbed it in the headlines. Unanimously indicating the Las Vegas arcade as the place of the massacre.

"That's not how it happened," the young cashier maintains, rubbing his hand almost lovingly along the cushion of an extremely beautiful antique pool table. The only one in the room, which is jam packed with video games.

Right now, in mid-morning, the machines are turned off and the partly closed shutter keeps the dim light cool and pleasant. The room has a vaulted ceiling and is full of recessed spaces, niches, and compartments. I try to picture it in full swing, with its white walls that dissolve the harshness of the neon light, the balls in the pinball machine bouncing crazily off the flipper, and down the metallic paths. And Tina, standing there, her chin hidden beneath the raised collar of her jacket, searching for a path through the electronic labyrinth.

"I used to see her around here, now and then," the cashier confirms. But he immediately goes back to the topic he cares about.

The massacre, he explains, was carried out a few meters further ahead, in another arcade ("closed ever since then"), with fewer games, less flashy. A shop like so many others, shoddily set up, a narrow hole in the wall with no signs, just a billiard table and two video games. But unfortunately, right next to the Las Vegas.

"An easy mistake to make."

But maybe the reporters also liked the arcade's name, which easily fascinates and has an evocative allure. The result is that the manager vainly continues to refute and protest the claim, but the Las Vegas is by now the place of the massacre in everyone's mind.

Is that why it's empty?

"It's not the moment to check it out," the cashier says dismissively. "It's summer. But in the winter, at this time of day, we're already packed. And we stay packed until ten thirty, eleven at night. Boys for the most part, but girls too."

"What kind of girls? Like Tina?"

He thinks about it warily, but with no hostility, his right hip leaning against the cushion of the billiard table. "The girls who have a job don't come here." He straightens up. "But no one writes books about them. Only about Tina . . . First interviews, then articles, and now a book."

Disapproval and envy mingle in his well-mannered voice. And now that he's gotten started he doesn't stop, launching into a full-blown indictment against the degeneration of the younger generation. A word of Sicilian dialect hardly appears in his Italian. Only the arrangement of the words in his way of speaking, the different word order, reveals the logic of a different language.

"Are they ever satisfied with what they have, perhaps? No, young people are never satisfied."

Do people get old this quickly on the island? That's the impression I get from listening to the Las Vegas cashier, who pulls himself out of the category of "young people" and gushes with nostalgia for habits and values of a bygone time that's impossible to believe is his own.

"They don't enjoy anything. It seems like they do everything as an obligation, spending money, going out and about. They rev up their motorcycles out of obligation, they pierce their ears out of obligation, they eat pizza together out of obligation. All it took before was being together, at a long table, and people were happy."

Kids who study at school on one side, and on the other,

"streetwise" kids. Once it was easy to distinguish between them. But now this difference no longer works either. They all have the same attitude, the same ribbed rubber shoes, the same motorcycle, and they're all taken in by the drug dealers stationed at the Quattro Canti.

"One distinction, only one, endures: the distinction between men and women."

And what about Tina? What is she, the first sign that this distinction is also losing its meaning? The cashier who doesn't want to call himself young weighs my question, and cautiously observes: "She was good at pool." He adds: "She would come with friends."

"Boyfriends?"

He takes some time before answering. "I doubt it. She had a way of doing things that was too masculine. Way too much. Could boys take up with her? I doubt it." He pauses. "She was too strange," he maintained, stressing "too." An entirely Sicilian way of expressing disapproval and suspicion about excess.

Graziella had also made a point of underlining this feature of Tina's, the harshness the girl always expressed when denying any romantic relationship: "Someone asked Tina, one time, if Nele, a small-time local boss, a fugitive, was her boyfriend. You've got to be joking . . . . What an insult! . . . From the way she answered, you'd have thought they'd maligned her. He's my sister's fiancé, she said. But it was obvious that something else about it irritated her. The very fact that someone might think she had a boyfriend. That was what she couldn't swallow. As if it diminished her, or unbearably degraded her."

"I haven't seen her for a long time," says the Las Vegas cashier, suddenly amazed at the thought.

"She was in prison."

"I didn't know," he blandly responds, shrugging.

"Then she was on house arrest. Now she's disappeared."

"She became a fugitive?"

"Disappeared," I reaffirm, against all my real convictions, just to test his reaction.

"A fugitive," he says assuredly.

"Disappeared," I repeat. "For no reason, apparently."

"But you don't run away for no reason." He looks at me. "For no reason . . . You don't run away, right?"

CHAPTER 18

The small villa was actually a bunker, with high walls around the perimeter that hid its facade, bulletproof glass in the windows, armored doors, and closed-circuit alarm systems. An impenetrable stronghold. A little fort in a remote location on the mountainous slopes of Etna, which went unused most of the time.

But now a lot of cars were parked in the part of the wide inner courtyard shaded by a pergola, several Mercedes, some Themas, and two off-road vehicles. The men shut up in the small villa had been discussing things for three hours by then. Outside, the bodyguards lit one cigarette after another while they kept their eyes on each other and watched over the movements on the small path that went around the house. Suspicion was palpable, a living presence.

Tina was also waiting outside, together with Janu, a

young man with the right credentials, trustworthy. The right man to be the driver for a fugitive. Nele often used him.

The walls blocked the view of the panorama, but from the guard posts next to the electric iron gate they could keep a watch on the uphill lane and Etna's slope. On one side stood forests of pistachio trees and blotches of broom, and on the other, lava rocks worn down by the wind. It was the first time that Tina had been on the road up the mountain, La Montagna. Black earth, different from the rough, loose rocks that she was used to. A horizon veiled by languid, mysterious mists.

From the gate they could see far and wide, and even catch a glimpse between the treetops of the asphalt highway at the bottom of the valley, and now and then the flash of a car passing by. Nothing coming from that side could surprise them.

"What a life," Nele vented as they drove uphill, looking at the deserted slopes. Perhaps that landscape, the contrast of the Mountain's undulating, silent slopes was what aroused his unusual talkativeness. "We're always having to count every bit of money like people on a salary. Snatching a bite here and there, like a mongrel hidden in the shadows. While there are some people who live it up in hiding. In a villa with a swimming pool or in downtown Palermo or the best cities. Cars at their disposal all the time, and men from everywhere taking their orders."

It wasn't right. The young men were also entitled to

an opportunity, to make their way. Too many differences between people who did the same work. Even though there were men who knew how to organize trafficking deals and others who didn't, men who knew how to make themselves heard and others who couldn't do anything else in life but plant a bullet between the eyes of a "target" whose name they didn't even know. In the end, the work was always the same for everyone.

Death, that's what our job is, thought Tina emotionlessly.

The days when she had her small gang, when everything happened as easily as a game and the group was a jealously protected space never shared with outsiders, seemed infinitely far away. Adults only cared about convenience. If murder was more convenient than robbery—less time to lose, fewer preparations, lower expenses—then murder became the normal practice.

Turning her back on the gate, Tina looked toward the villa. The sun was beating down on the glass of the closed windows. The meeting had already lasted a long time, and there was nothing, not a sign, not a hint, that might lead one to expect a quick conclusion.

"HOUSE ARREST IS HARDER than prison for these people. It may seem strange, but it's the truth."

Lawyer Laura Tilaro's office looks a little old, dusty, everything jumbled up. Similar to my own in every way. Piles of files on chairs, worn-down pencils and pens scattered all over except in the pen holder. A complete lack of formality that I've noticed in the offices of many women professionals. As if women at work get right to the substance of things, for lack of time or who knows what other reason, leaving men to take care of appearances. For me, it's a relaxing, absolutely congenial atmosphere.

"Prison is worse than drugs, it's addictive. Sometimes," Laura continues, "I have the impression they try on purpose to get into trouble, in a rush to go back to jail. It's the syndrome of the sailor when he sets foot on land after months of being at sea. He deeply desires that moment and then instead, he can't wait to get back on board. He can't get used to the rhythms of normal life anymore. Compile this with the difficulties of house arrest, for people who get by in haphazard conditions in houses that are more overcrowded than prisons. It can be real torture."

Laura is a beautiful woman who looks thirty-five years old. With a quick, efficient demeanor, like the makeup on her face, that suggests a mere hint of care and grace. She's married with a young son she's brought along to the office today, and who's having fun romping between one room and the other. To grab his mom's attention, the little boy has invented a really unique game. So now and then Laura's young assistant cries out, interrupting our conversation.

"He's going to jump, he's going to jump."

And each time, Laura repeats the same identical ritual. She leaps out of her chair, takes small running steps into the next room, and grabs the little boy, who has gotten up on a chair and is trying to climb out the window or the balustrade closing off the flight of stairs.

"As far as Tina is concerned . . ." says Laura, bringing the little boy back to his point of departure, "all this applies to her as much as it does to everyone. In the meantime, the stint in prison gave her more credit. It is, in some way, a mandatory step. By now this is well known."

"Excuse me."

With her flared skirt swaying around her tanned legs at every step, the assistant—a young, elegant university student, much more elegant than her employer—walks across the room to leave a file folder on the desk.

Laura glances through the pages inside the gray folder, her concentration ready and quick.

"It's difficult to be a criminal lawyer in mafia territory," she comments, to justify the interruption and smoothly shift to giving me friendly attention. "And especially so for a woman." But she smiles. There's something comic at the bottom of the situation. As she digs deep into each circumstance that comes to mind she can trace a vein of somber humor.

"It's as if they don't see me, even my own clients. One guy I got acquitted—and he listened to me present his defense in court and paid me, because I was his defense lawyer—well, after the sentence, he shakes my hand and rejoices, 'Yaaay . . . We got off. Imagine that. And without a lawyer.' Okay, so what was I? What did he think he was paying me for?"

She breaks off, her apprehensive eyes staring at the little boy who's trotting away.

"You wouldn't believe what it takes to collect the fees. They always try to get out of paying. It's not so much a problem of having the money as the fact that they don't consider it work, a service . . . Rather, it's something that enters into the mentality of doing favors, of exchanging things. At times it's also ignorance. I had to convince myself to stop saying 'I'll prepare the *fattura,* the invoice.' I avoid saying '*fattura.*' Because I would see those bewildered faces and some of them would beg me, please, that bad thing, no. For them the only *fattura* that exists is a spell, like those of the *magare* sorceresses, the women who practice magic."

She makes a correction in the margin of a page with her pencil, then closes the file. She sets it on top of a pile of papers. She picks up where she left off: "The real problem is the hard-case guys, the ones who take paying as an insult. They always look for something that's more involved than professional service. They'd like a lawyer who's complicit and compromised, subjugated. In contrast, the fee means that our relationship ends there, that there aren't any other interests in common. Then the intimidation begins. Right in front of my very eyes, in profound silence or chatting about this or that, the weather and the coffee—they're afraid of hidden microphones—they start turning my office upside down, breaking everything." She gives an exasperated snort. "It's not what you'd call a calm job."

"And yet you look . . ." I hesitate, but then return to the adjective that she'd denied: "Calm. Decidedly calm. All your anxiety is focused elsewhere, it seems," I say, thinking about how her little boy obstinately perseveres at creating dangers.

Laura sizes me up at a glance. "Lawyers . . . Don't forget that lawyers are like boxers. We like climbing into the ring. And when you lose, well, you still get to go home at night. For lawyers working with the mafia, it's an entirely different matter. Losing is dangerous. All it takes is the suspicion of a lukewarm defense, and . . ."

From the next room, the assistant bursts out yelling: "He's going to jump, he's going to jump."

Laura rushes off and reappears with her little boy on her shoulders. She puts him down at the starting line, and returns to her place behind the desk as if nothing had happened.

"But let's get back to Tina," she proposes.

"You were her lawyer."

"I defended her sometimes, when she was younger. I think it's a positive sign that up to now she's kept within the same typology of crimes: thefts and robberies. She has never been accused of mafia association. This means she hasn't advanced, that at least she hasn't become part of Cosa Nostra's affiliated work force. But now . . . Now she could be on the eve of a leap ahead in the organization."

The yell breaks out again: "He's going to jump, he's going to jump."

Laura stands up again, marches out, and bursts into the other room.

TINA RELUCTANTLY MOVED AWAY from the gate. She slowly went back, walking in her typical boyish manner, with her hands stuck in her jacket pockets, her shoulders hunched under the denim. Passing in front of the car, she remarked to Janu, who was smoking inside with the doors wide open to create a stream of air: "I'm thirsty."

She went around the house and opened a door that went into the kitchen. Inside, other bodyguards. A woman lying on a chaise lounge was painting her fingernails with orange polish. It was the first time Tina had seen her, but there had been a lot of talk about her. A boss's lover, that's what she was. And he was a boss who counted and could therefore dare to break the rules of behavior, flaunting dubious morals that the organization's rigid norms and customs didn't allow.

Any man of honor would have hidden the relationship, would have held it in the most intimate and strict confidentiality. Instead, he not only didn't hide that woman, separated and with two children, whom he'd been supporting for years. Worse still, he always brought her along with him, a habit that was quite frowned upon, and he let her drive the car. He allowed her to wait together with the bodyguards. The woman had an impassive, scornful face that kept everyone at a distance, and stopped tongues from wagging even more than fear of the boss's bad temper did.

An eccentric presence, but tolerated. Nevertheless, it fueled a hidden disdain for that man who compromised himself with a woman.

And yet all of them needed a woman—a woman's tacit acquiescence. In the men's straying, clandestine kind of life, women were the ones who opened up the refuge of an apparent, ephemeral normality. Who offered shelter and spoke the ancestral language of emotions. There had to be a person for them, somewhere, a person able to endure their absences, quick escapes, silences. There had to be a woman. They all needed one, in order to withstand it all.

And they all remained attached to someone, thought Tina. Nele had Saveria. Antonino had Giovanna. Only she didn't have anyone.

The woman lifted the brush from the little finger on her left hand and her prying eyes lit on Tina. Her blatant, curious stare irritated Tina. As if *that woman* wanted to size her up. She passed by her, glancing at her heavy thighs squeezed into her leggings. *Whore,* Tina disdainfully said to herself.

She opened the refrigerator, took the cap off a soda, and went back outside. Women were for consolation. But she didn't have anyone who could console her, and never would. Mixed up, unpleasant thoughts were agitating her. She didn't know why, but that woman with the orange fingernails made her more nervous than all the waiting around.

"Whore." She angrily got it out of her system again, leaning on the car and lifting the bottle to her lips.

A window on the villa's first floor opened and immediately closed again. Tina gave a start. She instantly reacted, tightening her fingers around the bottle's neck and squinting her eyes, as if to hold back a dangerous impatience that threatened to overwhelm her powers of resistance. The outcome of this meeting was important for her too, for her personal destiny.

Too many people on the organization chart of the "family" to which Nele belonged, the one he had "brought together" in the mafia through the oath and drop of blood when he was still a boy with little experience, were missing by then. The soldiers were there, but the bosses weren't anymore. Some were in prison, some had been sent far away by the State, and others had been killed. So now it was Nele's turn to hold the baton. It wasn't a question of an unreasonable demand, it was a normal request, part of their tradition. During that meeting, the "superiors" were supposed to give a definitive answer to the young man and formalize the passage of command.

If Nele obtained the command, for her too, for Tina too, that old, confused aspiration to be in Cosa Nostra acquired concreteness and real substance. She could get ahead, seize the opportunity that she'd pursued in vain up to that moment. Then perhaps that dark thirst for existing in the world that burned her throat would be allayed.

The door finally opened and the men started to come out. A glance at Nele's face was all it took for her to know that the outcome had been negative.

"They're taking more time to decide," he laconically informed her as they drove downhill, one bend in the road after another. Janu remained silent, concentrating on the driving.

They entered the highway. The smooth engine of the Mercedes didn't make a sound. The absence of noise made the rumbling in Nele's stomach seem louder and rending. The doctor's diagnosis was enterocolitis from nervous stress. But the only thing Nele had understood was that he had to put a Maalox tablet in his mouth and be patient. As always, he was the one who had to be patient. He spit out the Maalox. The taste of patience, of life dragging on, had become more unbearable than any pain.

Antonino was already waiting for them at the country house. To be careful, 'u niuru had arrived before them in another car. Their caution wasn't motivated by fear of the cops.

"Some trouble. Eh, do you like that idea? Let's make some real trouble for those *gentlemen*. We have to get organized," Nele began. An act of strength to make the respective positions clear. To dispel any ideas about putting off the answer and show everyone, the ones who could understand and the ones who refused to, on which side the power lay. So that everyone knows who they owe obedience and respect to. The plan was simple. But meanwhile they had to get more weapons and ammunition for a war whose length was difficult to calculate.

"We'll strike out on our own," Nele summarized, the Maalox leaving a white froth at the corners of his mouth. "We're the only ones who can negotiate our own business."

Tina nodded. For a while she'd been prepared to put everything she had on the line, her abilities and her life. She had no hesitation. Nevertheless, Nele's words tightened around her neck like a noose.

"YES, SHE COULD BE on the eve of making an important leap ahead in the organization," Laura pronounces.

She's busily going through drawers. She throws pieces of paper in the wastebasket, lines up pencils on the top of the dull, scratched desk. While she continues the provisional work of reorganizing, she explains her theory: "Two things make me think that. In the first place, she chose another lawyer when they arrested her. She didn't come to me, like she always had. She went to someone who is, so to speak . . . how should I describe him . . . 'specialized'? Someone who defends the small-time bosses and is a trusted lawyer for her clan. Or at least for the clan people say Tina worked for and could now have become an official member of."

We hear the little boy's shrill laughter and assistant's soft voice in the next room. Laura stops talking and perks her ears. A spontaneous, silent agreement holds us in suspense for a few moments. But no scream of warning demands her presence.

"The second element is her being a fugitive from the law.

It's not a matter of a simple violation of her house arrest. I really don't think that's it. It's something different, and it worries me more." She reflects a moment. "Your conversation with her friend, Giovanna . . . In a roundabout, indirect way, confirms it. It corroborates my doubts."

She stops messing around with the drawers and listens again. Almost alarmed, or maybe disappointed, at not being interrupted by the usual yell. On the other side of the door, the little child's voice tranquilly alternates with the girl's. An expression of amazed jealousy comes over Laura's face. Then she shakes her head, chuckling. "She's tamed him."

"An important leap forward in the organization," I urge her on. "What do you mean?"

"Tina isn't like everyone else." She leans her elbows on the desk and looks steadily at me. "Tina is a unique figure, with a strong, complex personality. What's more, she's internalized the image of herself that the media offered. So part of her is an act, and part is her real will to break out of the pack, to prevail, to affirm herself at any cost. A vicious circle has been triggered. And now it's impossible for her to back down."

CHAPTER 19

The crowd at the weekly local street market makes it impossible to walk freely, hemming everyone into a narrow pathway. A human snake slowly loosens its coils between the banks of merchandise stalls. Shoes, clothes, linens. The women from the old Sperone neighborhood and the new suburbs, the illegally constructed subdivisions of Settefarine, Margi, Aldisio, Scavone, Fondo Iozza, are all here shoving each other over rough lace panties and faux leather purses.

I move ahead, swept along by the crowd. At the allure of a certain material or knit top I don't even venture to put up the slightest resistance and try to stop. A glance of regret as the crowd's flow has already flung me far away, a safe distance from any temptation.

Every movement of the women around me raises a wave

of synthetic sweat from the acrylic fibers of their blouses and dresses. It beats against my body, gets into the pores of my skin, forces my nostrils open, invades my respiratory canals, smothers me. Gasping like someone drowning, I lift my head to reach the air. In this burst of movement I think I catch sight of Giovanna's cousin's shiny hair under a distant festoon of skirts hanging high. But I have to resign myself to the facts; I'll never reach her. I vainly struggle, using my elbows. The sieging crowd is too tight.

I continue pushing and becoming worked up, but only to overcome the irrational and depressing sense of waste that is beginning to obsess me. By now I'm spending entire days conducting useless interviews and planning senseless on-site investigations, waiting for phone calls, and bothering old friends or people I've never seen or known.

I had one aim in the beginning: to hold nostalgia at bay with the allures of Tina's story. But I chose a story that's gotten out of hand and won't leave me alone, that has trapped me inside. I can't even see the end of it. What is the end point, meeting Tina? Will that be enough? And when will that happen? Surely Tina already senses a change in the breathing of the pack of dogs hunting her down. Will she let me catch up to her?

But if that weren't possible, when will I allow myself to give up on it? When will I allow myself to abandon a story that I can no longer pursue?

I find I've even become superstitious, to keep myself from

giving up. I accumulate clues, premonitions. I imagine some of them are pieces of evidence. Being patient will be enough, I tell myself over and over again. Something is happening and it will explode soon. It's imminent. I feel it the same way you feel coming storms in the August air.

Meanwhile, Giovanna's cousin's head of hair has disappeared, overlapped by other heads of hair, other necks, other shoulders.

In a bend in the crowd, three or four Black men—the only ones I've happened across in Gela up to now—are selling fake Lacoste polo shirts. A light-skinned Arab—I can't identify any others, but it's difficult to spot them at a glance, thoroughly camouflaged in this natural environment that's absolutely akin to them—is offering straw hats instead.

The throng disperses when I reach the little huts selling fruit and vegetables, at the entrance to the street. One step more and the street is clear, the air scented with herbs. I feel like I've been hurled out, forcefully expelled from a reluctant belly. I feel a dizziness, counterbalanced by a sudden jolt of euphoria. I stop to breathe in the scent of the spices, the pungent aroma of the small bunches of oregano.

"Please wrap up twenty or so of them for me," I instruct the seller, who's shocked at my insane hoarding. But, unlike him, I have the insipid little supermarket bags, squalid surrogates for these aromatic delights, clearly in mind, inscribed in the memory of daily repulsion. I'm stocking up on flavors and scents for winter on the continent. Well then,

I tell myself, so I'm already thinking about my departure. I'm getting ready for the abandonment. And yet I'm sure that this time I won't yield to the seduction of parting. Not before I've seen the story that brought me back to the island all the way to the end.

"That little basket of black mulberries too." I'm caught up in the excitement of vindicating myself somehow this way. So excited that I can't resist urgent desire, and I hold out my hand.

With some fruit already in my mouth, I remember to ask, "Are they washed?"

"You're not supposed to wash them," he indignantly exclaims.

I shrug and enjoy the light sweetness of the mulberries.

"GO EASY WITH THEM, you're getting yourself all stained," Ignazio warns me from the other side of the sidewalk. But with a laugh of encouragement, and benevolent understanding. I pick up my purchases and walk ahead to reach him. He's busy too, holding bags and small plastic sacks, standing still in front of large baskets loaded with bread piled all in a jumble, exposed to the dust from the street and voracious flies. *Not very hygienic* is the first thing that comes to my mind.

But Ignazio comments, "Smell that wonderful scent in the air. *Iadduzza* bread, *circhitedda* . . . rooster-shaped *galletti*, round *ciambelle*. We still have our age-old breads made in their traditional shapes."

A rush of indulgence moves me closer to him, to his bald head and his obstinately positive preconceptions.

"You like Gela, don't you?"

"I'm not leaving here." He takes his wallet out of his pants pocket.

"You've wrapped yourself up real tight inside your cocoon." But at the bottom of my veiled, affectionate criticism, I discover a vein of envy, a need to have reassuring boundaries.

"I still see the things going on," he replies, without flaring up. "I haven't gone blind, even though it sometimes seems like that's the only remedy against becoming discouraged. But I continue to see things." He moves to the side to let a woman pass by and comes closer to me.

"In the north they complain—too many taxes. They make me laugh. I pay taxes. The same exact taxes. And I don't have sewers, I don't have water, I don't have schools, I don't have public services."

He has to fumble around a bit to put his wallet back in his pants pocket, with his hands hampered by the small dark paper bag with the bread inside.

"We're all wrapped up in a cocoon . . . But who knows whether a beautiful butterfly might emerge from the cocoon sooner or later. It's not the way it used to be, when the Christian Democrat Party even controlled the air people breathed. Things are changing quickly. Today, a young woman who enrolls in a university and commutes by train doesn't want fantastical stories. The beautiful stories about Greek civilization, the Arabs and the Normans . . . She wants to know why the train takes six hours to get her from Gela to Palermo."

By mutual agreement we head toward downtown. At every step I get a sharp whiff of aftershave.

"And you? What point are you at?" he placidly inquires. There's no more animosity, there's no bitterness in his interest, but rather a natural, thoughtful participation.

What can I answer?

"I'm inside the story by now," I say.

Ignazio frowns, and the wrinkles run up his forehead, clear up to the top of his bald head.

"There certainly must be people who don't want you getting in the way. You have to be careful." He shifts the bag of bread from one hand to the other. "They'll try to push you out. One can't expect . . . You're pursuing a fugitive. You can't expect celebrations and fanfare."

He slows down to face the uphill street. And also the story that suddenly flows free. "I always felt responsible for Tina somehow. I don't really know why. Maybe because I'd seen her when she was a little girl, or because I knew her grandmother. I never had any illusions about being able to save her, but . . . I tried to follow her progress, to not abandon her. And she accepted my presence up to a certain point. She trusted me. Then her brother-in-law, that Nele guy, entered the field . . . And someone wasn't pleased with the interest I took. They let me know that I had to stay in my place."

As he returned home from his doctor's office at school one day, he found his wife in tears in front of a bouquet and a card that said: *Condolences.*

"The hint was clear. I gave up. And I regret it," he murmurs. And all at once I understand that his bitterness—toward me too—stems from this, from his secret fear of having acted like a coward, of having behaved in a way that went against his deepest convictions, his very own moral imperatives.

"There's not just one Sicily, you know. There are so many Sicilys. Islands on the island. Each one indifferent to the other. They don't want to know each other. They don't even brush against each other. They're united only by a feeling of complicity. I . . . I thought I could break through the wall of reciprocal indifference. But I gave up. In the end, I gave up too."

Exactly halfway up the hill, a stumpy house sits on the curve in the street. The fresh washed clothes are fluttering in the shade, in the hollow circle of a future window.

"All of these empty floors in the building."

Ignazio slows down again, with the heavy breathing of a sedentary middle-aged man. I'm a little out of breath too. In my memories, I'd erased these hilly streets, with their ascents, descents, and round speed bumps.

"They're convinced that their children will fill them. But no one will ever go there. Never again. Could you imagine young people resigning themselves to living in there? The young are ashamed of their homes, of their poverty. They want to get out. Some of them become involved in politics. The kind of politics that pushes you toward social responsibility, I mean. The others . . ."

We're downtown by now. A small piazza with a beautiful, aristocratic building, its light-colored facade stained by the rust from the balconies, a harmonious structure that's losing its pure, clean lines as the stones corrode. An air of bygone times. Looking up, I can catch a glimpse of the rooms in the elite men's club: tall, gilded mirrors, a waiter dressed up in a formal white uniform who is already passing back and forth behind the French doors at this hour, men who are playing cards or are bent over the pool table. Always there, at the green table, day and night.

"Women burst into the club years ago," remarks Ignazio, mindful of my feminist battles and passions. "A big event, the club open to women. But it lasted just a short while." With clear satisfaction, he adds, "Due to the women's disinterest. They left just like they went in. Women, they don't have time to lose."

I wonder if his remark might hide some intentional contentiousness toward me. But meanwhile he's stopped walking in front of a small, narrow doorway that opens onto a very steep, dark stairway. He's arrived. This is his house. And now I'll find out how far his willingness to help really goes.

He doesn't invite me to come up this time either. He'll

never forgive me enough to let me into his family rituals again.

But he asks me, "Will you tell her story all the same? If you don't manage to meet Tina, I mean."

"Why shouldn't I tell it? In a way, I've already met her."

"Eh, you can't get out of this fix that easily. The story has to have a good ending." Ignazio can't resist making one last mocking, spitefully sarcastic remark. "The reader always expects a good ending that makes everything clear, written down in black and white."

WHITE. THE GECKO THAT popped out of the crack in the wall directly into the scene of her dream was white.

Tina woke up with a start, because she was no longer dreaming and that sharp image had pierced the night with unbearable violence.

She got up, groping her way in the darkness as she went to open the door that looked onto the countryside. She breathed in deeply. It was hours before sunrise and before the time set for the appointment with the men who were supposed to supply them with weapons and explosives. And perhaps it would be a lot of days and a lot of nights before the decisive test that would sanction their victory or defeat.

A slight blade of moonlight reached inside to rest on the floor, shining on a partially open bag, a transistor radio, a deck of cards, and a first aid kit. Tina bent over and put the packet of Travex tablets that had fallen out back where it belonged. Antihemorrhagic pills. More precious than a weapon.

As she went back toward the mattress, the dream came over her again, the clear flicker of a tiny tail flashing right in front of her.

The gecko had emerged from an opening in a wall, in the house on the alley. Completely white, the likes of which she'd never seen. It seemed naked, spit out of nothingness, out of a chasm where not even a sliver of light had ever reached to give it some color. Tina had taken the broom and used the handle to squeeze that tiny being, pale and slippery, up against the wall. It was so small that she had a hard time squashing it. Imprisoned below her, it started to sing. A faint, faint song that she could hardly hear, or rather, hear only in her dream, but painful, as if the gecko knew it was about to die.

CHAPTER 20

"I've been looking for you all day. Can you tell me where you've been?" Graziella is assailing me. With an exasperated expression she passes in front of me and plants herself in the atrium sitting room of the deserted motel. It's almost midnight.

I counter-attack. "At Falconara. It was a wonderful day."

And what's more, I feign a yawn. A performance I conduct for myself, not for Graziella. A way of confronting the unexpected encounter. In reality, I'm wide awake, even though I had already gone to bed and was about to turn out the light when the hotel reception desk called: "There's a woman who's waiting for you."

I pulled on my jeans and fixed my hair, while the sleep I had chased away again condensed around things and an acidic lump gathered in my throat. I closed the door to my second-floor room behind me, and made my way down the drowsy nighttime hallway. Then into the empty elevator, a chill along its cold metal grooves.

I found her standing, nervously tapping her fingers on the counter, her excitement barely held in check. Right there in person. In front of that unexpected apparition, I felt my body, my senses, my muscles, and my breathing, all of myself, emerge from the torpor of a day in the sun at the seashore. Suddenly I became electrified.

"Just perfect! Off you go on an outing at just the right moment." Graziella continues to reproach me. I realize that's another way to take her time, to stray off the subject. It's evident that something has happened. Some action, an event that is troubling the bubbly reporter for Telecittà.

"At this hour . . . What's going on?"

"You don't know anything? Really?" she scrutinizes me. I catch incredulity in her voice, which fades insensitively into veiled criticism, and then an open accusation, repressed indignation. As if Graziella suspected me of hiding something extraordinary from her, her of all people, who generously offered me her friendship and her collaboration. Some piece of news, a sensational scoop.

"You really don't know anything?" She presses me, unabashedly suspicious. Her attitude, incomprehensible and decidedly uncalled for, irritates me. Nevertheless, it has the power to make me fall into a state of guilty dismay. I shouldn't have gone so far away, I shouldn't have abandoned my post.

"What should I know?" I'm starting to worry. "Well, are you going to tell me what's happened?" But I immediately change my mind and stop her. "Wait."

The motel bar is closed. So I go back to my room, get two bottles of beer from the mini-bar, two paper cups, and return downstairs.

A huge muffled silence abounds, broken only by the voices of soldiers getting out of a patrol car. Total darkness lies beyond the windows; you wouldn't think an entire city was alive a few meters away. I linger to observe the scene. The soldiers come inside and go out, they go out and come back inside again, in a vain exercise of skill conducted in the light of a door that seems to open onto nothing. Graziella also observes them coming in and going out, going out and coming in.

"Sicilian Vespers," she murmurs vaguely. It's the code name of the operation that brought eight thousand soldiers to the island.

I recollect myself and set my spoils on the small, squat table, in the secluded corner of the sitting room.

"A beer?" Graziella disappointedly says, hesitating.

"Do you prefer some whiskey? Or gin?" I ask, ready to retrace my steps.

"No, beer is fine too. Sit down." She waves her hand impatiently.

But then we silently wait for the foam to go down, and silently take our first sip, peeping through a privacy screen of plants at the man on duty at the reception desk. His face, tilted toward a calculator, is yellow under the neon light.

Graziella looks back at me and begins, lowering her voice: "It went like this."

She adjusts her top's neckline, which slips to the side, revealing her bra strap. She lights a Marlboro.

Her account is unadorned, essential, and precise, like a press release.

"Great work," I congratulate her when she stops to take a breath. I don't know why, maybe because of an emotion I feel coming on, but I add in a light, paternalistic voice that is usually alien to me: "You have the makings for the job."

"Thanks," she says sarcastically.

"IT ALL STARTED YESTERDAY."

Graziella checks her watch. It hasn't struck midnight yet.

"Day before yesterday, in just a short while. In the late afternoon."

SEVEN P.M.

A certain Totuccio Spina shows up at the carabinieri station. A green shirt left unbuttoned on his bare chest and a large gold medal peeking out among the thick, curly hair. A fulsome drinker's stomach, drooping over his belt. Black hair hanging down on his neck, glistening with sweat.

By trade the man raises stock for slaughter. But his dealings aren't the cleanest. For some time he's been suspected of illegal profiteering, money laundering or weapons dealing. The greatest part of his profits most probably comes from these activities. At any rate, Totuccio shows up at the carabinieri station to report a murder.

He tells them that at five o'clock of that same day, he had gone out to the countryside with two friends to negotiate a purchase of sheep. A normal business transaction. When they arrived in the Zaibruca district, where they had their appointment with the clients, they were ambushed. There was a shootout. A gunshot hit and killed one of his companions, a certain Maurizio Riggio. The other one—Rosario Cafà, an outsider like the friend who was killed—managed to escape into the countryside. Totuccio also dove down precipices and cliffs, and finally, without knowing how and thanking our Lady of Grace, found himself on the highway. He walked a little ways before he got a ride to Gela.

This is the first version of events, Totuccio Spina's first story.

It's still light outside when the carabinieri conduct their investigation of the crime scene. There's no need to fan flashlights over the area. Besides, Totuccio Spina's story was very detailed, with exact directions, exceptionally precise descriptions: the branches of the path, the carob trees, the landslide that had transformed the profile of the rocks, widening the jagged mountain crests. There aren't any ambiguities in his reconstruction of the events and places.

The carabinieri find the Renault 11 right away, the front

of it smashed in from a recent accident, and a little further away, Riggio's body, its legs stiff in an unnatural pose. On the ground, they recover six shell casings from a twelve-caliber rifle, four from a handgun and at least nine from an automatic weapon. More than the place of an ambush, it's a real battlefield.

Up to this point, the findings fit with Totuccio's statements.

But, hidden a few kilometers further ahead, the carabinieri also discover a beat-up Fiat Croma with holes in it. Inside, two more bodies. The dead men are Antonino 'u niuru and Nele. Tina's brother-in-law. Nele 'u killer.

"That was his nickname. Did you know that?" Graziella asks me.

"No, I didn't know."

In the Fiat Croma's trunk there is sixty million lire in hundred-thousand lire bills, and in the glove compartment there's a set of keys, a packet of Maalox, a military handgun. There's a lot of money—three million lire in cash—in their wallets too and a photo of a beautiful brunette girl, in Nele's wallet.

The discovery and the personality of the two fugitives cast a different light on the shootout and make Totuccio Spina's story ambiguous, incomplete, or a lie.

The man seated behind the reception counter stands up, yawns, walks clear to the motel door, and is spellbound looking outside, into the night.

THE SLOPE IS GENTLE, but enough to take in a sweeping view, to the right and left, in front and behind, clear down to the narrow path, so narrow that two cars can't go side by side. Dried clods of dirt, smooth boulders that reflect brighter lights. There aren't any trees, except for a spot of carob trees far away; you can see clearly far into the distance. Because of these characteristics, this place was chosen as the meeting spot, and to be a neutral zone, that wasn't in territory controlled by any clans.

With the front of the car pointed downhill, the Fiat Croma has been standing at the top of the hill for more than half an hour. It's not very hot, but the sun still beats down overheating the inside of the car. Nele stands behind the wide-open back door of the car. He's fiddling with a cigarette he can't decide whether to light or not. Antonino is sitting in the driver's seat. He dries the sweat off his hands—big hands, with a few hairs on his knuckles—on the steering wheel cover made of synthetic fur. He has his shirt cuffs unbuttoned and the sleeves slide up, revealing a tattoo that from a distance looks like a dark birthmark, and up close proves to be a spectacular archaic monster, its back painted scale by scale. Both of their minds are fully focused on the necessity of keeping watch over the details of the place and time. No other thought distracts them. Their eyes burn from looking at the horizon and the hill, naked at the sides of the path.

When the Renault begins to come up the hill, Nele and Antonino have to squint to overcome the blinding glare and

288 • MARIA ROSA CUTRUFELLI

see the profiles outlined behind the back windshield. Who is that man sitting next to Totuccio? In the back seat there's another head swaying slowly back and forth, in short movements. They can't give names to the faces that become clearer as they pull out of the distant shade little by little and the car moves ahead.

The Renault is still several meters away. It climbs up toward the Croma, slowly advancing, nose toward nose.

"Who is that man?" Nele wonders out loud. He's still squinting his eyes tightly in an effort to identify him. His left hand raises the cigarette to his mouth while his right hand flicks the toothed wheel of the lighter. All at once an instinctual alarm stiffens his body. The small flame flares in a brief shot of fire. Nele freezes. But it's too late. A wrong move on his part, so amateurish. A little habit that automatically kicks in. An error that's his loss because he has both hands occupied and can't get the gun out of the glove compartment. And it's precisely this moment that the killers choose to jump out of the car, and shoot.

THE BEER HAS BECOME warm. It doesn't look very inviting, oily inside the paper cups. Graziella gulps down a sip and makes a face. But she continues to drink it.

"Wait, that's not all."

She dries her mouth on the back of her hand—a coarse gesture that I've never seen her make—and continues:

"Rosario Cafà, Totucci's friend, the one who narrowly

survived the shootout," she specifies, "comes back to Gela, to his friend's home, only at about seven in the morning."

The carabinieri are already there, ready to interrogate him. At first the man is taken aback, then, when he's strong-armed, in front of the evidence, he confirms Totuccio's story and explains that he couldn't get a ride. He had to return on foot.

But the two men's depositions continue to be contradictory. They give different accounts of the same event, one refuting the other. Even the reconstruction of the ambush and the events of the escape undergo modifications and substantial variations as the hours go by.

"Ultimately it's inevitable. They'll be arrested for withholding information and aiding and abetting."

"Totuccio finds a ride right away, the other one wanders around all night," I summarize and hesitate. "It seems . . . I don't know . . ."

Graziella's bangs are also moving doubtfully back and forth.

"I think what happened was the exact opposite of what the two accomplices maintained. The ambush, for a start. Who says that they weren't the ones who committed it and not the victims? And there was probably another car waiting for them on the highway. I believe that's precisely how things went, and that both of them lied about it. They had a plan. But it didn't work. Not completely. They didn't show they were sufficiently capable. And Caffà was forced to come back on his own. Maybe because he had to chase through the countryside . . . all night . . ."

She lowers her chin and moves around restlessly on the couch while her slender shoulder slips out of her light blouse again.

"The news is coming out drop by drop. But . . . The key character is this Totuccio Spina. He started collaborating all too easily."

"An infiltrator?"

My mind races to formulate questions, to sketch hypotheses. Then it stops, frightened, incapable of continuing coherently. The rush of facts, the jumble of events takes away my lucidity, disorients me. I really struggle, following Graziella's reasoning. There's a question I'd like to pose, but I still don't dare. What does all of this mean for Tina? How is she involved, if she is involved?

"An infiltrator?" I repeat.

Graziella smiles in reply. "You don't infiltrate the mafia. Never happened. Not in Sicily, at least. The links are too tight. When they say the mafia has control over the territory, that's exactly what they mean. There's no space for foreign bodies, for infiltrators. The only space possible is the space of breaking omertà, for people who are on the outside or on the margins. And for the ones inside, informing. Or becoming a *pentito*, turning state's evidence."

"So this Totuccio . . ."

"The most probable hypothesis, at least the one that

seems most probable to me, is that this is a case of someone who was playing both sides between two clans, or between a mafia clan of stiddari and one of Cosa Nostra. This is possible, it's already happened. Totuccio Spina betrayed Nele and delivered him to the killers. And now he's scared. Because maybe those guys have shown they don't really appreciate a traitor. A traitor never deserves gratitude. So Totuccio turned himself in . . . out of fear, I imagine. Driven by fear, without carefully calculating the consequences. But now, if he wants protection, he can only collaborate with the police."

In fact, he was quick to change his story, admitting that they had gone to the Zaibruca district to negotiate a shipment of weapons and two-way radios.

"Sheep! Far from it!"

And now Totuccio Spina is singing like a canary. If he is to be believed ("but, as you can entirely understand, it's not official information . . . rumors, nothing but rumors"), Nele wanted to put together a group of his own, taking advantage of the fact that the bosses of the "family" are all in jail and the expert killers have been forcibly relocated by the State.

"He wanted to strike out on his own, do you understand? Acquire power in his clan in order to climb to the top management of the organization. But it couldn't go well for him. He was nothing, Nele, nothing mixed with nothing."

I'm surprised by the vehemence and disdain with which she says the last words.

"It's his fault," Graziella says accusingly. Her passion and fervor seem exaggerated, excessive to me. "It's that little nobody's fault if . . . Well, according to Totuccio Spina, together with Nele and that other guy, that Antonino 'u niuru, there was also Tina."

"Tina?"

"Tina," she confirms, quite certain.

That's the point. We've reached it, finally. This piece of news is why Graziella waited for me late into the night. To her, as to me, Tina evidently represents something. Her story roils our emotions. Her fate is not insignificant to us.

"Maybe Cafà didn't get to her. Maybe she managed to escape with her life."

"What makes you believe that?"

Otherwise, she reasons, Cafà would't have come back. If he did, it was to let them know that the hunt wasn't successful and had to continue.

"In any case, now Tina doesn't have any alternatives."

We both look at the bottom of our glasses where a few drops of yellowish beer still linger. Without lifting her eyes, Graziella continues, lowering her voice even more, as if hiding the logical thread of an unpleasant and unwelcome reflection:

"Her betrayal is worse than Totuccio's, if that's even possible. She sided with a loser, a guy who concocted things that were too big for him. She's being hunted down, chased by everyone. The police. The clans. She can't withstand being on the run. By now no one is able to help her, the risk is too great."

"She could give herself up," I venture to say.

"She could . . . But prison is anything but safe. It doesn't guarantee staying alive."

Her face lights up with a strange emotion. She sadly says, "For the men in what used to be her clan, it's as if she were already dead. There aren't any appeals in Cosa Nostra. For them, a crazy little straggler like Tina *'a masculidda* . . . is barely an *ammazzatina*, just a two-bit hit."

The night manager has returned behind his counter. His stool is turned sideways, and I notice he's sitting a certain way to keep an eye on us. He looks tired. Perhaps he's waiting for us to leave so he can go to sleep.

But Graziella hasn't finished yet. She hasn't said everything she had to say. I sense from her attitude, from the way she raises her shoulders, unexpectedly and enjoining, that she is preparing herself to confront a new round.

WHEN SHE REACHES THE shade of the carob trees, Tina slows her flight. With stiff fingers she undoes the collar of her denim shirt, which is strangling her, blocking the blood pulsing in her neck. She looks around.

"Where can I run?"

The attack of panic is sudden and violent. All of a sudden the landscape seems like an enemy, too open, without any shelter. Every cleft, every hiding place, is a trap. The smooth, grey boulders don't offer any cover and reflect the blinding lights of her own fear. Her eyes can't decipher the terrain, identify an escape route. Escaping is impossible. It's crossing the threshold blocked by her father's body all over again. One can cross over the threshold one time, but never again.

Something has jammed inside her.

Tina continues to see only the burst from the machine gun that moves from Nele's body to the Fiat's windshield. She continues to see Antonino, who has already catapulted out of the car and responds to the gunfire before being hit as well. She continues to see the two killers, whose jackets bulge over their bulletproof vests. And she still feels her body bend and burst forward like a spring.

Her rigorous, obstinate daily training pays off. Her legs, her arms, are loose, agile, fast. They don't betray her. In just an instant her right hand slips the nine-caliber Beretta out of her pants belt while the other hand releases the brake and puts the gear in neutral. The Fiat starts moving blindly down the slope. A few meters and just before impact she throws herself out of the car as well.

On the ground, with both hands, she aims at the head of the killer closest to her.

"Turn around," she yells. "Turn around, I'm taking your photo."

Now she finds herself in the shade of the carob trees and doesn't know how she got there—moved by some magic from one place to another. She listens hard to catch her pursuer's footsteps. But what she hears is only the beating of her own heart, right in the middle of her forehead, in the furrow that separates her eyebrows.

The first time. More than a thought it's a flash, a burst. She had never shot at a human target. That was the first time. And she hit the mark. Tina puts the Beretta back inside her belt and cleans off her hands, rubbing them up and down her pants several times, a mechanical, unconscious gesture.

Where can I run? is her only thought. There's no place for her anymore. But now he's nearby and there's the sound of labored huffing from another breath, over there, inside the thicket of trees.

Her resolution explodes with sudden lucidity: *I'll never let them get their hands on me, never.*

And now she clearly sees her escape route, one step after the other through the countryside.

GRAZIELLA LEANS TOWARD ME. "Everyone knows . . ."

I instinctively move back.

"Everyone knows," she says, moving still closer, "that you're looking for her. Her relatives, her friends. *L'abbanniasti* . . . You yelled it from the four corners of the earth. Tina surely knows too."

"And so? What does it matter by now?"

"Perhaps . . . perhaps she might get in touch with you."

There's her real motive. Now Graziella's more genuine interest is revealed; she has a professional interest, when it comes right down to it. That's what I owe her presence here to, in the middle of the night, and her persistence at the beginning, her questions about how much I already might know or might not know yet.

But her passionate involvement isn't only a calculated professional action. After all, I too am moved by something analogous. I can understand her.

"Why should she get in touch with me?" I reply, without hiding my annoyance at that absurd, entirely senseless conjecture. An absolutely improbable eventuality.

The same thing Giovanna was thinking perhaps, when she said, "You reason well," while she was drying my hair. "You can talk sense into her." But then Tina was just a girl who had violated house arrest, nothing more than that. Everything was still possible. But now?

"You're looking for her, you want to write about her." Graziella starts at it again, her voice conciliatory. "That gives her prestige."

The argument is impeccable. I gave her prestige. This means that I have power over her. While she, in turn, willingly or unwillingly, has acquired power over me. Over my imagination, my time, and therefore my life. There's an exchange. A bond.

And a precise responsibility, Graziella piles it on. Mine. By letting myself be captured this way, I set in motion an irreversible mechanism. I put Tina at the center of a story that is no longer only hers, or ours.

"And then, more simply . . . You're not from this place, you're not mixed up in local . . . matters. But people know who you are, where you come from, and what you do. You're the right person, if Tina would want to get in contact with someone."

"In short, in this case my exile would be a guarantee." I find a way to joke about it.

"Your exile?" Graziella looks up, perplexed. But this is not the time to explain the carabinieri captain's theory of the various Sicilianicities to her.

"It's nothing, sorry."

The flash of perplexity disappears. "Now she has nothing left to lose," she reasons. "Talking to you, in fact, could be useful to her. If she were to look for you . . ."

"If she were to look for me . . . ?"

"I'd like to know before the others do."

CHAPTER 21

The house in Settefarine has its own particular usefulness, with the entrance looking out over the neighborhood and the rear windows—the only ones in the entire building—that watch over the highway. On the one side, the immense illegal kasbah, where no one sees or says anything. On the other, a wide view to spy any threats coming from the outside, from the world that opens up beyond the border of the road. A perfect house for fugitives and criminals.

But when the threats originate inside, in the narrow streets and the ditches cutting through the land, then everything changes. And the house can prove to be a trap with no escape for Giovanna, who lives there, and for her dangerous guests.

"One night. Just one night."

Tina knows this hiding place can't last very long.

For now she's alone, and that reassures her. Giovanna

is observing the wake at her mother-in-law's home. And Saveria is crying her eyes out elsewhere. Two wakes without the dead. The bodies of the two fugitives are still lying in the morgue, waiting for the coroner and autopsy.

"A love without any Jordan almonds. Love with no wedding."

Giovanna's lifeless voice was the greatest sorrow for Tina. Nothing else matters to Tina except her impotence in Giovanna's eyes. Hers more than Saveria's, her grandmother's, or her mother's. And she's ashamed and suffering over this impotence. Instead of all of the rich, splendid things that she'd dreamed of for her friend, Tina brought her this gift— the news of a death and the threat posed by her presence.

"A love without any Jordan almonds," Giovanna began repeating obsessively. "And a funeral for the excommunicated," she said, while folding towels in her cramped hair salon, going back and forth without a moment's peace, straightening things up, arranging rollers and curling irons.

It was clear that she said it thinking about herself, not him. What is mourning without the ceremonies? A void of suffering. And memory clutches onto things, onto wedding favors just like funeral announcements on black-bordered posters; it wants its representation, its show.

A sliver of sunlight still illuminates the room. In order to erase Giovanna's voice echoing inside her, Tina turns on the radio and looks for some music. She keeps the sound low, so it doesn't go beyond that last patch of light. She takes a deck of cards out of the bedside table and sets up a game of solitaire on top of the blanket. At the foot of the double bed, there's a baby carriage. On top of the chest of drawers, a baby bonnet from a layette and an old stub from a Toto-calcio soccer pool betting sheet beside it.

The objects of family life, the music, and cards help Tina reflect, push down her fear, fold it up again and put it aside like a dress that's been worn. Meanwhile a thought is slowly rising to the surface, its outlines becoming increasingly clear. Already recognizable. Already, almost, a decision.

THE SHOWER IS A cascade of prickling needles whose sadistic sharp points tap down on my skin, red from the sun's rays and dried out by the sea water, and jump off again. I try to delicately lay the rough motel towel over my shoulders. It's evening again. Hot, solitary, unpleasant.

My notebook with all of my notes sits on the bathroom shelf, along with a forgotten tape recorder I never used. Right away, from the very first day, it unexpectedly seemed like a useless appendage of ostentatiously fake irrelevance.

I roll the shutters way up and move the drapes, while the dust hidden in the folds of the material scatters in the sun's sinking rays. The faded, sad houses and large service center with cars parked in line under the canopy come into view. The radio in the police car right under my window crackles with incomprehensible orders.

I look without seeing, like any other resident of this city.

And I don't even make comparisons with the past anymore. It's as if I'd never been away from this place. The emotions of a distant yesterday have welded together with those I feel now. Time has compressed into a single block. A sensation that I don't like. It seems like I've lost a perspective that I worked tirelessly to achieve; how can I still pretend to be in exile and allow myself absent-minded thoughts of regret, of bittersweet nostalgia? The island is keeping me firmly enmeshed in its present.

I sit down, listlessly open my notebook, and fiddle around with my paper and pen. Just to pass the time. In contrast to the tape recorder, my notebook is indispensable for me. It forces me to focus my attention, to remember the untrustworthy fleetingness of emotions. Because a familiar place where you've lived and loved and made choices that changed the course of your life appears simple—too simple—to understand, and it can deceive you.

The telephone rings. Roused as a trembling runs through me, I slowly lift the receiver.

"Did they inform you about it? Did you read the newspapers?" asks Laura, the lawyer, at the other end of the line.

The disappointment I feel when I recognize her voice makes me realize that I'd hoped for and believed in Graziella's prediction. My impatience is gnawing away at me. I want to finally hear the voice that I've imagined in its full range of tones, detected in all of its most secret modulations. Even if she might ask me to justify my stubborn intrusiveness, for my piratical raids on a life that doesn't belong to me.

"Yes, they informed me."

My excitement quickly dissolves, taking away all my strength. I remain on the edge of the bed, my head bent, lost in contemplating the dirty green carpet with its shabby fibers, some darker stains, some threads that stick out of the weft. I remain there, sitting, waiting for a voice that would tell me, *here I am, I've crossed the border, I'm not your character anymore.*

I wanted to force my way inside this story. And now I find myself a prisoner of something that I don't control and don't determine.

Tina also, I think, is a prisoner of a situation that she no longer controls. But her fear certainly isn't an abstract phantom, like mine. Will that count in her decisions, and how much? On this island, fear is lasting and tenacious. A natural element. A way of life that is transmitted from father to son, mother to daughter. To the point of spilling back into desire and becoming a habit one feels like satisfying and needs to satisfy all the way, to the very end.

An excessive, risky involvement. I know all at once that this isn't my fear. I'm not afraid of the involvement. On the contrary. I'm afraid of not having the appointment.

HER HIP, WHERE SHE had hit the ground rolling out of the car, is hurting. The bruise pulsates as if her heart had moved down to the center of her body's suffering. Sitting like that makes it even worse. Tina lifts up her top. Her flesh is swollen, the skin torn. She slowly spreads on a little lotion while the pain shoots into her chest and takes her breath away.

Several hours, a night . . . How much time does she have to organize her movements?

The possible choices, in any case, are few, clear, and without any alternatives. Whether living on the run or in prison, sooner or later the vendetta will strike her. That's a certainty. Her death has become a job for someone to take care of quickly and efficiently.

But how much life—and what kind—could she have left until then?

Tina doesn't even think about being an informant or and becoming a *pentito*, a State's witness. She's not interested in the protection the State gives to people who talk, her life shattered all over again, and living who knows where. All those troubles in exchange for an act of infamy. It's not worth it. It's only of use for people trying to fulfill a vendetta, any kind of vendetta at any cost. Tina knows that a lot of people talk not because they love life, but because, yet again, they have an inextinguishable desire for reprisal.

No acts of infamy, of breaking omertà . . . But then what remains, if not the inescapable certainty of a death that someone is already planning for her?

The room is dark by now, but Tina doesn't turn on the lights. It's better that the home appears uninhabited to curious eyes. This small precaution stirs an unexpected tiredness in her. Acts of caution have become the very essence of her life. Daily habits. Gestures that have been repeated too many times. She's ready to burst with impatience. Surviving—what kind of prospect is that?

Standing back from the window, she checks the empty land, the deserted plain.

"*You all aren't laying a hand on me.*

Maybe the invisible men pursuing her are nearby, but it doesn't matter anymore. Tina has found the solution and is already organizing her performance.

"I alone can take my life in my hands," she says aloud. "I alone."

And she feels invincible, invulnerable.

"IT'S FOR YOU."

The night porter's voice is coldly professional. The other voice, in contrast, has a slightly hoarse timber that I hadn't imagined.

"Do you know who I am?" Without waiting for a response, she orders: "At six. Sharp. Very sharp," and she explains where. Then she laughs. Incredibly, she laughs.

"Bring me a present. Tomorrow I turn twenty."

THE NIGHTTIME IS LEAVING.

The night porter stays behind the windows of the front door to watch me while I cross the service center and approach my car.

An aimless ride in the car, like long ago. A ride to make the appointment arrive more quickly, to bring it closer.

At this hour even the low walls of the promenade are deserted. A shadow slides onto the sand and disappears underneath the pylons of the Conchiglia resort. Maybe someone going to shoot up while looking at the sea, in the solitude of an empty beach.

There's not even anyone at the tourist marina. A cement clearing. Two or three boats and some cabin cruisers swaying slowly on the dark water. They use them for the same things as country homes, for huge Sunday meals, moored in the boiling heat of still water and cement, facing a precipitous landscape that they no longer see.

I slow down in front of the sparse soaring palm trees beyond the swimming club's white, sunken walls. A pool, open-air ballroom, and five million lire in annual dues. This is where the middle class in Gela treats itself to the illusion of an exclusive place, a worldly life. But Gela isn't Palermo, where the two societies—the legal one and the clandestine one—can never even meet or, if they meet, can keep up the pretense of not recognizing each other for a while.

I step on the brakes. I stop the car, leaving the engine running; its rumbling—a low, imperceptible murmur—keeps me company. I rack my brains over that unexpected request. Surreal.

What gift can I ever think up for a girl like Tina in this sleepless night?

CAREFUL NOT TO LET the water slosh out of the plastic bowl, Tina goes up and down between the kitchenette and the bathroom. Distant gurgles are all that comes out of the faucets, and so to fill the sink a long job of transporting water is necessary. But the reserve tanks of water are full, as always, as a necessary precaution. Giovanna is often forced to dip into that reserve to rinse out her customers' hair.

Tina takes off her clothes from the waist up to wash herself. The water falls from her hands onto her small breasts, her pectoral muscles, well-developed like an athlete's, on the warm hair under her arms, on her strong yet slim limbs. Then she takes off her pants and rubs the sponge on her legs over and over again, between her thighs, around the feathered edges of the bruise that's spreading on her right hip. Dirty foam is now floating in the sink.

She combs her hair back with the wet brush. A red blotch, an annoying circle with raised edges, appears on her temple, where her skin becomes almost transparent, defenseless. Tina lingers, staring at it. She finally shrugs and continues to smooth back her hair, making it lie flat on her head. A rubber band holds it tightly in a short ponytail. Her movements are rhythmic, euphoric; they're the gestures of a girl who is getting ready for her birthday party.

If it weren't for that blotch on her temple, nothing would

lead one to believe she had any anxiety, or fear. Tina had learned to turn fear upside down so well, to look inside it for the dark, thrilling pleasure of excitement.

She piles her sweaty, dirt-crusted clothes in a corner. But naturally, in Giovanna's closet there's not even one piece of clothing suited for her: just skirts and blouses with embroidered designs, see-through fabric, gold flourishes. Feminine adornments. Tina softly sighs and shakes out her denim jacket well before putting it on again. Downstairs, in the entrance hall that's used as a garage, she has her motorcycle. That's the essential thing.

Finally, she stretches her hand out toward the gun. She hesitates. She had learned to use that weapon with so much perseverance and now it has something foreign, mysteriously hostile about it. But she can't leave it there, in Giovanna's home; it's a weapon that shot at a man. At Nele's murderer, and at the same time, at Francesco's murderer. When she'd learned the name of that man from the radio, a shiver ran through her with the realization that vendetta and betrayal were linked together. A single knot. Exactly how the wizard of the Nile had foretold. Francesco was avenged. But she had lost her opportunity.

The barrel brushes against the bruise and presses on her hip, but it's an inevitable weight that Tina can't get rid of anymore. And so she smooths back her hair, and straightens her jacket again. She just has to wait until it's time for the appointment. Her performance needs a spectator, like sacraments need a priest. And light. At least the light of dawn, in the absence of a spotlight.

THE SUN STARTS TO heat the dry grass, to drive the smells out of the dust, the heaps of garbage behind the homes and at the sides of the roads, the Petrolchimico towers, and the flat fields that the fires have sprinkled with black dewdrops.

I enter the partially asphalted road that runs to the ghost junction and rises toward the high span of the overpass. I have to go into the junction, get onto that monumental sketch of a highway, travel a stretch of it, up to the bridge supported by two pylons—the meeting place.

Access to the elevated span of the overpass—already in ruins during the design phase—is prohibited. But I still don't see any barriers. I push ahead, shifting down a gear. In any case, there must be a way to pass through. I remember seeing cars up there. And in fact, where the road starts to rise, there's the barrier; boulders and supports that were removed long ago, and block part of the roadway, a pure testimony to an old, vain attempt to close it off.

Beyond the useless barrier, a bumpy but operable path. I go further, holding the steering wheel with both hands. I'm on the bridge now, which abruptly ends right across from the side entrance—the workers' entrance—of the Enichem company. At the widening in the path, at the highest point of the overpass, I stop the car. The guardrail is low, just a thin strip, a grille, and a corroded metal sheet.

I get out of the car and right away the wind wraps around me. Beneath me, suspended in a sheer mist, appears a sweeping view of the horizon that extends from the plain to the sea, a curve that contains all of Gela: the ruins of the Acropolis and the industrial complex's tongues of fire, the isolated, sparse green of the palm trees, the downtown, the working-class neighborhoods, and over there, the Bronx. To my right and to my left stand the two ramps that uselessly rise, uselessly descend, simulating a highway junction.

And finally, the bursting roar of an approaching motor-cycle breaks the silence of dawn. At first there's just a figure against the light that blends into the lines of the motorcycle and leans to the right or to the left according to the holes, bends, and detours caused by the road's surface. Then the denim jacket, which the wind billows out on the sides and back. Then a pale face, unrecognizable behind a pair of large dark glasses.

The motorcycle slows down, pulls over to the side, and stops. We're face to face, Tina and I. Me, standing a few steps away from the car, her, sitting straight on the seat, her feet planted against the asphalt.

Despite the wind, my hands are sweaty. My mouth can't even form a greeting. I just stare at her. She lifts her glasses, moving them up onto her smooth, pulled back hair. Right away I gaze into a look I know so well. The reckless, pro-vocative look, though wounded by a strange melancholy, of that fourteen-year-old girl, which had captured my attention on the page of a daily newspaper.

That's what makes me remember her request.

"I have it with me," I simply say, as if there weren't anything more important to talk about. "The gift."

The idea came to mind while thinking of Graziella's story, her attempted strategy for slipping into the opening created by Tina's natural vanity. I fling open the Fiat's door and get the dossier, which has all of the newspaper clippings I gathered even before deciding whether to dive into this story or not.

Tina's hard look crumbles for an instant at the sting of emotion. She sets the packet on the handlebars and, without getting off the bike, slowly leafs through it, lingering on the photos. She didn't turn off the engine, so to stop the wind from blowing away the pages, she has to use her elbow while she performs complicated maneuvers using just one hand. Underneath the light fabric of her pants, I can sense her legs straining, the tension stiffening her tendons from her calves to her ankles, helping her keep her balance. When she has finished leafing through the whole file, she closes the folder and holds it out to me. I spontaneously gesture to refuse it, and she sticks it in my hand by force. Then she pulls back, leans herself on the handlebars with her forearms, and in that detached position, she says, "You keep it. You'll need it."

Her voice isn't as hoarse as it was on the phone, but it's just as soft and guarded. And yet the control she feigns through her tone of voice, attitude, and entire body doesn't seem to arise from coldly governing over the situation but, on the contrary, from the desire to hold back and hide an excess of passions and conflicts.

After that short, concise statement, Tina falls silent. She doesn't say a word. It seems like she's waiting for me to make the first move.

And so, "You came looking for me," I remind her.

"You," she interrupts, "were looking for me."

"But this time, you came looking for me," I insist. "Why?"

She reacts like a smartass little girl. "I got curious."

But there's something in her look, a restrained euphoria, an excitement that makes me uncomfortable, upsets me, and holds me back. What would happen if I asked her some question that was out of place? Would her self-control become more rigid, or would it break into pieces like the shatterproof glass that dissolves into myriad slivers when struck in a particular spot?

The dark lenses come down, hiding her gaze.

"I have a gift for you too," Tina quickly says. She sits back as if she were about to leave again, before adding, "I want you to feast your eyes on my gift. And for you to make it into a beautiful story."

She revs the engine and really takes off. The wind blows the dirty exhaust fumes in my face. Surprise immobilizes me as I'm nearly on the verge of leaping. It keeps me nailed down on the spot, arms wrapped tightly around my dossier, watching the motorcycle's course.

I see it speed up with difficulty, but then it gives a jump, leaps, and speeds along as if it wanted to hurl itself against the futuristic landscape drawn beyond the bridge, against the tangled roads that intersect, rise up, come together, depart and return to each other. Yellow and black road signs, road number four, number three, number two, indicate the intersections of an industrial zone that was never put into operation, a city lost even before it was born. In the background, empty parking places, never repaired, the skeletons of warehouses.

The motorcycle continues to speed ahead. I see it leaping forward, rearing up and skidding on the uneven terrain. It's traveling as if it had a long speedway ahead of it. It races toward the parapet, toward the fragile obstacle of the guardrail. And it doesn't stop.

CHAPTER 22

The Gela-Catania highway is behind me by now. The Caltagirone mountains and the amphitheater city sitting on the three hills that looks down on the gravel beds of rocky torrents are behind me. The gardens on the Catania plain are behind me.

I'm crossing through the decayed outskirts of Catania, the "Milan of the South." A sad area, shaped by "structural" deviance, as the sociologists say: an immense, anonymous mafia hotbed. Here it's another city, that makes it impossible to imagine the existence of a different Catania, elegant and sumptuous with its Baroque buildings of the 1700s, its monuments made of pink glittering lava.

The air coming in through the open window of the Fiat gives no relief. It's a dizzying blast of hot air. The only bit of refreshment is the scent from the small bunches of oregano bought in Gela at the Tuesday street market, which escapes from the plastic bag resting on the passenger seat.

I stop at a diner on the road that runs along the sea and goes directly to the airport. It's my return trip.

The place is new, clean, vaguely pretentious. Nevertheless, it has an unfinished air about it, something temporary that makes my heart ache. The short pergola looks out on a yellow wasteland, abandoned, seeming to invoke the attack of property speculation.

I can no longer see what remains of the beautiful Sicily, though it's still a lot, after the devastating fury of excavators and government mismanagement. All that remains in my eyes is this inescapable desolation.

The moment of another separation, of a further farewell has really arrived.

I'm going away, I think with relief, while I wait for the waiter to take my order. This feeling of impossible completeness always pushes me out of Sicily, in a painful yearning for escape. The same yearning that binds me to Sicily in an eternal return. Elsewhere I'm in exile, but I can't remain on this island of shadows and ghosts—emigrants, fugitives, murder victims, living in hiding and *lupara bianca* with no trace of the slain, small-time murders and monumental crimes—on this island that is open to every invasion and closed around its secret pain. I don't have enough strength. I don't have the heart for it.

And not even for a simple thing like looking through the

newspapers I bought before getting on the road. I have them here, beside me. I compulsively touch them, rearrange them, check them, and touch them again as if they were a fetish prepared for an arcane ritual. But I can't bring myself to read the news reports about Tina's death, in so many versions and variations.

Yet, here it is, a great deal of material for my dossier. Rich material, so very rich. Articles, photographs, interviews, comments—a real press success.

Graziella was the first one to reconstruct everything. Point by point. And she had an exclusive interview with me, "the only eyewitness," for Telecittà. Without a doubt, Tina would be more than satisfied. A successful show. Great acting.

But I'm tired. Truly tired of this show, much more than of the words that I was forced to pronounce. More than of the questioning and giving a statement at police headquarters. It didn't take much of my time, after all. I didn't have a whole lot to say, nothing concrete, nothing that could be useful to an investigation that, in contrast to my own, required evidence, facts that were verified and demonstrable.

But it was only in that moment, only when I had to explain, to rationalize, and to justify, that I realized Tina had bet on me as her last card dealt by destiny. Her last opportunity. And she hadn't been afraid that I might betray her in the ways I could have betrayed her: missing the appointment or showing up in "bad company."

I'm tired, and yet beneath my tiredness there's room for a sense of quiet, of fulfillment. I'd say even an answered prayer. So I couldn't hold back my impatience when Graziella said goodbye to me and murmured, "Sad."

Mimmo nodded, agreeing.

"What?" I asked sharply. Not because I couldn't guess what they felt, but to show I disagreed right away.

"Dying that way," she said, amazed at having to explain.

"Why? On the contrary."

Both of them looked at me as if I were crazy. And maybe they're right, because there's a voice inside me that keeps repeating that in some way, in some contorted, desperate manner, this is a story with a happy ending. Tina, after all, got what she wanted. Even if only for a short while—the time it takes to read an article or listen to a news report. In her delirious pride, Tina knew how to create a way to exist, to make space for herself and enter the collective imaginary.

That's what she aspired to, a dream of existence. But she was only granted the perversion of the dream.

I turn the small fork around and around on the plate without making up my mind to bring it to my mouth.

An affirmation of herself. Cruel. All the more cruel the more ephemeral it is. But Tina's young years didn't take this into account. I alone think about times long-ago, when songs resonated on the lips of puppeteers and storytellers. I alone am filled with regret over the present, memory that lasts a second, the flash of an image on a television screen, entrusted to pages that barely last a day.

And a book too . . . How long can a book last? As long as the song about the legendary Baroness of Carini, whose secret love story ended in her violent death?

All of the newspapers published a photograph. I saw it, unintentionally. A white piece of material that covers something on a closed road, beside a row of prickly pear trees and a mound of landfill. Off in the distance, the blurry Petrolchimico tanks. Everything is in this photo: the story of Tina and the story of Gela. But the story of one is the story of the other, and together they form the story of Sicilian unhappiness.

The flash of a car passing by on the road beyond the pergola dazes me, while I remember the first time that I saw the photo of fourteen-year-old Tina.

I put the photo aside, among other clippings, fragments, news items. But something inside me was secretly, unconsciously working away at it, until it exploded all at once. I decided to write about her without asking myself the reason why. I knew I would understand the reason during the work. I was perfectly conscious of one thing alone—that every time one chooses a story to tell, one story among so many, one also chooses a compromise.

The restaurant bill is in front of me, inside a light green paper folded over on the tablecloth. I open my purse to look for my wallet. It's late. All of the rituals, the motions of departure are still ahead of me: returning the rental car, the line at the check-in counter.

I'm going away once again. But this time, I'm taking double the spoils with me—the scent of oregano and the story of Tina, who didn't want her twenty years.

TRANSLATOR'S NOTE

I still had everything under my control, was respected and gave the orders. Damned cops, damned judges.   —Angela Russo

Don't fuck with me . . . I have to be there when you unload the stuff, I have to watch over my own business.   —Maria Serraino

With the full powers of fiction and fact, *Tina, Mafia Soldier* takes readers deep inside the life of a mafia girl who fights to assert herself in the deadly Sicilian Cosa Nostra, and make her mark on the world. This focal point and the interlacing of imagination and historical truths make the novel as unique today as it was when first published in 1994, amidst public uproar over women's active participation in violent mafia operations reported in the daily news. From the late 1980s through the early 1990s, women in Cosa Nostra, the Camorra and 'Ndrangheta, the three primary mafia organizations in Italy, dominated the headlines, the stories of their lives revealed through interviews, court documents, and statements given by witnesses to their crimes. The special issue that the weekly news magazine *Europeo* dedicated to women in the mafia in December of 1990 typifies the explosive media attention. It hit the newsstands with a loud yellow cover that framed headshots of three "Mafia Women," as the caption in giant block letters announced: Rosetta Cutolo, Emanuela Azzarelli, and Ines Barone. In contrast to the wholesome image of the middle-aged Cutolo and prim Barone, both glancing to the side, the adolescent Azzarelli stares straight into the camera. Below a mop of short hair, the girl's languid dark eyes and full lips look somber, but there is hardly a trace of the arrogance or brutality that made her "a star of the young gangs that filled [Gela] with bloodshed, holding it under siege, as well as a celebrity of international mass media" (*Europeo* 8). In fact, the press dubbed Azzarelli the "Bonnie of Gela" after the famous American gun moll, due to her exploits as the respected boss of a gang of male minors working for Cosa Nostra. In *Tina, Mafia Soldier*, Maria Rosa Cutrufelli brings together psychological, social and criminal elements from the life stories of diverse mafia women, and Azzarelli's in particular, to create kaleidoscopic images of Tina the mafia soldier, viewed through the multiple perspectives of family, the law, mafia men and the narrator's discoveries.

MAFIA WOMEN EXPOSED

For many Italian readers, the revelations in the *Europeo* exposé and others detailing women's involvement in the decisions about criminal operations and their execution created the idea of a radical change in the mafia. However, from their beginnings in the late 1700s and early 1800s, the Camorra, 'Ndrangheta and Cosa Nostra have been distinguished by developing effective strategies of adaptation to changing social, economic and political conditions, which affected female roles in the clans as well. As a rule, the mafia does not allow women to be initiated as affiliated members or become the official boss of a clan. Furthermore, countless *pentiti*, members of the mafia who "repented" for their crimes and provided testimony to prosecutors, maintained their wives and mothers knew nothing about the business. Such statements, along with mafia women's own manipulation of gender assumptions and the stereotype of the southern woman as silent and submissive, created a cover for a range of increasing responsibilities shouldered by mothers, wives and daughters in mafia families. In the 1800s, for example, over 575 female precursors to Rosetta Cutolo and Maria Licciardi of the Camorra were found guilty of such mafia activities as running illegal lotteries, prostitution rings and loan sharking businesses, while their strong-willed female counterparts in the 'Ndrangheta, armed and dressed like men, committed robberies and rustled livestock. During the massive 1920s trial of over 200 mafiosi in the Madonie clans, seven women were charged with racketeering, aiding and abetting fugitives and handling the accounts. Since the expansion of the drug trade in the 1970s, when Maria Serraino of the 'Ndrangheta and Angela Russo of Cosa Nostra ran their family networks with iron fists, female roles include contraband and counterfeit goods dealings; collecting extortion money and managing clan accounts and investments in both illegal and legal businesses; mastering web-based operations for controlling and communicating with clan members, and organizing deals for trafficking in weapons, humans and drugs. In cases where male bosses are in jail or fugitives on the run, women may command the clans by proxy.

In the history of adaptive changes to women's criminal roles, their public exposure in the early 1990s reveals important innovations in response to changes in Italian society and culture, as well as problems within the mafia itself. In the wake of the Maxi-trial in Palermo, which in 1986 began the prosecution of over 450 members of Cosa Nostra, of whom four were women, numerous mafiosi chose to turn state's evidence, and divulged invaluable information about the organization's structure, members and crimes. In response to the wave of defections, dubbed "*emergenza pentiti*" (*pentiti* emergency), Cosa Nostra took strategic action. The bosses encouraged and coerced clan women to act as public relations experts with the media. In spectacular performances, mothers, wives and daughters contacted news agencies to speak out. They proudly voiced unwavering loyalty to the mafia and their belief in the values of honor and respect, while disowning their men who broke omertà. As the wife of one *pentito* declared, "Better for him to be dead than a *pentito*." Such messages were addressed to both the general public and members of Cosa Nostra, and intended to convey the stability of the organization, assert internal control and launch a threat to potential traitors.

Among the women who represented the "feminine" face of Cosa Nostra to the press, Emanuela Azzarelli had unique features. Most important, she did not engage with the media as the loyal daughter in a mafia family, groomed to become the obedient wife of a mafioso. On the contrary, at fifteen, she spoke as a boss of the criminal band of Via Abela, which worked with the Madonia clan of Cosa Nostra doing jobs in the extortion racket, robberies and arson. At the same time, in public appearances she played upon ambiguities created through her way of dressing, gestures, words and silences. Right after her arrest in December of 1990, for example, she told the police "You and the journalists are ruining me, you're making me into something I'm not." The role of performance in the creation of public mafia identities is artfully depicted by Cutrufelli, evoking the desire for freedom, going beyond all imposed limits. Indeed, Azzarelli, along with a

few other female adolescents, signaled a new social phenom-
enon of girls who armed themselves and acted to acquire
honor and respect by imposing their will on citizens in the
community through the use of physical violence, and thereby
gain standing in Cosa Nostra. This emergent trend inspires
Cutrufelli's gripping psychological development of the ideas,
desires and fears driving the female mafia mind, which is
anchored in vivid depictions of life in Gela, a city besieged
by warring members of Cosa Nostra and Stidda, a mafia
organization made up of mafiosi who had been expelled
from Cosa Nostra clans and reorganized. Although Gela
had never been a mafia stronghold, the construction of the
Petrolchimico oil refinery in the early 1960s created prime
conditions for members of Cosa Nostra in nearby Riesi and
Stidda to capitalize on lucrative opportunities in land speculation, illegal construction and public works contracts. Vying
for power over the city, the criminal organizations exploited
children as an expendable labor force for committing thefts,
extortion, arson and murder in what became an outright war
fought in the city streets in the late 1980s. In comparison to
other Italian cities with high concentrations of mafia clans,
the deadly gunfights and bombings were unprecedented
for their brutality, frequency and the numbers of children
involved. From 1987 to 1990, over one hundred people died
at the hands of the mafia in Gela, which had a population of
90,000. In spare prose, Cutrufelli portrays one of the most
horrific attacks, the "Children's Massacre," which claimed

eight young lives and left at least seven wounded on 27 November 1990. During the intense cycle of attacks and counterattacks, other young adolescents just disappeared, tortured, killed and their bodies set afire or dissolved in acid to avoid leaving any evidence, a form of murder known as *lupara bianca*.

Over the last thirty years, stories about Cosa Nostra, the Camorra and 'Ndrangheta have proliferated in Italian literature, film, and media, putting greater attention on the roles of women as well. Nonetheless, key myths and fantasies about mafia women and the crime organizations themselves remain entrenched in the cultural imaginary. Looming large are the mythic images of the obedient wife devoted exclusively to caring for children, and her antithesis, the powerful, rich mafiosa, untouchable because, according to another fallacy, the mafia doesn't kill women or children. Cutrufelli's *Tina, Mafia Soldier* dismantles such notions. Moreover, the unique mingling of creative imagination and historical truths exposes the violent system of oppression that denies mafia women and men, as well as honest citizens, the liberty to make autonomous decisions and live free from perpetual threats of deadly aggression.